"Will it hurt?" his question w... a part of his innocent act

Dylan nodded. "The future has to be born, Kane," he said, "and birth is traumatic. But it will be brief, and the new world awaits you once it's done. You need never look back, never regret. God will be with you."

Kane gritted his teeth as he watched Dylan bring the stone closer. Then he felt it brush against his skin, its surface cool, and for a moment the ex-Mag tensed.

"Relax yourself into it," Dylan advised. "Don't fight it."

Dylan pulled his hand back slowly, leaving the stone balanced on Kane's outstretched arm. The stone was resting against Kane's wrist now, in the groove that was made there at the heel of his hand. Kane watched as the stone rested there, doing nothing out of the ordinary. And then he felt it move, like an insect's tiny feet tickling against his wrist, and he almost laughed. The movement was so slight that, in the gloom, he could not really see it. All the same, he felt it, felt as it rolled and turned, inching around in a slow turn at the base of his palm.

Suddenly, Kane felt a strange kind of pain, his skin splitting at his wrist with a burning sensation. It reminded Kane of the way that chapped lips feel in cold weather, a hotness around the wound. He watched as the stone rested at his wrist, watched as it seemed to become slightly smaller. It was sinking, Kane realized— sinking into his flesh, burrowing there like an insect.

Other titles in this series:

James Axler
Outlanders®

TRUTH ENGINE

A GOLD EAGLE BOOK FROM

WORLDWIDE®

TORONTO • NEW YORK • LONDON
AMSTERDAM • PARIS • SYDNEY • HAMBURG
STOCKHOLM • ATHENS • TOKYO • MILAN
MADRID • WARSAW • BUDAPEST • AUCKLAND

Recycling programs
for this product may
not exist in your area.

First edition August 2011

ISBN-13: 978-0-373-63871-0

TRUTH ENGINE

Copyright © 2011 by Worldwide Library

Special thanks to Rik Hoskin for his contribution to this work.

Printed in U.S.A.

The rules of the finite game may not change;
the rules of an infinite game *must* change.
—James P. Carse
Finite and Infinite Games

The Road to Outlands—
From Secret Government Files to the Future

Almost two hundred years after the global holocaust, Kane, a former Magistrate of Cobaltville, often thought the world had been lucky to survive at all after a nuclear device detonated in the Russian embassy in Washington, D.C. The aftermath— forever known as skydark—reshaped continents and turned civilization into ashes.

Nearly depopulated, America became the Deathlands— poisoned by radiation, home to chaos and mutated life forms. Feudal rule reappeared in the form of baronies, while remote outposts clung to a brutish existence.

What eventually helped shape this wasteland were the redoubts, the secret preholocaust military installations with stores of weapons, and the home of gateways, the locational matter-transfer facilities. Some of the redoubts hid clues that had once fed wild theories of government cover-ups and alien visitations.

Rearmed from redoubt stockpiles, the barons consolidated their power and reclaimed technology for the villes. Their power, supported by some invisible authority, extended beyond their fortified walls to what was now called the Outlands. It was here that the rootstock of humanity survived, living with hellzones and chemical storms, hounded by Magistrates.

In the villes, rigid laws were enforced—to atone for the sins of the past and prepare the way for a better future. That was the barons' public credo and their right-to-rule.

Kane, along with friend and fellow Magistrate Grant, had upheld that claim until a fateful Outlands expedition. A displaced piece of technology…a question to a keeper of the archives…a vague clue about alien masters—and their world shifted radically. Suddenly, Brigid Baptiste, the archivist, faced summary execution, and Grant a quick termination. For Kane there was forgiveness if he pledged his unquestioning allegiance to Baron Cobalt and his unknown masters and abandoned his friends.

But that allegiance would make him support a mysterious and alien power and deny loyalty and friends. Then what else was there?

Kane had been brought up solely to serve the ville. Brigid's only link with her family was her mother's red-gold hair, green eyes and supple form. Grant's clues to his lineage were his ebony skin and powerful physique. But Domi, she of the white hair, was an Outlander pressed into sexual servitude in Cobaltville. She at least knew her roots and was a reminder to the exiles that the outcasts belonged in the human family.

Parents, friends, community—the very rootedness of humanity was denied. With no continuity, there was no forward momentum to the future. And that was the crux—when Kane began to wonder if there was a future.

For Kane, it wouldn't do. So the only way was out—way, way out.

After their escape, they found shelter at the forgotten Cerberus redoubt headed by Lakesh, a scientist, Cobaltville's head archivist, and secret opponent of the barons.

With their past turned into a lie, their future threatened, only one thing was left to give meaning to the outcasts. The hunger for freedom, the will to resist the hostile influ-ences. And perhaps, by opposing, end them.

Chapter 1

"The rules of the finite game may not change; the rules of an infinite game *must* change."
—James P. Carse,
Finite and Infinite Games (1987)

Kane awoke in darkness.

His head ached, a dull sensation as if from too much sleep. He was ravenous, too, and his mouth was dry, so dry it felt as if he had been chewing sand.

Kane felt the rough, cool rock beneath his crumpled form and realized he had no recollection of how he had come to be here, wherever here was. He was lying on his side, the rough surface pressing against him. His muscles ached with a cold burn, like the onset of influenza.

Slowly, Kane rolled onto his back, stifling a groan of pain as his body protested the movement, settled as it was on the rocky ground. He lay there, gazing up into the darkness, his breaths coming out as forced bursts. He tempered his breathing, waited for his eyes to adjust to the gloom.

Kane knew he was a large man, muscular yet well-proportioned. He kept his dark hair trimmed short, and more than one person had told him his penetrating, steel-gray eyes seemed full of challenge and fury. His upper body was powerful, with broad shoulders and a firmly defined chest, and his arms and legs were rangy, giving him something of the appearance of a wolf. His was a body suited to stealth and swift movement, a body built to respond. His temperament was like that of a wolf, too. On the one hand, Kane was a natural pack leader, yet on the other, he was a loner who preferred to handle things his own way rather than worry himself with the concerns of others. It was this latter quality that had defined Kane's life, from his younger years as a Magistrate in the barony of Cobaltville, where he had gone from enforcing the baronial law to rebelling against it, to his subsequent role as a Cerberus exile. The Cerberus rebels had pledged to defend humankind against the insidious threat of a race of aliens called the Annunaki.

Kane was trained in many combat arts, at home with gun and knife, and just as deadly with his fists. In short, he was a magnificent specimen of what man can make of himself.

Or at least he had been.

Now, he lay on the stone floor, his body bruised and aching, scarred even through the armorlike weave of the skintight shadow suit he wore. Whatever had hit him had hit him hard.

At least his breathing was normal now; he could be thankful for that much. His guts seemed to churn, his stomach rumbling in complaint at the lack of sustenance.

"How long have I been here?" Kane wondered aloud. And more to the point, just where the hell was here, anyway?

Lying on his back, his breathing slow and regular, he reached out with his senses, letting what information he could detect flow into him like an empty receptacle. Kane was renowned as a remarkable point man, having an almost Zenlike oneness with his surroundings in any given situation. There was nothing mystical about this ability; it was merely the studied use of his five natural senses with a focus and surety that few people would ever achieve.

He was in a small, enclosed space. He could tell that much without even moving. There was no breeze, just the lightest drafts moving about him. The air seemed normal enough, although it smelled a little of sweat and all those other scents humans create when held in an enclosed space for any length of time. As he realized this, Kane wondered when he had last urinated; his bladder ached dully. His stomach rumbled again with the thought, reminding him of its emptiness.

He could not detect any breathing other than his own, and suspected he was alone.

His eyes were adjusting now, getting used to the darkness he had woken to. There were rocks above him, he saw, and along the walls to either side of him. It seemed he was in a small cave, hidden away from the sun.

His mouth was terribly dry. His tongue felt as if it was swelling up, and his breath had a solid harshness as it passed through his open mouth. He took another breath and could taste the dryness, and something rotten in his throat.

With a grunt of effort, Kane pushed himself up, forced himself into a sitting position. He felt cramps run across his stomach muscles, realized he had been lying in one position for far too long.

"Just how long was I out?" he muttered.

At first his legs did not want to move, and he almost fell as he tried to stand erect. This wasn't like waking from sleep, Kane noted. It was more as if he had been in some kind of coma. His lack of any immediate memory confirmed that feeling.

Automatically, he reached up and brushed at the wayward strands of hair over his face. He felt the stubble, a rough line running down his jaw, like a bed of tiny needles. He thought back, tried to remember when he had last shaved. It seemed like less than a day ago, just before he and his team had taken the mat-trans leap to Louisiana to fight with the queen of all things dead, but he had at least two days' growth of beard now, maybe three. It was closer to a beard now than stubble. Somehow time had slipped by without his noticing.

Kane stood, pins and needles running through his toes as he did so, his feet numbed by the boots he wore. His body felt heavy, as if he were waterlogged, an old thing dredged from the river.

Gradually, he made his way to the wall, walking like a geisha girl, with tiny steps as though his feet were bound. He felt sick.

There was so little light, yet he could see the structure looming ahead of him. Kane reached out with his right hand, noticing the absence of weight there for the first time. He had had a Sin Eater stored in a wrist holster, a handgun that reacted to a specific flinch of tendons to deliver the formidable weapon straight into the user's grip. The blaster was gone. Kane ran his left hand along his arm, felt the torn strands of leather there, the remnants of the holster that had been violently ripped from him, stripped away at some point he could no longer recall.

Then Kane pushed his fingers against the wall before him, pressed his palm flat against it. It was cold and rough like the floor and the ceiling.

He walked along three paces until he found another rock wall in the gloom, their meeting point creating a right-angle corner. He was in a cavern, then, a cave of some sort, just as he had thought.

"Where the hell am I?" Kane muttered as he peered around, his eyes struggling to make sense of the darkness.

Systematically, he ran his hand along the wall, staggering in slow steps, feeling sensations gradually return to the numb muscles of his legs and feet.

It appeared to be a cave. Yet there didn't seem to be an exit, which made little sense. How had he come to be here, in a cave with no door?

There was the interphaser, of course. Like the mattrans, the interphaser worked to transport people instantaneously through the quantum ether to new locations. Had he used an interphaser to get here?

Kane knelt down, sweeping his hands across the rough floor, brushing the sand and dust as he sought the little pyramidal shape of the interphaser unit. It wasn't here. Nothing was here. Just him and the clothes he wore, in a room without a door.

His stomach grumbled again as he struggled back to a standing position, peering around him at the dark cavern. This was it. He was alone, trapped in an impossible space.

So, is this how it ends, Kane asked himself, *or simply how it begins?*

Chapter 2

Brigid Baptiste's eyelids fluttered open, revealing two emerald eyes. Her eye color was so vivid it seemed almost luminous in the darkness, like a cat's eyes. Even as her eyes flickered open, Brigid winced, feeling the pain spike across the left side of her face. Something had hit her at some point, and the ache was still there when she moved.

In her late twenties, Brigid was a striking woman. Her figure was trim and athletic, its curves enhanced by the tight-fitting shadow suit she wore as she sat on the single chair in the darkened room. Her green eyes peered out of a beautiful pale face with a high forehead that signified intelligence, while her full lips promised a more sensuous side. Her face was framed by a cascading wave of red curls that reached midway down her back. Her usually flawless skin was mussed and dirty right now, and a bruise had formed around her left eye socket, an angry yellow crescent from cheek to brow.

Warily, Brigid moved her head, looking about her. She was in an enclosed space, but it was too dark to distinguish much else. The ceiling was high, reaching at least two stories above her, and the walls looked rough in the semidarkness, though it was hard to discern details.

She tried to stand, only to find she was trapped in places, her arms restrained behind her, her ankles bound somehow to the chair. There was a deep ache in her shoulders, she realized as she tried to shift; she had been here a long time, locked in the same position.

But where was here? Brigid thought back, trying to remember how she had come to be in this place. Even in the poor light, the walls looked rough, uneven, and Brigid guessed they had been carved from rock, probably some natural formation. There was a slight breeze, too, the most miniscule movement of cool air about her face, making her skin ripple with goose bumps.

For a moment, the beautiful, red-haired warrior struggled, working through the dull ache in her limbs as she pulled against her bonds. Though she could move her head, she seemed to be stuck fast. Her arms were pulled down and back, held behind her with some kind of wrist ties. Her legs, too, were fastened in place, bound at her ankles to the legs of the chair. It was hard to see what the chair looked like. It felt hard and unforgiving, with no padding to provide support or comfort.

As she struggled against the bonds, her grunts echoing in the still cavern, Brigid became aware of another presence. She stopped, automatically quieting her breathing as she scanned the area about her.

She had missed it the first time, and she almost looked right past it again, her gaze gliding over the shape poised before the rocky wall. But there was a figure carved of rock and almost perfectly camouflaged, its form visible only because of the uneven shadows it cast. It stood over to her right, and Brigid kept her head straight ahead, peering at the form from the corner of her eye so as not to give herself away. It was hard to decipher, for the thing was so well hidden it seemed almost to be encoded into the rock wall itself. She traced its shadows, the way they played at the edges of the bulky form, which was tall, seven feet or more. Brigid realized that with the ceiling so high, it was hard to judge the thing's height accurately, but she also knew what it looked like—for she had seen it before.

She thought for a moment, recalling her previous encounter with this would-be god of stone. It gave no reaction to her waking, appeared to be dormant itself.

"I can see you," Brigid announced, her voice like a bell in the quietness of the room.

She waited, but there was no response from the figure in the darkness.

Warily, Brigid turned her head toward the figure hidden in the shadows. It had been easier, somehow, to see it from the corner of her eye, like a trick of the light. Brigid rolled her head, working at the stiffness in her neck as she tried to assess the figure. She estimated that it was standing ten feet away from her, its back pressed against the wall.

"I said I can see you," Brigid repeated, "Lord Ullikummis."

For a moment there was no reply, and she wondered if the great stone being was asleep, or perhaps dead. Then, as she watched, a tracery of fire seemed to ignite across the figure in thin streaks, each orange glow affirming the shape of the majestic form and lighting the cavern around it.

Brigid steeled herself as the figure moved, stepping away from the rock wall with one powerful stride. His legs, like his body, appeared to be carved from stone, with rivulets of lava glowing through cracks in their dark, charcoal surface. He had no feet; his legs just seemed to widen at the base like the trunks of mighty oak trees. Each step was heavy, a stride with purpose, such was the gravity that this creature projected in his fearsome movements. He was humanoid in form, standing a full eight feet tall, but appeared fashioned from rock—not like a statue, but jagged and rough, like something weathered by the elements, a confluence of stones smashed together by the environment into this horrifying, nightmarish form. Two thick ridges reached up from his shoulders, curving inward toward his head like splayed antlers. The head itself was a rough, malformed thing, misshapen and awkward, with just the suggestion of features hacked into its hoary surface.

Brigid found she was holding her breath as the hulking man-thing stepped closer. Though she had seen this monster several times before, the immensity of his form remained intimidating.

Then he stopped before her, at last opening his eyes— two glowing portals of magma within his rock face—to stare at her.

"You seem ill at ease, Brigid," the figure said, and his voice was like two rock plates grinding together. As he spoke, his open mouth revealed more magma, glowing like a beacon in the darkness of the cavern.

This creature was Ullikummis, dishonored son of Enlil of the Annunaki. Thousands of years before, the Annunaki, a lizardlike race, had come to Earth in an effort to stave off the boredom that their near-immortal lives and absolute knowledge engendered. Blessed with infinitely superior technology and a callous disregard for other species, they had appeared as gods to the primitive peoples here, and the stories of their interfamily squabbles had become the stuff of mythology to the lowly indigenous species called man. The Annunaki had walked the Earth for hundreds of years, basking in the glory of their false-idol status, treating humankind as their personal playthings, to do with as they wished.

Their reign on Earth lasted until they ultimately became bored with the deception. Soon after, Overlord Enlil, a malicious and selfish creature even by Annunaki standards, set out to destroy the Earth with a great flood, sweeping away all evidence of mankind's existence and leaving the planet as one would a fallow field, ready for renewal in the next season. However, Enlil's purging failed, thanks primarily to the intervention of his own brother, Enki, who had become soft-hearted and felt that humankind's tenacity deserved rewarding. Since then, the Annunaki had been watching humans and guiding their destiny, manipulating them from the shadows, until finally revealing their presence on the Earth less than two years ago.

Since then, the Annunaki overlords had been driven back into hiding through a combination of their own squabbles and the efforts of a brave band of human warriors known as the Cerberus rebels. But the threat had left a terrible legacy in the form of Ullikummis.

The son of Enlil, Ullikummis had been genetically altered so that he no longer resembled the reptilian race he represented. Described in ancient records as a sentient stone pillar, Ullikummis had been conceived purely to act as his father's personal assassin, trained from birth in the arts of killing, that he might dethrone Teshub, the so-called god of the sky. When Ullikummis had been shanghaied by a group of Annunaki led by Enki, Enlil's kindhearted brother, Enlil had been forced to disown his son to distance himself from the assassination plot and save face. Thus, Ullikummis had been banished to the stars by his own father's hand, where he took a slow orbit through the Milky Way in the stone prison of a meteor.

Three months ago, Ullikummis had returned to Earth in a fantastic meteor shower that had all but destroyed Cerberus's orbiting satellite communications arrays. By the time the Cerberus techs had their monitoring equipment up and running again, the rogue stone god had taken his first steps in building an army to hunt down and destroy his father, who remained in hiding on Earth. Accompanied by Cerberus personnel Falk and Edwards, Brigid Baptiste had been part of the three-person field team sent to investigate the crash site of Ullikummis's meteor prison, and she had found herself recruited into a nightmarish training camp called Tenth City, where only the strongest could survive. Within that training camp, Mariah Falk had almost committed suicide at the stone god's command, while Edwards had temporarily lost his mind. With the help of her Cerberus teammates Kane, Grant and Domi, Brigid and her field team had been freed and the training camp destroyed. Ullikummis, however, had somehow evaded death, his whereabouts undetected by the Cerberus rebels.

The hideous stone god had briefly reappeared while Brigid, Kane and Grant investigated an undersea library along with oceanographer Clem Bryant, but they had seen nothing of Ullikummis since then.

Brigid's mind raced back, trying to recall how she had ended up here, in this cave, trapped before the brooding form of the stone god. Her mind began to fill in the blanks, but before she could sort it out, Ullikummis reached for her with one of his mighty stone hands and tenderly brushed his rock fingers down her left cheek. They were cold to the touch and rough, like the stone they resembled.

"You were hurt," Ullikummis said, his uncanny eyes glowing more brightly for just a moment. "Does it hurt still?"

Brigid pondered the question, wondering if this was

some kind of trick. Finally, she spoke. "Yes," she admitted. "It hurts a little."

"It is nothing," Ullikummis assured her. "The human form can endure less than the Annunaki, but this wound is but a trifling thing. Do you wish to see it?"

Brigid's eyes met her captor's, if that was truly what he was, and she nodded very slowly as his fingers remained pressed against her skin. "Please," she said.

Ullikummis pulled his hand back, and began to stride away across the space behind her. She waited, bound to the chair, and her heart raced in fear as she heard the creature of living rock pacing across the stone floor, his steps echoing like hammer blows.

As Ullikummis's mighty footsteps faded into the distance, Brigid took a moment to gather her thoughts. She had a remarkable gift of eidetic recollection, more popularly known as a photographic memory. Brigid was able to remember the smallest details of anything she had witnessed. The last she could recall, she had been with the other members of CAT Alpha—Kane and Grant—as their atoms were digitized and sent across the quantum ether via the mat-trans unit, a teleportation device in use by the Cerberus operation. The three of them had emerged in their home base of the Cerberus redoubt to a scene of carnage. The overhead lighting had been sparking, and the nearest of the computers was shattered, blood smeared across the shards of its monitor screen. There had been shouting, too, and gunfire, and Brigid and her companions had been forced to assess the situation in less than two seconds, realizing their help was needed urgently.

Eight hooded strangers were in the operations room, where the mat-trans unit was located, and they were in the process of destroying the equipment there while

Cerberus personnel tried to fend them off. As Brigid scanned the area, Domi's pure white albino form had dropped from an overhead vent and leaped across the room, bouncing from work surface to work surface like streaking lightning as a stream of bullets—were they bullets?—whipped through the air at her. Beside Brigid, Kane was already drawing his Sin Eater pistol, the 18-inch muzzle of the weapon unfolding in his hand as it was propelled from its hiding place beneath the sleeve of his jacket.

Agile and girlish, Domi blasted a stream of shots from her Detonics Combat Master, firing behind her as she leaped behind one of the computer terminals. In a second, the glass screen of the terminal shattered as one of the enemy's projectiles struck it, shards bursting across the desk as the circuits fizzled and died.

Grant was still in the doorway to the mat-trans chamber behind Brigid, and she heard him call out one word—"Duck!"—before he began picking off the hooded strangers with rapid blasts from his own Sin Eater weapon, even as Kane hurried to help Domi.

Brigid was in motion then, too, reaching for her own blaster where it jounced against the swell of her hip. She selected her first targets as, bizarrely, a stream of what appeared to be pebbles raced through the air toward her at high speed. As soon as her TP-9 had cleared its holster, Brigid snapped off her first burst of return fire, felling one of the mysterious strangers, who wore a hood to cover his features. The figure went down, tumbling backward as the bullets struck his body.

Brigid was turning, finding her second target even as her semiautomatic shook in her hand with recoil. But as she spun she noticed something unnerving from the corner of her eye: the figure she had just shot was pulling himself up off the ground, pushing the hood from his face. He was still alive.…

Back in the cave, Ullikummis's footsteps grew loud once more, and Brigid focused her thoughts on the present. The looming stone creature came around to stand before her, and he held a rectangular object almost five feet in length. Brigid watched as the stone colossus set it before her, turning it to face her. It was a freestanding, full-length mirror with a swivel mechanism to adjust its tilt.

"Are you able to see?" Ullikummis asked, changing the angle as he spoke.

Brigid peered at her reflection in the mirror, saw the yellow crescent on her cheek despite the gloom. "Yes," she said.

Nodding sullenly, Ullikummis stood back, and he seemed to wait patiently while Brigid examined her face in the mirror. It wasn't quite a black eye; the blow had been just a little too low for that. Instead, it had left a nasty bruise, along with some swelling, but there didn't appear to be a cut or abrasion.

Brigid looked up into the glowing orbs of Ullikummis's eyes. "Why am I here?" she asked. "And where are we?"

He looked back at her, his face an expressionless mask of rock, like a cliff ruined by erosion. "In time," he replied, in that terrible voice of grinding stones. And that was all he said.

Brigid watched as Ullikummis walked past her once more, watched his retreat reflected in the mirror. The glowing veins that webbed his body faded as he disap-

peared into the shadows of the cave behind her, the re-
sounding strikes of his footsteps fading to nothingness.

Brigid watched the reflection of the blackness for a
long time.

Chapter 3

Kane struggled to order his thoughts as he stood alone in the cold-walled cavern, trying to remember how he had arrived there. It was hard to think straight. His head ached, not with a throbbing but with a tautness that felt like a clenched fist, as if somehow his hair was too tightly woven into his scalp.

His mouth was still horribly dry, and the ex-Magistrate was conscious that he was woefully dehydrated. His stomach hurt, too, hurt with emptiness.

Kane pushed past the pain in his skull, forced himself to examine more closely the space he found himself in. Pacing it out, Kane estimated it to be a rectangular shape of approximately eight feet by six—small but accommodating so long as he lay on the floor the right way. The floor itself was hard, unforgiving rock, but there was an uneven carpet of sand, enough to cushion the contours of his body and so provide a little comfort while he slept.

The sand reminded Kane yet again of the dryness in his mouth, but there was nothing to drink here; it was just a cave, empty but for its lone occupant—himself. Cold, too, since his shadow suit's regulated environment had somehow failed.

"It's a prison," Kane muttered. "I'm in a cell."

But who had put him here and why? No, those questions weren't important, not yet. Those were questions that Kane could address when he needed to. Right now, he needed to find the answer to a far more fundamental question—*how* had they put him here? Because if he could figure that out he might have a chance to escape.

The room was sealed, and more than that, it was solid. The walls reached all the way around with no signs of a break, he discovered as he ran his fingers slowly along them, high and low. But his captors had managed to place him inside, so there must be a way out; there had to be.

Kane peered up then, the thought occurring to him with slow inevitability. An oubliette—that could be it. A dungeon with its access point in the ceiling, out of reach of the prisoner. He had seen them before and admired the simplicity of the design, imprisoning a man merely by removing the ladder that led to his freedom.

But no. As far as he could see in the gloom of the cavern, there was nothing up there, just more rock running across the ceiling, like clouds on an overcast day. He reached up, found that if he stretched he could just scrape the tips of his fingers against the stone. It seemed solid enough, not a hologram or an optical illusion. Bending his knees, Kane sprang into the air, slapping his palm against the ceiling. It was solid, giving back no echo to suggest any hollowness beyond.

For the moment, at least, he was trapped.

Kane moved to a corner of the room, unzipped his fly and relieved himself, the pressure in his bladder finally insisting upon release. The stench of his own urine came to him, stronger than he expected. After he was done, he covered the puddle of urine with sand like a cat. He wondered if he was being foolish, if this was the only liquid he would get here, and that, no matter how repellent the thought, he would need to salvage it to combat dehydration.

No, Kane told himself. *If they wanted to kill me they*

would have done so. I'm alive because someone wanted me to stay alive.

But the thought didn't ring entirely true. To end up here, he had been defeated, and it was possible that his foe, whoever that was, had such a callous disregard of his opponents that he had locked Kane here to starve, a slow ordeal that would lead to madness and death.

Kane's nose wrinkled at the acrid stench of urine, and he sat as far from the damp sand as he could, resting his back against the cold rock wall. With no way in or out, he let his thoughts drift, struggling to recall what had happened, to piece together how he had ended up in this pitiful predicament.

They had returned from Louisiana, he remembered that much….

THE FOG AROUND THEM was beginning to clear, and Kane, Grant and Brigid found themselves standing within the mat-trans unit in the Cerberus ops center in Montana, the familiar brown-tinted armaglass materializing behind the swirling transport mist.

"Good to be home," Kane said, brushing back his wet hair.

Brigid Baptiste nodded as she tapped in the code that would release the lock and allow them to exit the mat-trans chamber. The Cerberus redoubt had served as the hub of teleportation research and development for over two hundred years.

Brigid's hair clung to her face, still damp from her encounter with the queen of all things dead in the Louisiana redoubt. "I need a shower," she told Kane as the door slid open before her. "A warm one this time, with soap."

"Sounds good," Grant agreed as he rubbed his aching shoulder.

A few years older than Kane, Grant was a behemoth of a man, tall with wide shoulders and ebony skin. His muscles strained at the weave of his shadow suit. A Kevlar trench coat hugged his shoulders and draped down like a bat's wings over his legs. His dark hair was cropped close to his scalp and he wore a gunslinger's drooping mustache over his top lip. Like Kane, Grant was an ex-Magistrate from Cobaltville. In fact, he had been Kane's partner in the Magistrate Division, and over the years the two had fallen into an uncanny simpatico relationship during combat. Grant had been recruited into the Cerberus operation along with Kane when the two of them had gone rogue from the barony, after learning it threatened the well-being and natural progression of humankind. They seemed to be somehow closer than just combat partners or friends—they were more like brothers.

Grant rolled his shoulder as he followed Kane and Brigid from the mat-trans chamber and out into the familiar ops room with its huge Mercator map dominating the far wall. What confronted the three Cerberus warriors was a scene of carnage.

Something had paid Cerberus a visit.

Something bad.

The room was a mess. The overhead lighting flickered and flashed. The two neat aisles of computer terminals were wrecked, and Kane saw the glass of monitor screens littering the floor as he dodged beneath a hail of bullets launched at him and his companions. No, not bullets, he realized as they rattled against the desk he had dodged behind—they were tiny chips of rock flying through the air.

Already Kane was moving, his hand preparing to receive the Sin Eater pistol he wore in a wrist rig on his right arm. The fabled sidearm of the Magistrate Division, the compact pistol elongated to its full length of eighteen inches as it was powered into his waiting palm. Once it was there, Kane's index finger met the gun's guardless trigger, reeling off a swift burst of fire at the hooded interlopers in the room. A storm of 9 mm titanium-coated bullets sped across the ops room as Kane darted for cover, trusting his colleagues to do the same. His attack was met with another hail of stones.

When the rain of tiny rocks ceased, he popped his head up over the side of the desk and began assessing his targets systematically. Kane counted eight strangers in an eye blink, all of them dressed in dirty cowls that covered their heads like a monk's habit. They were hurrying through the room, striking out at the last few Cerberus personnel who opposed them as they smashed the remaining computer terminals, using clubs or just their fists. Even as Kane watched, the blond-haired comms op, Beth Delaney, was knocked to the floor by a savage, backhanded slap from one of the strangers. She toppled over with a loud crack of breaking bones.

Through the chaos, Kane spotted his colleague Domi leaping for cover, her agile, alabaster form flying through the air like some crazed jack-in-the-box.

"Domi, what's going on?" he demanded.

Ten feet ahead of him, the albino girl looked down the aisle, pinpointing Kane by his voice. A true child of the Outlands, she was a strange-looking individual, barely five feet tall with chalk-white skin and bone-white hair. Her tiny frame was more like a teenage girl's than a woman's, her small, pert breasts pushing against her maroon crop top. Besides the top, Domi had on a pair of abbreviated shorts pulled high at the hip and leaving the full length of her dazzling white legs exposed.

As was her habit, she was barefoot. The albino woman's weird, crimson eyes flashed as they met Kane's down the length of the computer aisle. "Took your sweet time getting here, Kane," she shouted. "We're under attack! They took Lakesh."

"Dammit!" Kane spit.

Dr. Mohandas Lakesh Singh, known to his friends as Lakesh, was Domi's lover, and the founder of the Cerberus operation. A fabled physicist and cyberneticist, Lakesh was a freezie—which was to say, he had been born over two hundred years ago, in the twentieth century, bringing his incredible knowledge of the mat-trans system, along with a sense of freedom almost forgotten by humankind, here to the twenty-third century. Lakesh had helped establish the Cerberus operation, and had been there with Kane at the start. While their relationship had not always been one of absolute trust, Kane respected the man and knew they needed to have him in command. Moreover, Lakesh's exceptional knowledge could prove to be a weapon in enemy hands. Leaving him hostage to the machinations of these mysterious interlopers could very well prove the end of the Cerberus facility as Kane knew it.

He became aware of other gunshots behind him, and he turned to see Grant vaulting over a nearby desk and meeting one of the hooded strangers with both feet, knocking the creep backward.

"We were out in the field," Kane explained. "No one alerted us to—"

Domi cut him off with a gesture of her hand. "There was no time," she explained. "These weirdos seemed to come from nowhere. Screwed with the power, screwed with our comms."

"How did they get in?" Kane asked, mystified. The

mountaintop redoubt was well protected from intruders, so a force the size Domi's words implied should not have been able to waltz in easily.

She glared back at him, a snarl appearing on her alabaster lips. "What am I, the answer girl?"

"Hold that thought," Kane instructed as he spotted one of the strange robed figures scrambling toward him from the other side of the desk. Kane leaped from cover, blasting off a stream of shots at the approaching intruder, felling him. The stranger toppled as the bullets struck, crashing over a desk before landing in a heap. A little way along, Kane saw Domi reappear from her own hiding spot and snap off three quick shots at another of their foes, while behind them both, Brigid Baptiste was putting up her own defense with her TP-9 semiautomatic.

"Any idea who they are?" Kane asked.

"No, no and no," Domi snapped, as if guessing his next questions. Then she did the strangest thing—leaped over the desk before her, the Detonics Combat Master spitting fire at her target even as he fell.

"He's down," Kane called as he ran to join her, leaping over the fallen body of a Cerberus tech. "No need to expose yourself."

"No, Kane, you not know," Domi explained, slipping into her strange, clipped Outlander patois as she glared at him over her shoulder.

But he did. In that moment, he saw the man Domi had felled in a volley of bullets get up, and brush himself off as if her shots had meant nothing. Instantly, a feeling of dread gripping him, Kane turned to see his own foe—the one he had shot and presumably killed—struggle back up off the desk, return to a standing position, the spent bullets dropping from his robe like snowflakes.

"What are they—armored or undead?" Kane asked as he drilled the figure again with 9 mm bullets. "'Cause I have had my fill of undead for one day."

"Not undead," Domi told him. "But dead inside. Nothing hurts them."

Kane spun as another shower of stones hurtled toward him, and he saw now that their enemies were using simple slingshots to launch the projectiles at exceptional speed. It was almost as if the stones themselves could gather speed as they cut through the air. Sharp edges slapped at the protective weave of the shadow suit Kane wore beneath his torn denim jacket as he held his arm up to protect his face. The stones ripped his sleeve, sending pale blue threads flying like seeds blown from a dandelion. Kane pulled the remains away, tossing them aside. When he drew his arm back, he saw that the superstrong fiber of the shadow suit beneath it was torn, and needle-thin streaks of blood ran through it where his bare skin had been exposed. The weave of his suit was akin to armor, so whatever these people were throwing was exceptionally tough.

Kane ran at the hooded stranger who had just thrown the wad of stones at him, vaulting over a desk and bringing his Sin Eater to bear on the woman as she reloaded her catapult from a small pouch tied to her belt. He snapped off another shot as she placed the ammunition in the sling she held poised, and her own shot went wide.

Across the room, Grant was involved in his own scrap with one of the intruders, shoving the hooded man's fist aside before blasting him in the face with his Sin Eater. His opponent collapsed, a plume of dark smoke pouring from beneath his hood.

"You hit them close enough," Grant announced, "and they'll go down." He didn't need to shout. Instead, he had automatically engaged the hidden subdermal Commtact unit that was connected to his mastoid bone.

Commtacts were top-of-the-line communication devices that had been discovered among the artifacts in Redoubt Yankee several years before. The Commtacts featured sensor circuitry incorporating an analog-to-digital voice encoder that was embedded in a subject's mastoid. Once the pintles made contact, transmissions were picked up by the wearer's auditory canals, and dermal sensors transmitted the electronic signals directly through the skull casing, vibrating the ear canal. In theory, if a user went completely deaf he or she would still be able to hear normally, in a fashion, using the Commtact. Grant, Kane and the other members of the Cerberus field teams had Commtacts surgically embedded beneath their skin, a relatively minor operation that allowed them to keep in real-time contact in any given situation.

Kane picked up on Grant's advice, jumping over the nearest desk as another volley of stones whizzed across the room at him. He was on the slingshot bearer in an instant, high kicking the guy in the face. It felt like kicking a wall, and Kane staggered back with a grunt.

The man stared at him, eyes burning from beneath his hood. "This is the future," he stated, his voice eerily calm. "Submit."

Kane thrust his right fist forward, slamming it up into the stranger's gut. "Sorry, that ain't going to work for me, buckaroo," he growled as he unleashed a burst of bullets into him.

The man keeled over as the blast took him, dropping to the floor like a discarded bag of compost even as the woman Kane had just shot clambered to a standing position behind him.

"Point-blank them," Kane instructed, looking about

him to catch the attention of the other Cerberus personnel in the room. "It's the best way."

Then he was back facing the woman who had tossed stones at him just a half minute before, the one he'd thought he had dispatched. Kane whipped the Sin Eater up, driving it toward her face, but she moved fast in the flickering overhead lights, slapping the muzzle of the blaster aside even as Kane squeezed the trigger.

His shots went wide and she drove a powerful fist at his jaw, connecting with such force that his ears rang. When Kane looked up, the woman's hood had dropped back and he saw her face for the first time. She was older than he had expected, with lined skin and crow's feet around her eyes—probably in her late forties or early fifties. There was a blister dead center on her forehead, and Kane found his attention drawn to its ugliness for a distracting instant.

The woman grabbed a small lamp off the nearest desk, its cable sparking as she wrenched it from the socket and swung it at Kane's head. He regained his composure just in time, using the muzzle of his Sin Eater to deflect the projectile. Then he drove the pistol forward and blasted a stream of bullets into the woman's throat and upward, peppering her face. He did not like doing this, but there was something eerily wrong with these interlopers, who acted with such single-mindedness that they seemed to be automatons.

Somewhere behind Kane, Brigid Baptiste had found herself trapped between two of the slingshot-wielding strangers. As the one to her left flung a handful of tiny stones at her face, she dropped to her knees, feeling them pull at her hair as she managed to duck just in time. The stones struck the other attacker like buckshot, knocking him to the floor. Then Brigid kicked out, striking the first man behind the ankle and bringing him to the ground. As he fell, Brigid whipped up her semiautomatic, blasting a stuttering burst of bullets into his torso.

Behind her, a third assailant had grabbed something from one of the debris-strewed desks, and she turned just in time to see him throw it at her head. It was a two-inch-high, circular object—a magnetic desk tidy designed to hold paper clips and drawing pins while they weren't being used. Brigid reared back as the thing hurtled toward her, cried out as it struck her just beneath her left eye.

She fell backward, and for a moment her vision swam. She ignored that, bringing up the TP-9 and peppering her attacker with bullets as he charged at her. The man fell forward, his long robes wrapping around his legs as he tumbled. Brigid leaped over his fallen body, hurrying across the room even as another of the strangers lunged for her from his position on the floor.

Ahead of the titian-haired former archivist, another of the strange hooded figures had plucked a slingshot from his robe, and he leveled it at Brigid, preparing to shoot more grit at her. Suddenly, there was a blur of movement as Grant thrust his elbow into the interloper's back, jabbing at his kidney. Grant snarled in pain as he connected, but the hooded stranger fell, crashing into a wall.

"Either they're wearing armor," Grant theorized as Brigid joined him at the next aisle of desks, "or they aren't human."

"They're certainly strong," she agreed. "Could they be some new form of Nephilim?"

"Shit knows," Grant spit. "Let's keep moving."

Nearby, Kane was looking around the room, with Domi at his side. Among them, the foursome had at last managed to dispatch all eight of the invaders.

Farrell lay in a pool of blood on the floor, his gold hoop earring glistening crimson. Part of the Cerberus team, Farrell sported a shaved head and a neatly trimmed goatee. Right now, his face was bruised and bloodied, and his eyes were closed.

"Farrell?" Kane demanded. "You okay?"

His teammate groaned, and Kane checked him more closely. He had a nasty cut at the back of his head where he had been coldcocked, but the wound appeared to have stopped pouring blood.

"You'll be okay," Kane announced, since his Magistrate training extended to basic medical knowledge. Farrell wasn't listening; he was at best semiconscious.

Across the aisle, Brigid and Grant did a similar check on the prone form of Beth Delaney. There was an ugly slash across her face, but she seemed otherwise okay.

"We have to find Lakesh," Domi insisted, hurrying toward the doors beneath the Mercator map, which covered an entire wall of the ops center. Somehow, the streams of light that usually snaked across the map had all been replaced with an eerie red glow.

Kane glanced about him. There were several other Cerberus people in the room, and he had a nasty feeling that at least two of them weren't breathing. But Domi was right. They needed to keep moving, to worry about the living first. If Lakesh was still here somewhere, and still alive, then it looked as if it was up to Kane's makeshift army to save him.

The foursome hurried through the doors, emerging into the redoubt's central corridor. The hallway appeared to be carved through the rock of the mountain, its high ceiling held in place by a network of thick metal girders.

Nothing could have prepared them for what was waiting out there now, on the other side of the door.

KANE OPENED HIS EYES, his breath coming with a suddenness that seemed to snap him out of his reverie. He was sitting on the floor of the cavern that had become his cell, his back pressed against the coolness of the rock wall, and for a moment he wondered just what it was that had shocked him so.

Then he heard it again.

There was a noise off to his left, coming from the wall itself. He strained, trying to make out what the sound was. It seemed to be some kind of scraping or grinding, as if two great rocks were being forced together.

A few months back, Kane had been involved in an escapade that had featured a subterrene, a kind of boring machine that could cut tunnels through rock. Although it was muffled, the noise he heard now reminded him of the subterrene's underground approach.

He got up from the floor, easing himself further into the darkness, as far away from that scraping sound as he could get. He was suddenly very conscious of the fact that he was trapped here in an eight-by-six cell, and if something was coming through that wall, he had no realistic way to avoid it.

Chapter 4

Grant was ready when the hidden door slid open. There, framed by the light that spilled into his cavelike cell, stood a man carrying a tray of food. The meals were bland and simple, a pitiful scoop of some kind of watery gruel or porridge, with barely any taste, each portion little more than a mouthful. Grant had been slipping in and out of consciousness for an indeterminate time, but they had left the food for him. He had forced himself to choke it down as he tried to recover his ebbing strength. When they last came, just a few hours earlier, to clear the trays, Grant had feigned sleep, listening for the sounds of movement and pinpointing the hidden door's location in the rock wall.

Now, as the door opened and the person he thought of as his captor entered, Grant pounced from the shadows like a jungle cat. His meaty paw raced through the air, deflecting the plastic tray of food even as he drove his shoulder at the man's rib cage with a low follow-through. The tray clattered aside, smacking against one of the solid rock walls even as the man in the doorway was knocked backward, losing his footing in a graceless tangle of limbs. As he fell backward, Grant dropped with him, driving a savage punch into his captor's jaw. His fist connected with a loud crack, and the man's head bopped backward, his skull knocking against the rocky floor.

Poised over his captor, Grant drew back his arm for

another blow, watching as the man's eyes lost focus and his head rolled from side to side. He was a young man, probably still in his teens, dressed in a simple robe, with a dusting of bristle on his chin where he was encouraging a tidy growth of beard. For a moment, the youth's head seemed to sway, then his eyes focused on Grant's and the alarm in them was clear. As the youth opened his mouth, Grant struck him in the face, slapping his head back into the hard flooring once again, striking with the force of a hammer blow. With a pained grunt, the man stopped struggling and slipped into the warm embrace of unconsciousness.

Swiftly, Grant patted down the now-still form. He himself had been stripped of his weapons along with his Kevlar-weave coat when he had been placed in this strange, cavelike cell, just the straps of the wrist holster still in place around his right arm where his Sin Eater handgun had once rested. He had been left in his boots and shadow suit, the latter torn along both arms and his left leg, its armor-like weave damaged but still durable. There was a bump on the back of his head, too, a swelling just below the crown where he had taken a hard knock.

The unconscious body lay motionless as Grant patted the youth down. He held no obvious weapons, just a little pouch tied simply to his waist on a cord. Grant opened it and peered at its contents in the orange-hued light that spilled in from the corridor. The pouch contained a handful of stones, most so small they were little more than grains of sand. Grant had seen these people use the stones as weapons, throwing them from their hands or via little slingshots, but he could locate no slingshot on the guard's person.

Grant remained there for a moment longer, resting his weight on his foe's body as he looked warily around him.

He peeked outside the cell, and saw that he appeared to be in a dim tunnel carved out of the same rocks as his cell. The ceiling was low, and it arched to a peak in an asymmetrical way, the rough walls scaling down to form a narrow width that could just barely accommodate two men walking abreast. To his left, the tunnel ended abruptly in a wall, while it continued on down to his right, the walls apparently solid, with no signs of any other caves. That didn't mean spit, Grant knew—he had observed the way they opened the door to his own cell. It was like some kind of flowing rock that slotted perfectly over the entry to the cave, masking its presence with remarkably precise engineering.

The tunnel was lit indifferently by indented patches on the wall that flickered like burning embers. Keeping his movements appreciably silent, Grant rose on tiptoe to examine the nearest of these glowing indentations. The patch appeared to be a clear stone with a sliver of magma burning at its core. Its appearance reminded him of a child's marble, the way a streak of paint is held in place within the glass.

As he examined the strange light fixture, Grant heard a noise from the end of the tunnel, and immediately recognized the sound of approaching footsteps. He stepped back from the weird light source, his ebony skin and shadow suit helping him blend with the thick shadows of the corridor. The body of the man who had come to feed him was obvious enough if they were looking for it, but it might take them a few seconds to notice it in the semidarkness of the tunnel, half sticking out of the open cell.

Grant watched as two figures appeared at the far end of the tunnel, like dark shadows moving across the volcanic magma lights. They were talking, and while Grant couldn't hear every word they said, they appeared to be discussing the forthcoming relocation of their captives.

Captives—plural, Grant realized. Then he wasn't the only one. He had no idea who these people were, but they acted as some kind of prison guards for him and the other captives; that much was obvious. He watched as they came closer, stilling his breathing as they came within earshot.

"Life Camp Zero will welcome them all in time," the warden figure to the left was saying. "Some of them are beginning to understand already."

"They all will in time," the other replied, his voice hoarse, as if he was suffering from a sore throat. "The future's opening up to us, my brother. It's all just a matter of t—"

Abruptly, the man stopped talking, and Grant watched warily as he trotted the next few steps forward, having spotted his comrade lying on the rocky floor of the tunnel.

"What the heck's going on here?" the guard demanded, pressing his fingers to the man's neck and feeling for a pulse.

Behind him, his companion seemed stunned by the sudden change in tone, and he took a moment to gather his wits, peering into the empty cell where Grant had been held. "That's Lance, isn't it?" he said. "He was on food detail…."

"Someone didn't appreciate dinner," the first man said, and he looked up along the tunnel, gazing frantically into the darkness.

Grant came at them both then like a runaway train, the reinforced soles of his booted feet slamming against the rock floor as he charged. His hands reached down and grabbed at the one who had checked for his fallen companion's pulse, wrenching him off the floor even as he struggled to stand up of his own volition. In an instant, Grant had tossed him up against the low ceiling, where his skull smashed with a loud crack. There was something eerily familiar about the move, the thought nagging at Grant for a fraction of a second, like a single flash of lightning, unexpected and bewildering. Then he watched in satisfaction as the guard flew through the air against his partner, both of them crashing to the floor like falling skittles.

Like the one who had come to feed Grant, the two men were dressed in simple clothes, hooded robes with nothing out of the ordinary about them, their dirty uniformity the sole indicator that they shared an allegiance.

"Where am I?" Grant snarled as he loomed over the two struggling guards.

Though physically capable, neither of them appeared to be any great challenge to the huge figure Grant cut. But to his surprise, the second of them—the one at whom he had thrown the first—reared back and launched himself forward, springing from the floor in a flash.

Grant shifted his weight subtly, falling just a little backward as the man lunged at him, swinging a balled fist at his face. Grant dodged, letting the fist swish through the air past him before he reached out and snagged his wrist. With a crack, he snapped the bones, and the guard hissed in pain.

Grant bounced lightly on his heels, readying himself for the next attack. "You want, we can keep this up till I've broken both your arms," he warned. "Or you can just answer my question."

In response, the man smiled, his dark eyes meeting Grant's. "I am stone," he replied.

And then he was upon Grant again, his left arm

swinging through the air with phenomenal speed. Grant batted the punch aside, taking a step back as he did so. The man's first attack may have been of poor quality, but he seemed to be getting into it now—deflecting that second punch had felt like batting aside an iron bar. Furthermore, Grant wanted to finish this quickly before the noise of the scuffle attracted any further attention.

His opponent was hindered by the broken wrist, and his right hand flopped at an uncomfortable angle as he struggled. Still, he seemed incredibly powerful and single-minded in his attack now, fighting more like a machine than a wounded man. Grant ducked, avoiding the arc of the next swinging punch, and drove his hand up and forward, connecting with the man's jaw with a ram's-head blow. The guard's teeth clamped shut with a horrible clack and he staggered back a half step. Grant was already following through, thrusting his left knee into his solar plexus with such swiftness that the man folded in two like a snapped twig. Grant stepped back as his opponent smacked into the wall behind him, then keeled over, a wave of disorientation obviously overwhelming him.

Grant moved swiftly, dismissing his struggling foe as he hurried down the tunnel, leaping over the other one, who was still recovering from being thrown against the ceiling. Boots striking against the hard stone, Grant rushed past the glowing pods of light winking eerily within the wall cavities.

As he ran toward the junction in the tunnel, confused thoughts rattled his mind. Who were these people and how had they trapped him—an ex-Magistrate, of all people? His memory of how he had come to be here was blurry at best, but the torn shadow suit and the evidence of his being stripped of his weapons suggested that he had come here as part of a Cerberus field mission.

He struggled to remember how it had happened. Had he been with Kane? With Brigid? His memory was a closed book to him just now; he couldn't seem to pinpoint anything at all.

Grant was an ex-Magistrate, trained in the arts of combat. His captors, though fast, appeared to be normal enough. He should not find himself like this, trapped in a cell, with no memory of how he had come to be here. It seemed ludicrous.

At the end of the tunnel, he found himself with two options, left or right. He looked back and forth for just a moment, trying to discern any difference between the choices presented to him. Bland rock walls ill-lit by magma lamps on either side—no choice to speak of.

He was trapped like a rat in a maze, he realized, with no idea which way to turn.

He glanced behind him, saw his foes rolling on the floor. Then he made a decision on instinct, turning right and hurrying down the tunnel, while keeping his movements as quiet as he could. He needed to put as much space as possible between himself and the three people he'd left outside his featureless cell, and the more turns he took, the more difficult he would be to track down.

Right, then left, then another right, keeping up a zigzag pattern, boots slapping against the floor of the empty tunnels carved from rock. An open doorway led him to a stone stairwell, eerily lit by the same magma pods.

Here and there, Grant found low walls, some barely reaching to his knee, and he leaped over these, wondering at their purpose. It seemed that the labyrinthine cavern was a natural feature, adapted for use as a prison block, yet the shifting walls gave him the distinct impression there was more to it than that.

Grant ran on, frequently peering over his shoulder to check that he wasn't being pursued. Turning a corner, he found himself in a wider tunnel, its ceiling stretching approximately twenty feet above him. He peered up into the gloom, seeing the stalactites that lined the ceiling, scarcely visible in the dull glow of the magma pods lining the walls at irregular intervals. This tunnel stretched a long way, and Grant saw two of the now-familiar hooded figures moving toward him, some distance away. He pulled back, pressing his flank to the wall of the tunnel he had emerged from.

The hooded figures walked toward him, talking in low mumbles. Hidden in the gloomy shadows, Grant prepared himself, bunching his hands into fists. It was hard to think clearly for some reason; he felt as though he was recovering from a hangover. Was it the lack of food, perhaps? Or was something else affecting him here?

Grant was about to pounce upon the robed figures when they turned off the main tunnel, into a side corridor in the opposite wall. The entrance was almost hidden in shadow, the lighting here was so poor.

Grant reached over, tapping his finger against the nearest glowing orb of magma. Close up, it seemed to flicker, as if it were alive. The light became brighter for a moment as the lava within the pod was drawn to his hand, then it ebbed back to its dull glow as he moved away.

"Weird," he muttered.

Carefully, Grant made his way out into the main tunnel once more, looking all around him. Jutting rock walls were place here and there like hurdles on a race course, low to the stone floor. At one end, perhaps a dozen paces from where he now stood, there was an open archway, the low rocks overhanging in a jagged pattern.

From beyond that arch, the eerie orange glow of lava seemed brighter.

With as much stealth as he could muster in his tired body, Grant padded toward the archway. Edging up to it, he put one hand on the wall there and peered at the scene beyond.

Beyond the opening was a large cave, where several more of the hooded figures were moving about. Waist-high ridges of rock cut across the space in two curved lines, with breaks in them here and there. Grant's attention was drawn to something over in the far left corner of the room. Lightning bolts seemed to flash there, behind a screen of misted glass, and he recognized with a start that it was a mat-trans unit, with fingers of rough stone cladding branching across the armaglass like a creeping vine.

"Where the hell am I?" Grant muttered.

A mat-trans, he thought, turning the fact over in his head. If these people had a mat-trans, then here was a chance for him to escape, to bring help. If he could access that device, he could return to Cerberus and bring his allies to shut down this hellhole. Or he could take a quantum jump to New Edo, call upon his lover, Shizuka, and her fearsome Tigers of Heaven, to back him up as he closed down this perverse prison. He wouldn't need to program in the correct coordinates for the mat-trans unit—he could take a random leap, then recover at that destination, once he was out of the vipers' nest. But to access that unit in the first place would mean somehow crossing this room without getting caught. He could wait it out, maybe, skulk in the shadows until such time as an opportunity arose. The prison guards were all dressed in shapeless hooded robes, and if Grant could snag one of these, he could likely pass unchallenged for a short while at least, until word of his escape from his cell became widespread. Or he could fight it out now, take on the eight figures in this cavern, but in his hungry, weakened state that could be suicidal.

In the far corner of the cave, the crackling lightning ceased and the mist inside the mat-trans unit began to dissipate. Another robed figure appeared within it, and Grant watched with interest as the figure stepped forward through the opening door, greeting others in the room with friendly authority.

Grant stepped back from the archway as the new arrival turned in his direction and began walking toward him, with two of his similarly dressed companions in tow. *Dammit, they're coming out here,* he thought.

The ex-Magistrate turned, heading for the access tunnel he had recently used, only to spot the three figures he had left by his open cell.

He turned back, looking across at the far side of the tunnel, to a branching corridor where the other figures were disappearing. A moment later, he ran through that doorway and found himself in another rock-walled tunnel. This one ended in a sharp turn, and Grant heard something from the far end as he rushed along it. Pulling up short, he leaned against the wall and peered around the corner. A bank of elevator doors was embedded in the rock. The glistening steel was at odds with the cavernous tunnel, reflecting the glowing pods of magma like fire.

Grant peered behind him for a moment, checking that he wasn't being followed, before he turned back to examine the situation.

As he stood there, the farthest set of elevator doors slid open and a familiar figure stepped out.

Chapter 5

The wall behind shook Kane as he pressed against it, vibrations carrying from the other side of the tight cave. The wall before him, eight feet away and almost lost in darkness, seemed to be rocking, as if struck by a quake.

Kane watched as the wall began to shift. And then, to his astonishment, it seemed to part before his eyes, more akin to liquid than something solid, like the Red Sea's fabled parting before Moses. Where once had stood a solid barrier, now there was a gap running from floor to ceiling, easily wide enough for a man to fit through. Light filtered dimly through this impossible doorway, the orange-red of flowing lava.

Kane was about to take a step forward, wondering what new trick this was, when two figures appeared at the edge of the doorway, their features hidden, backlit by the lava flow in the tunnel beyond.

"Kane."

It was a man's voice, firm and solid, with a slight accent.

"Yes," Kane replied warily.

The figures strode through the doorway, and Kane saw that both wore hooded robes that hid their features. He waited, pressed back against the wall, assessing the shapes their robes disguised, automatically checking behind them for more people. The one in front was a man, tall and well-built, with wide shoulders and a swagger to his step that spoke of power and confidence. Behind him was a thinner figure, also tall but more shapely—obviously a woman. Behind them, silhouetted in the doorway, Kane noticed a mongrel dog following them with weary disinterest, stopping to sniff at the new doorway and the floor and walls.

"Well, it seems you know me," Kane said, "but I'm a little at a loss. Care to bring me up to speed?"

The couple stopped before him, and Kane watched as they pushed back their low-hanging hoods, revealing their faces in the dim orange glow of the lava flow beyond the cave. To his surprise, Kane recognized both of them, although it took a moment to place the man's features.

He had short, dark hair and a hard face with tanned skin. He was in his forties and had grown a beard since Kane last saw him. His right ear was mangled now, but Kane recognized him as one of the farmers who had been indoctrinated by the Annunaki prince Ullikummis in Tenth City, out in the wilds of Saskatchewan, Canada.

Kane thought for a moment, struggling to recall the farmer's name. Dylan, that had been it. But Kane's team had freed the man, released him from the mind worm that had controlled his thoughts. What the hell was he doing here, holding Kane captive? Was it some kind of misguided revenge? It made no sense.

Standing behind Dylan was a beautiful woman whom Kane had last seen many months ago out in the Snake-fishville desert close to the fishing village of Hope. In her early twenties, the shapely woman had long, dark hair and hazel eyes like pools of chocolate. Her olive skin showed a tan, and there was something altogether entrancing about her, the way she carried herself, the swell of her breasts and the casual sway of her round hips. This beautiful woman was called Rosalia, and when Kane had last seen her she had been a bodyguard in the employ of a group of immoral profiteers who were trading in pirated DNA. Kane's team had burned down that operation, halting the threat of reborn baronies in the process, but evidently Rosalia herself had escaped. She looked more tired than Kane remembered, tired and drawn. But then, Kane suspected that he, too, looked pretty exhausted just now.

"This is your future, Kane," Dylan began. "The world changed while you weren't looking, and you've woken up to the new reality. Rejoice."

Kane smiled in self-deprecation. "New reality, huh? Just how long was I asleep?" he taunted.

Dylan ignored his frivolity. "Your team, Cerberus, waged a war upon the Annunaki," he stated, as if this fact was commonplace. "The Annunaki were your betters, of course, but you stood up to them, managed to disrupt their plans and, in your limited and infantile way, stymie their progress."

"Well, I do what I do what I do," Kane muttered.

"That is to be commended," Dylan affirmed. "Though primitive, your efforts repelled the hated Overlord Enlil and the others of his coven. But you did not stop him entirely. Enlil still lives and his power base is growing once more, on the banks of the ancient Euphrates."

This was news to Kane. The last time he had seen Enlil, the lizard-faced monster was trapped aboard an exploding spaceship called *Tiamat*.

"The future requires men like you," Dylan continued, "men of good standing, to extinguish Enlil's threat once and for all."

Kane ran a hand through his hair as he considered the proposition. "This all sounds good…Dylan, isn't it?"

The man nodded. "First Priest Dylan of the New Order," he clarified.

Kane locked eyes with him in challenge. "And whose New Order is that?" he asked, his interest piqued.

"Lord Ullikummis," Dylan said. "Our savior. He has seen the great works you have done. You, Kane, have faced Enlil when he was Baron Cobalt, Sam the Imperator, and as Enlil himself. And no matter what face he presented, you have always sought to stop him, to strike that face."

"Well, what can I tell you?" Kane said. "I'm a face striker."

"Lord Ullikummis studied the history, saw your works," Dylan repeated.

Kane realized what the man was referring to. Less than two months before, Kane had been part of a team sent to protect an undersea archive called the Ontic Library. According to their information, this archive was the storehouse for the rules that governed reality, hosting a sentient data stream that contained and ordered all of history, down to the smallest minutiae. When Kane's team had arrived, they'd found Ullikummis working his way through the data, where he'd appeared to be searching for evidence of his mother, Ninlil, whose rebirth had been the source of much conflict between Cerberus and the Annunaki overlords. In accessing those records, Ullikummis would have learned of the role of Cerberus, and the almost archenemy status that existed between Enlil and Kane. Ullikummis himself was an adept assassin, so little wonder that he would see the benefit in recruiting Kane's skills if he planned to do battle with Enlil and his armies.

"He wishes you to join him," Dylan concluded.

"You know, I'm really not a big joiner-upper," Kane

replied flippantly, "but you thank the big guy for the offer."

"The world has changed," Dylan repeated. "Sooner or later, you will submit. Take this path now, and it will be easy. You will become a lieutenant in his army. You will live like a king when the world is reshaped, with a barony of your own, and all you need do is pledge your fealty to Ullikummis."

Kane looked away, girding himself, hiding his fist behind him as he bunched it in the shadows. "It sounds so easy, but I've got a better idea—that you surrender."

Dylan almost spit, he was so surprised by the demand. "Surely you can't be serious, Kane. Look around you. Look at what you've been reduced to, you and your people. You've lost. You're lucky that he even kept you alive."

Kane held the man's gaze as he spoke. "You and your boss's little army surrender now," he snarled, "and I'll go easy on you."

Dylan sniggered. "You're a fool, Kane. A blind fool. You cannot stop the future from happen—"

Kane struck suddenly, swinging his arm forward and punching the man in the face with his balled fist, forty-eight hours of frustration and rage finding primitive release in that one blow. He staggered a step backward in surprise and Kane was on him in that instant, swinging his other fist at Dylan's face even as the first priest of the New Order tried to fend off the blows.

Rosalia, the woman who had entered with Dylan, moved then, taking two swift paces forward before high kicking Kane in the face with professional detachment. The blow knocked the ex-Magistrate back against the wall, and Kane felt his head spin with nausea as the rusty taste of blood filled his mouth.

Behind the woman, somewhere close to the open door, the dog yipped before assuming a low growling, clearly irritated.

When Kane looked up, he saw the dark hair of Rosalia as she pressed her face close to his. "Don't be a fool, Magistrate man," she hissed.

It was good advice, Kane knew. He was weak from lack of food, and his body was still recovering from some battle he could not fully recall. Or perhaps he could. The name Ullikummis had triggered something in his memory, and he was just beginning to remember what had happened in Cerberus's main corridor.

Kane discarded the nagging memory for the moment, struggling to stay on his feet as he leaned against the rough wall.

Dylan stepped close to him, standing over him but not bothering to strike him. "You will learn the error of your ways in time," he said, "and you will come to embrace the New Order. The Life Camp is calling you, Kane. You cannot begin to imagine how the world has altered, how different it is becoming."

The priest turned and paced toward Rosalia, who waited at the doorway, her dark eyes fixed on Kane's pitiful figure as he slumped against the wall, gingerly fingering his lip, which dripped with blood.

"The world is changing," Dylan said yet again as he stepped through the door. "Your time—the age of Cerberus—is over."

Then he was gone, and Rosalia followed him, the dog trotting along at her heels. Kane watched as the strange stone doorway slid back into place, the magma glow of the space beyond obscured by a rock wall. Once more, Kane was locked in a cell with no exit.

"First priest, huh?" he muttered as he wiped at the blood that trickled from his mouth. "Didn't I know you when you were just the understudy, you self-important prick?"

Chapter 6

Grant hunkered down in the shadows of the tunnel as the silvery elevator doors in the rock wall slid apart just a few feet from him.

Striding from the elevator, much to his surprise, was the familiar form of Edwards, an ex-Magistrate like Grant himself, and a member of the Cerberus outfit. Edwards was tall and broad shouldered, with hair cropped so close to his scalp he appeared almost bald. His lack of hair left his ugly, bullet-bitten right ear on show. Like the other people Grant had seen here, Edwards was disguised in a dark fustian robe, its hood pushed back from his head as he scratched his ruined ear. Grant was relieved to see a friendly face, and he realized immediately that the ex-Magistrate must have had the same idea as him—disguising himself in one of the enemy's robes so that he could scope out this prison. The thought struck Grant that maybe Edwards was part of a larger rescue party, and he waited for a moment to see if anyone else would emerge from the elevator cage. No such luck.

Or maybe Edwards had come with Grant, whose memory was so scrambled it was hard to recall how he had come to find himself in that cell. Maybe they had infiltrated together and Grant had been captured. Maybe his long-trusted partner, Kane, was somewhere nearby, too.

Grant watched as Edwards reached for the hood of his robe, pulling it down over his face.

"Edwards," he whispered, stepping out of the shadows to reveal himself to his Cerberus ally.

Edwards turned to look at him, his face an emotionless mask.

"Man, am I glad to see you," Grant continued, as he took a step forward, keeping his voice low. "I guess they caught us both, huh?"

With the speed of a flinch, Edwards's right arm snapped out, his fist clenched. Surprised, Grant tried to avoid the blow, but he was too slow. With the solidity of stone, Edwards struck him across the left cheek, sending him lurching against the nearest wall.

"Whoa, whoa! Cool your jets, man," Grant cried. "It's me—Grant. I ain't one of them."

Edwards's blue eyes focused on him, and his brows knitted in an angry scowl. "Yes, you are," he replied, following his first punch with a vicious left cross.

Grant was so surprised, he didn't have time to avoid that blow, either, and he grunted as Edwards's knuckles rapped the side of his face, knocking him even farther backward. Grant stumbled as he tried to stay upright.

Edwards's hood fell back from his face, and before Grant could protest, the shaven-headed figure drove another punch at his skull. Grant deflected it with a grunt, batting the swinging fist away with his outstretched hand.

"Edwards!" Grant cried as the fierce ex-Mag came at him with a savage right jab. "It's not a trick. It's me. They had me in a cell but…"

Edwards wasn't listening, Grant realized. Not exactly renowned for his even temper even in the best of circumstances, his teammate had built up a head of fury now, and was coming at him with the relentlessness of a thunderstorm, driving punch after punch at his face and torso, years of Magistrate training making his body a lethal weapon. Grant held up his left arm, blocking Edwards's latest blow and turning it against him, making his fist snap back and cuff himself across the nose. Edwards ignored it.

Grant leaped backward, putting a few feet between them. "Look, I don't know what's going on, but you keep up this ruckus and we're going to get ourselves caught and tossed back in our cells."

Edwards dipped his head, and for a moment Grant thought he was acknowledging the point he had just made. But no—he suddenly charged again, his boots slapping against the rocky floor. The tunnel was too narrow, Grant realized; he had no chance to step out of this maniac's way. Even as that fact sank in, Edwards's shoulder was slamming against his ribs, forcing Grant to give ground. There was nothing for it, he knew. Edwards was out of control, and he would have to fight back, restrain him if the man was to see sense.

They had fought before, when Edwards had been under the influence of the faux god Ullikummis. Grant recalled how Edwards had been singular in his purpose then, too, when Grant had infiltrated Tenth City with Kane and Domi to rescue Edwards's scouting party. As Brigid had explained it, the architecture of the metropolis had been designed to grip the inhabitants' minds in stasis, forcing them to do the bidding of Lord Ullikummis. It had been a subtle and strange form of brain control, and the implication that it had been employed across the globe and was inherent in the design of every city ever built by man was worrying, to say the least. But like so much that the Cerberus warriors had encountered since Ullikummis had returned to Earth, the implication remained unexplored while other problems commanded their attention.

Grant stumbled backward once again, almost toppling over one of the strange ridges that broke up the tunnels. He stepped up onto it before kicking out with his other foot, slamming the charging Edwards across his breastbone. His old colleague staggered back, his arms windmilling as he fought to keep his balance.

As he stepped down from the low stone wall, Grant heard other sounds coming from the tunnel at his back, the noise of hurried footsteps as prison guards were alerted and rushed to grab their escapees. If he hadn't been sure before now, Grant knew at that moment that he needed to stop this insanity or dispatch Edwards quickly and come back for him later.

"Just listen to me for a moment," he urged. "Try to think. They have a mat-trans. I saw it. If we work together we can—"

But Edwards didn't seem to be listening. He had stepped back slightly, and Grant noted how he was lowering his center of gravity in preparation for delivering a nasty double kick. A moment later, Edwards's right leg swung forward, slamming hard into the cartilage at the back of Grant's knee before sweeping up to connect with his face. Grant held his position as the first blow struck, not quite placed to pop his kneecap, though Grant knew he had to put that down to luck. He was more concerned by the second blow, anticipating it and deflecting it with both hands.

Edwards's foot came back down to the floor, but he was already spinning, driving his left knee upward toward Grant's groin. Grant stepped aside and his opponent's knee missed him by the smallest of margins.

Then he saw the opening in Edwards's defense, and he grabbed the material of the man's tunic in his left hand even as his right fist powered out, striking him across the cheek. Grant cried out as his fist connected, for it felt as if he was striking a solid wall.

"What the hell?" Grant spit as he followed up with his right fist again, swinging it in a powerful cross.

Edwards took the blow to the side of his face without even blinking, the whites of his eyes flashing red in the dim magma glow of the inset lights.

Grant glanced back down the tunnel, saw the approaching forms of the three guards he had dispatched outside his cell. "Dammit, Edwards," he said, turning back to his old colleague, "there's no time for this shit. You have to trust me or we'll both end up dead."

"Don't you get it yet?" Edwards snarled in response, his leg kicking upward at Grant's face. "Haven't you figured out where you are?"

Grant dropped low as Edwards's foot brushed past his jaw, kicking out his own foot in a sweep designed to knock Edwards's legs from under him. The blow struck hard, and Edwards sagged against the far wall of the tunnel, collapsing to his knees with a grunt of pain.

"Why didn't you tell me?" Grant growled at the ex-Mag, leaping toward Edwards's toppling form, his fists bunched.

"Look around you," Edwards growled, indicating the rough walls and the flickering volcanic lights. "You're in hell now, Grant. And you're here to stay."

Grant stopped short, his fist poised to strike Edwards in his wickedly grinning mouth.

The man took advantage of his momentary hesitation, driving his foot up across his foe's jaw, knocking him backward. Grant cried out as he rolled away, tumbling across the rough tunnel floor beneath the glowing embers of the magma lights. His mind was racing, trying to piece together what Edwards had just told him. Could it possibly be true? Wasn't hell just some crazy old myth, like all the others he and Kane and Brigid had exposed across the globe? Another primitive belief based on nothing more than ignorance and superstition?

From behind, the three people Grant had come to think of as prison guards hurried toward his fallen form, their feet clattering on the hard floor. The lead figure was pointing at him, his finger jabbing the air.

"Stop him!" he called.

Standing over Grant's sprawled form, Edwards smiled, his teeth glinting orange in the eerie glow of the volcanic lights. "Already ahead of you," he assured the prison guards. "This little puke ain't gonna cause us no more trouble."

"Sorry, Mojambo," Grant snarled, "gonna have to rain on your parade here." Then he leaped from the floor, driving himself at Edwards like a wound spring.

Grant struck out with both fists, slamming one into the underside of the man's jaw, even as the other pounded into his solar plexus. Edwards yelped with pain, toppling over into a fetal crouch. Behind him, the three hooded guards rushed forward, and Grant turned to face the newcomers.

"Grab him," one of the guards ordered, "quickly!"

Instantly, Grant went on alert. He struck out blindly with his fist and caught the first of the men across the chest. He followed up with a low punch to his gut, striking with such force that the slender man doubled over, spitting gobs of blood as he tumbled to the floor.

Then the second one was upon him, and Edwards had recovered also, pushing his muscular form off the rough rock floor. Grant spun, booting the first in the face in a roundhouse kick that left him facing the ex-Magistrate again, whom he identified as the more dangerous foe.

As Grant turned, the third guard rushed at him, holding something in his bunched fist. Instinctively, Grant raised his left arm to block the blow, which had been intended for his skull. Flames of pain rushed through his forearm, and Grant screamed in agony, his voice high and strained.

Then Edwards socked him in the jaw, even as Grant tried to block him. It was like being hit in the face by a hammer, such was the power behind Edwards's punch.

Grant staggered back, found himself stumbling against the rough tunnel wall, his ankles catching on one of those low ridges. Then the guard struck again, and Grant saw that he held a sliver of rock shaped like a blackjack, and was using it to strike out at his foe.

The tunnel before Grant seemed to whirl, the elevator doors to spin, and his vision blurred as he was set upon by the two men. He kicked out blindly, and felt his toe connect with one of his attackers. The dark form fell backward, toppling over and slamming into one of the walls with a thud. But the other one struck Grant again, kicking at his chest and face, forcing his head back against the hard floor of the cavern.

Grant was conscious of how the sounds around him changed, becoming distant as his skull struck the rock again. He reached out, trying to push his opponent away, but couldn't seem to locate him through the miasma of his fuzzy vision. Then he felt another hammerlike punch, and his head snapped back once more.

And as Grant sank into unconsciousness under the rain of blows, he heard Edwards laugh.

"Welcome to hell, bitch," his old colleague guffawed. "Enjoy your stay."

The rock walls…the glowing magma within them… it all seemed to make some perverse kind of sense in that instant. Grant couldn't recall how he had come to be here, but maybe Edwards was right. Maybe he was trapped in hell. Maybe they all were.

Chapter 7

Brigid waited a long time in the empty cavern, tied to the chair with nothing but the mirror for company. She tried to remember what had happened after she and her companions had arrived at Cerberus via the mat-trans and engaged with the hooded intruders, but every time her mind thought back on it, she found herself distracted by something in the mirror, certain she could see someone stalking toward her from behind. When she looked more closely, she saw it was nothing, just the dark shadows of the cavern playing tricks in the faintly swirling magma lighting.

And yet she could not relax. The mirror was like a ghost thing, an object sent to haunt her, to render her in a permanent state of anxiety. Perhaps that had been Ullikummis's plan all along, to leave her with this simple torture, this way to seize her mind, her most powerful weapon.

So she watched the mirror, studied her reflection. Her cheeks were dirty, scuffed with grime. There was a crescent-shaped bruise dominating the righthand side of the face in the mirror. She remembered now how the magnetic desk tidy had been thrown at her, smashing her so hard she had felt the ache in her teeth.

But outside the ops room, it had been worse. There had been blood, washing down the walls and across the floor, a ghastly glistening sheet of crimson a half inch thick, enough to turn her stomach. She, Kane, Grant and Domi had stopped dead in their tracks, horrified by that sea of red swirling around their feet.

The lighting of the tunnel-like main corridor had been strobing on and off, illuminating the high rock ceiling in a firework staccato, flashing against the steel girders that held the roof in place above them.

Amid the pulsing lighting, Brigid had seen several figures lying motionless. She'd recognized Henny Johnson lying facedown in the pooling blood, her short dark bob matted against the side of her face. Automatically, Brigid had hurried over to the woman, her boots splashing in the wash of blood.

"Henny?" she'd asked, rolling the woman's head. "Henny, are you—?"

She'd stopped. Henny's eyes were open, but there was no acknowledgment on her blood-drenched face. Above her lifeless eyes, a wicked bruise showed across her pale forehead, and there was a clear indentation in her skull above her right eye. She was dead, struck by a stone.

Gently, Brigid had closed Henny's eyelids, giving the armorer what little dignity she could in her final rest.

"Life spilled," Domi had said, lifting one bare foot and looking at the blood oozing into the cracks and ridges between her toes. "Nasty shit."

"What happened to the power?" Brigid asked, glancing to Domi as she stepped away from Henny's fallen form. Domi had been the only one of them on site when the attack had begun; she was their only hope now of piecing things together.

"They attacked like locusts," she explained. "Swarmed through the redoubt before we could respond. I watched on the monitors as they surged through the doors like a tidal wave. A tidal wave of people."

"It makes no sense," Brigid argued. "How could they just walk in?"

Domi raised her hands in a gesture of defeat, the Detonics Combat Master still clutched in her right fist. "They did—that's all I know. It was so quick, Brigid. You wouldn't believe."

"They must have planned it, then," Grant growled from where he was checking on one of the rooms that led off from the main artery. The room was empty, but the thin pool of blood was spreading across the floor even here.

Kane turned to Domi as the foursome continued hurrying along the wide corridor, he and Grant checking the side rooms with brutal efficiency in a standard Magistrate sweep pattern. "They must have got to the generator," he surmised. "That's why the lights are on the fritz. But I don't get it—why didn't anyone stop them?"

"We tried, Kane," Domi told him hotly. "There are dead people all about—you notice that?"

Kane stopped, looking about him as if for the first time. The blood, the bodies, the ruin of familiar places. It seemed faintly unreal.

"Kane," Grant called, standing in the doorway of one of the rooms. "You need to see…"

Kane had hurried over to join his partner, Brigid and Domi just a step behind him. Grant was standing at the door to a closet used for storing cleaning supplies. The light inside the cupboard was flashing on and off, making a tinkling note each time it winked on. Inside, Cerberus physician Reba DeFore was crouched on the floor, pulling her knees in close to her face. She was sobbing in silence, her shoulders shaking as she tried to stifle each cry.

"Reba?" Kane asked. "DeFore, it's me. It's Kane."

The medic looked up, her brown eyes rimmed with red as she peered through the untidy mess of her blonde hair. DeFore had always taken special care with her hair, forming elaborate creations with the ash blonde tresses, different every day. Kane had never seen her like this.

"Reba?" Kane said again, his voice gentle. "Come on, it's okay. What happened here? What happened to you?"

As he stepped forward, Kane felt the liquid under his heel, and realized that Reba DeFore was sitting in a pool of blood. She continued to shake as he approached her.

"He's here," DeFore said, her voice breathless with fear. "I saw him."

Brigid was standing in the doorway, listening to their companion's words. "He who?" she asked.

"The stone man," DeFore explained.

Brigid could still remember the chilling sense of dread in DeFore's tone, as if a part of her sanity had been stripped away.

BACK IN THE CAVE, there was movement in the mirror. Brigid shifted in her seat, feeling her tension rise as she warily watched the huge stone figure appear from the shadows. It was Ullikummis, the glowing strands of lava glittering across his charcoal flesh.

Brigid tried to turn, but couldn't shift her head far enough, and was forced to watch the reflection of the great stone god striding toward her in the dim light. He stopped directly behind her, peering over her head at his own reflection in the mirror.

"You see the mirror?" Ullikummis asked.

Brigid studied the reflection of his craggy stone face looming out of the darkness above her own. He looked damaged, the stonework more ruined than she remembered, as if hit with buckshot, or a dead thing eaten by worms.

"Yes." She nodded, the word little more than a breath.

She saw the stone colossus move his hands then, reaching behind her until she felt his hard, cool fingers pressing against the nape of her neck.

"What are you doing?" she blurted, unable to keep the fear out of her voice.

"Watch the mirror, Brigid," Ullikummis replied, "for in it is contained your future."

Brigid felt something drag along the nape of her neck, bumping over the vertebrae there where it pressed against her skin. It felt like needles, or the feet of an insect playing along her spine.

"Please," she said, cursing herself for showing weakness in front of her enemy.

Then she felt something jab at her skin, and she stifled a cry of pain. Something was pressing into her, pushing against the flesh at the back of her neck.

"Please stop," Brigid cried. "Please tell me what—"

Ullikummis met her eyes in the mirror as he worked something at the top of her spine. "You have fought with the Annunaki for the longest time as apekin measure," he stated, as Brigid felt the hidden thing burrowing into her flesh. "Have you never wondered what it is like to be one of us?"

Brigid screamed as something clawed beneath her flesh, plucking at the ganglion of nerves that wrapped around her spine.

"Are you aware of casements, Brigid?" Ullikummis asked.

She couldn't answer. Her mouth was frozen open in

silent agony as the sharp thing, whatever it was, continued to pull at her beneath her skin.

"Other worlds," Ullikummis continued, "a theory of alternatives where futures may be played out differently."

Brigid had heard of the theory, had been privy to it on occasion, where a future with Kane as her lover had been foreseen. She tried to focus her mind on the words Ullikummis was saying in his gravelly tones, tried to reach past the pain as her body struggled against its ties.

"I was taught by a wise Annunaki named Upelluri," Ullikummis told her, his voice like the grinding of stone. "Upelluri once explained to me how the Annunaki differ from humans by explaining their simple-minded concept of the casements. He said that naive and short-sighted philosophers had misinterpreted them, treating the different vibrational frequencies as one would the rooms of a house. Instead, Upelluri had compared it to looking in a mirror."

Brigid rocked in place, wailing in pain as the thing burrowed through her spine, seeming to tear at her very being. "Please," she howled. "Please stop." Her breath was coming faster and faster, a runaway steam locomotive hurrying to disaster.

Ullikummis reached forward with one hand, clasping her head by the crown, holding it rigidly in place as she tried to squirm, forcing her to look into the mirrored glass.

"You see your reflection," Ullikummis explained, "and behind it you see the reflection of the cavern beyond, and the cavern in the mirror appears to have depth. But in reality, the whole thing is but a picture on a flat, reflective surface, with no more depth than the surface of a blade of grass."

Brigid stared at her reflection, at the thing that loomed behind her, even as pain surged across her back like fire.

"Close your eyes," Ullikummis instructed.

She tried to shake her head, to tell this nightmarish thing that walked like a man no.

"Close your eyes," Ullikummis repeated, "and the pain will pass."

Her breathing was coming so fast now, the steam engine jumping the tracks and hurtling off the cliff. The pain was oblique, an impossible thing to calculate, to comprehend. She closed her eyes, praying it wasn't a trick, praying that Ullikummis was not toying with her as a cat toys with a mouse.

"This world," she heard Ullikummis intone, "this galaxy with all its depth and color and difference—this is but the image on the surface of the mirror to the Annunaki. That was how Upelluri explained your ways to me."

Brigid waited, eyes closed, feeling the thing rummaging beneath her spine, like a rapist's hand tugging at the hair at the nape of her neck, plunging her down, down, down. She whined, a gasp coming through clenched teeth.

"Don't fight," Ullikummis instructed placidly. "Relax, Brigid."

Brigid struggled to hold herself still as the burning continued, trying the whole while to pretend it wasn't happening, that it wasn't there.

"You fought with my father," Ullikummis said thoughtfully, after a long pause. "I saw this when I imbibed time in the Ontic Library. You fought with my father, and others of our race, of the Annunaki."

In her fixed position in the seat, Brigid squirmed as the pain shifted, reaching down her back like claws.

"I saw there," Ullikummis continued, "that you have exceptional knowledge for an apekin, a…" he stopped, as if trying to recall the word "…human. And yet you never questioned what it was you fought."

"Tried," Brigid replied, the single word coming out as a gasp between her gnashing teeth.

"They acted like you," Ullikummis said. "My father and the other overlords were aliens to your world, yet they behaved like you, like actors on a stage, dressed in masks and rubber suits. Humans in everything but appearance," he mused, adding as if in afterthought, "and perhaps stamina. Yet you never questioned this."

"They had technology," Brigid began, her words strained. "They differed from—"

"No, they did not," he interrupted. "The Annunaki are beautiful beings, multifaceted, crossing dimensions you cannot begin to comprehend. Their wars are fought on many planes at once. The rules of their games intersect only tangentially with Earth and its holding pen of stars. What you have seen is only a sliver of what the battle was, and the Annunaki have shamed themselves in portraying it thus."

Brigid listened, wondering at what Ullikummis was telling her. She recalled travelling to the distant past via a memory trap, and seeing the Annunaki as their slaves, the Igigi, perceived them. They had been beautiful, just as Ullikummis was telling her, shining things that seemed so much more real than the world around them, colored beings amid a landscape of gray. But when she had faced Enlil, Marduk and the others in her role as a Cerberus rebel, they had been curiously ordinary. Yes, they were stronger, faster, supremely devious, but they were—what?—the thing that Ullikummis called them? Actors on a stage? People dressed in masks and rubber suits like some hokey performance designed for children? Had Brigid and her companions been taken in by a performance, a show designed to entertain the feeble-minded?

As Brigid considered this thought, Ullikummis spoke once more in his gruff, throaty growl. "They started their current cycle as hybrids, half human, half advanced DNA. The human part clings, holding them back. If you saw the true battles between the gods, if you had witnessed the ways they fought across the planes millennia ago, you would never even recognize the creatures you fought as the Annunaki—you would think them a joke."

"Why are you telling me this?" Brigid asked, baffled.

In reply, Ullikummis gave a single, simple instruction. "Open your eyes, Brigid."

She did so, found herself staring into her own green eyes in the mirror as the agony in her back abated, faded to nothingness. The mirror was like a drawing, a picture that could be falsified, that owed no one the truth.

Brigid let out a slow breath, felt her heart still pounding against her rib cage. The pain in the back of her neck was gone as if it had never been.

"Do you understand now?" Ullikummis asked, his voice coming from above her head.

Brigid nodded. "I'm beginning to," she said.

Chapter 8

There was a deep vein of pain in Mariah Falk's left leg, down at the back of her ankle. A couple months ago, she had been shot there, and now the coldness of the cell was getting into the old wound.

Wincing, she opened her blue eyes and reached down, rubbing her leg to relieve the aching numbness.

Falk was a slender woman in her midforties, with short brown hair streaked with gray. Though not conventionally attractive, she had an ingratiating smile that served to put others at their ease. A highly trained geologist, Mariah was one of the brain trust of experts who had been cryogenically frozen at the end of the twentieth century and now formed a significant part of the Cerberus staff.

Right now, however, she found herself lying on the rocky floor of a cavern, where she had been brought by Ullikummis's loyal troops. Mariah remembered being transported here, and for the past two days she had waited patiently as the hooded troops had brought her basic meals of watery gruel. The food tasted foul and she suspected there was barely enough nutrition to sustain a person, but what option did she have? She was trapped in a cell with a door that appeared only at her captors' request, with no warmth, barely any light other than the faint disk in the wall that offered a dull orange glow like a sodium streetlamp.

Ullikummis. He had brought this upon her. In a round-about way, he had been the one to cause her to get shot in the leg a few months earlier, as well, for it had been during her indoctrination into his regime in Tenth City that Mariah had sustained the wound.

But why her? She wasn't like Brigid Baptiste or Domi. They were warriors, soldiers in the war against the Annu-naki. But Mariah was just a geologist. She had no place being here, locked away in a cell, treated like something inhuman. Soldiers playing soldier games, that's what this was.

But then Mariah remembered the soldier game she had become embroiled in forty-eight hours earlier, the same way she had remembered it a hundred times before while lying on this cool, unforgiving rock floor.

SHE HAD BEEN SITTING in the canteen waiting for Clem Bryant when it began. The Cerberus canteen was never a lonely place; there was always something going on, some group just coming off shift or wolfing down breakfast—be it six in the morning or six in the evening—prior to starting their shift.

Mariah sat at one of the tables with its shiny, wipe-down plastic top, a book propped open in her hands, watching the world go by. Now and then she would spot someone she knew stride through the swinging doors and head over to the serving area, and they would wave or nod in acknowledgment before she went back to her book.

Sometimes it was weird, Mariah reflected, living in the future. She was a freezie, a refugee from the Manitius moon base who had been woken two centuries after her own time and forced to adapt. Mariah was quite happy to chug along at her own pace, studying rocks and offering insights into the changes in soil structure that had been wrought by the nuclear war of 2001. Still, it was a strange thing to be living in the future. The book she was reading, for instance, was a relic of another age, for the mass production of literature for entertainment had somehow fallen by the wayside during Earth's darkest days, and the barons who had risen to control America had frowned upon such frivolity. Perhaps, Mariah thought, they had been scared that people might use books to expose the truth, to encourage the free-thinking that the baronial system had almost managed to stamp out. The barons had turned out to be the chrysalis state for the Annunaki overlords—little wonder they were afraid of freethinking and the sharing of ideas. Things could be hidden in books, even in the most innocuous fiction.

Mariah chuckled to herself. Perhaps not this particular fiction, she mused as she admired the cover painting of a handsome, broad-shouldered man in a doctor's white coat consulting a chart with intensity, while the pretty nurse in the foreground bit her lip and looked concerned. It was a done deal that the two of them would get together just in time before the final page, to live happily ever after—the novel's pink spine promised that, even if the book itself strived to add tension to the romance.

Mariah looked up, eyeing the door that led into the kitchen area. Did she and Clem have a pink spine on their book? She hoped so. She had been getting closer to him over the past six months or so, spending more time in his company.

Clem Bryant was a fascinating mixture of contradictions. On the one hand he was polite, well-spoken, sophisticated and urbane, able to verbally fence his way out of any situation. On the other, he had a spiritual side that seemed to be at odds with the image he presented to the outside world. The first time Mariah had realized this was when Clem had taken her on a trip—a date, really—to the steps down to the River Ganges, where he had explained to her about washing away one's sins. Mariah had been taken aback by this, as Clem had always seemed so straight-laced. And yet it seemed to fit with his personality perfectly. He gave off the impression of having an amazing sense of inner peace. A freezie just like Mariah, Clem was an oceanographer by trade, but had found his true vocation as a cook in the Cerberus kitchen.

As Mariah watched idly, the staff door to the kitchen swung open and he came striding toward her, carrying a plate of something in his hand. In his late thirties, Clem was tall and slender, with dark hair swept back from an expanse of forehead, a carefully groomed goatee on his chin. Though he looked typically well-kempt, Clem's white apron was speckled with cocoa powder. He greeted Mariah with a broad smile as he took the seat opposite hers.

Mariah glanced down at the plate, which he'd placed between them, and saw it contained a little stack of brownies dusted with icing sugar. "Chocolate brownies, Clem?" she asked. "I've never seen these on the canteen menu."

Clem gazed at her, his intelligent blue eyes peering into hers. "Well, one has to shake up the menu now and then or become stale," he said with a raised eyebrow. "But I require a guinea pig to test the first batch. Any suggestions?"

Mariah held one hand above her head excitedly. "Ooh, pick me, pick me!" she trilled.

He laughed, pushing the plate toward her. As he did so, the doors to the canteen crashed open and one of the Cerberus security detail—a woman called Sela Sinclair—came running into the large room.

"We're under attack," she shouted, her eyes wide with fear.

"What th—?" Mariah muttered. But before she or anyone else in the room could respond any further, the doors slammed open on their hinges and seven mysterious figures in hooded robes spread out into the room. The strangers launched small stones out of something held in their palms, and the stones seemed to race through the air, picking up speed as they hurtled toward their victims. Two struck a diner in the back before he could even react, and his head exploded as a third stone smashed through his skull.

Sela Sinclair dropped and spun, raising the M-16 she held and blasting off a half dozen shots in quick succession. The weapon had an underbarrel grenade launcher, a little bulky, but designed for maximum damage. Sela herself was a wiry, lean-muscled, dark-skinned woman with a perpetually fierce expression. A noble warrior and efficient combatant, she was ex-USAF and had been part of the Cerberus Away Teams since their formation.

The woman's shots struck the lead pair of hooded figures, and the one to her left fell, his robe sweeping up like a sail catching the wind. Then incredibly—impossibly—the figure sat up and pulled himself back to a standing position as if nothing had happened. Mariah felt a lump in her throat as she tried to swallow, watching the scene unfold before her.

Another of the hooded figures swept his hand through the air, unleashing more of the small, sharp stones. They whistled slightly as they whizzed through the air, shattering drinking glasses and embedding themselves in the walls even as quick-thinking Cerberus personnel dived for cover.

Sela rattled off a swift volley of shots, scampering beneath a table even as the hurtling stones hit their next victims. She cursed as she watched several of the diners drop as the pebbles struck them, falling facefirst into their meals or tumbling from their chairs, their eyes wide in shock. The stones were traveling at the speed of bullets, somehow picking up velocity once they had left their wielder's hand. There was no time for Sela to worry about the victims now; she had to deal with these interlopers who had followed her up the stairs, had to defend as many people as she could.

A number of the Cerberus personnel were battle hardened, and all of them had been trained in basic combat techniques. Immediately, the two-man team closest to Sela were on their feet, asking what they could do.

"Are you armed?" she asked as she leaped between tables, her bullets ripping through the hooded shrouds of the interlopers.

Several people in the room said that they were, producing four pistols and a combat knife between them. As Mariah and Clem watched from the far table, Sela's shots struck another of the intruders—only for the man in question to continue walking forward, brushing the shells aside like raindrops.

"Come on, Mariah," Clem urged, leaping from his seat.

"Where are we going?" she asked as the battle raged behind them.

"Kitchen," he told her, grabbing her wrist.

Mariah hurried to keep up, her feet slipping on the tiled floor of the canteen. "What the heck's going on?" she asked, glancing back as Clem pulled her through the swinging door into the cooking area. Something else was following the hooded strangers through the door, something tall and bulky, its footsteps shaking the room.

"I don't know," Clem answered, hurrying over to the stove and grabbing a bubbling saucepan by its handle. Other cooks were hurrying about the area, wondering what was going on as they heard the gunshots and the barrage of stones pelting the walls.

The word went out immediately—Cerberus was under attack. Several of the kitchen personnel grabbed cooking items, wielding them like weapons as they hurried outside, determined to help. A kitchen hand beside Mariah grabbed a vicious-looking meat cleaver and hurried through the door.

"We should have heard the alarm," Mariah complained. "Why wasn't there an alert?"

Clem looked at her anxiously as he adjusted the heat on the hob. "Perhaps these visitors hit the PA system first," he suggested.

"But there are—" Mariah began, pitching her voice loud over the sound of a grenade being launched outside.

Clem cut her off. "Mariah, I need sugar. Top cupboard."

She stood there helplessly for a moment, trying to make sense of his request. Outside, the tarantella of bullets and stones rattled against hard surfaces.

"Sugar," Clem repeated, raising his voice but never sounding angry or rushed.

Mariah opened the cupboard he had indicated, pulled out a large container marked Sugar.

"What are you making?" she asked as she handed it to Bryant. "I don't think this is really the time to start baking a sweet, Clem."

"You saw those people," he reasoned. "They brushed aside Sela's bullets." On the stove, the saucepan of boiling water bubbled as he poured sugar into it. "In prison, they call this napalm. Boiling water and sugar—sticks to the skin and burns, just like its namesake."

Clem dipped a Pyrex mixing jug into the bubbling saucepan and filled it before reaching for a nearby mug with his other hand. "Come on, Mariah. Time to sound the horn and get in the hunt."

As if caught up in a whirlwind, she grabbed the steaming cup he passed her, and followed him back into the canteen. "Clem, I think you should know something…" she began.

Clem was already through the door to the eatery, the steaming contents of the mixing jug slopping against its sides as he ran. His shoes slid on the tiled floor as he skidded to an abrupt halt, hardly able to believe his eyes. There, striding across the room like some animated cliff face, came Ullikummis, rogue scion of the Annunaki. He was bent down, his misshapen head ducked so as not to scrape against the ceiling, which seemed suddenly low in his presence. The rock lord's feet slammed against the floor, cracking tiles and leaving dents with each mighty step. Even as Clem watched, a Cerberus staffer called Watts, who had joined Sela's makeshift army, was cast aside, the Beretta in his hand blasting shots into the ceiling as he was tossed feet over head by a mighty backhand slap from the stone giant.

"Oh, my goodness gracious," Clem exclaimed, the words coming in an abrupt tumble like a thunder strike.

"That's what I was about to tell you," Mariah said as she stood at his elbow. "Ullikummis is here."

Both Clem and Mariah had encountered the stone-clad Annunaki before. Her unfortunate meeting had occurred in Tenth City and resulted in her being very nearly indoctrinated into Ullikummis's war cult. Clem had met the rock monstrosity later, during the exploration of the undersea Ontic Library, which housed all history and knowledge. Now they faced him once again, as his hooded troops rushed about him, clearing aside Cerberus personnel in swiftly fought battles.

Suddenly, the overhead lights flickered and died, and for a moment the cafeteria was plunged into darkness, the only light coming from the horizontal slit windows located high in one wall. In the darkness, Ullikummis became a glowing network of lava, the streams outlining his body like some ghostly stick man, his eyes two fiercely glowing orbs.

Mariah watched the would-be god's mouth open, a shimmering orange in the darkness like the heart of the sun, as he spoke one word: "Submit."

Mariah heard Clem respond automatically, and she felt a strange sense of pride. "Never."

Then, with a plinking sound, the fluorescent tube lighting flickered back on as the emergency generator kicked in. But the light kept dimming, threatening to shut down again.

Close to the far wall, Sela Sinclair was fending off two of the robed figures. She had lost her M-16 in the scuffle and was now wielding the Beretta 9 mm that she habitually wore at her belt, holding it in a two-handed grip as she pumped bullet after bullet into the torso of the one of the strangely garbed figures. The stranger slowed, knocked sideways by the impacts, but would not go down.

Sela adjusted her aim, closed one eye as she targeted the figure's forehead, which was hidden beneath his low-hanging hood. "Fuck it," she muttered, blasting a 9 mm

Parabellum bullet where she knew the man's head must be. The bullet cut through the man's hood, and he staggered in a two-step jig before falling to the floor.

By then, his companion was on Sela, his hand sweeping up in an underarm throw. She sidestepped as a half dozen tiny flecks of stone leaped from the sling in his hand and rushed at her. The stones rattled against the wall behind her even as Sela turned the Beretta on the robed man and snapped off a shot straight into his face, as she had his companion. The figure made no noise as the bullet struck, but Sela smiled grimly when he staggered backward, crashing into the nearest table and sending dirty plates flying as he fell.

She was already searching for her next target, ejecting the Beretta's empty cartridge and slapping in the new one she had retrieved from her belt pouch. To Sela's surprise, the figure she had first shot pulled himself up off the tiles and made to grab for the pistol in her hand. She reacted immediately, instinct taking over as she lifted the barrel out of the man's reach and drove the toe of her right boot at his face. The kick made contact and the man shook, caught as he tried to get up off the floor. Sela grunted, feeling a shuddering through her leg. It had been like kicking a solid brick wall.

To Sinclair's left, the second figure was rising from the table, as if she hadn't shot him just a few seconds before.

What the hell are these people? she wondered. Sela had witnessed a lot of strange things in her position with Cerberus, but she had never seen anything that appeared quite so ordinary and yet utterly invincible. *It's as if they're made of stone,* she realized, and her eyes flickered automatically to the towering creature who blundered through the canteen—Ullikummis.

Then the first attacker was upon her, and Sela was driven back against a table as the Beretta jumped in her hand, blasting shot after shot into her foe's gut. It was no good. No matter where she shot them these stone men would not drop, not for long.

Sela yelled in pain as she rolled over the table-top and slammed against the floor. As she landed, the other hooded figure vaulted over the table and landed on her, driving his knees into her chest. She expended her breath in a gasp, felt her attacker's fist strike her face once, twice, thrice, knocking her head back against the hard tiled floor. She struggled beneath the hooded figure, trying vainly to shift his weight and free herself from his attack. Then a blur at the corner of her vision caught her attention, and she turned just in time to see her other attacker run at her and kick, booting her full in the face.

Sela Sinclair's nose exploded in a bloom of blood, and her vision went dark as she faded into unconsciousness.

Elsewhere in the cafeteria area, other members of the Cerberus team were falling to the strangely unstoppable intruders. Clem Bryant was ducking and weaving as one of the robed figures lunged for him and Mariah. Like Sela's foes, this figure threw a handful of stones he'd pulled from the pouch at his belt, and Clem shouted an urgent warning for Mariah to duck. She did so just in time, though several of the stones clipped her shoulder as she tried to get out of their way.

Mariah examined her shoulder, saw that the standard-issue white jumpsuit was torn and there were threads of blood appearing where the stones had—what?—grazed her? It felt like something more, and she reeled in horror as she saw one of the pebbles burrowing into her flesh. With a yelp, she grabbed for it, plucking it out of her skin even as it threatened to disappear.

Before her, Clem pulled back his attacker's hood and tossed the boiling sugar solution—the homemade napalm, as he had called it—into the enemy's face. The figure beneath the hood looked human, quite a handsome young man, in fact, albeit with a stern set to his square jaw. He screamed as the boiling liquid struck, and Mariah watched in amazement as Clem's foe crashed to the ground, clutching his burning face.

"What did you…?" she asked, suddenly recalling the mug in her hand.

"The sugar makes it stick to your opponent," Clem told her briefly. "Like a scalding that just won't stop."

Mariah swore, staggered at the man's ingenuity. Clem—a cook and deep-sea diver—had somehow figured out something that could stop these incredible intruders who had infiltrated their home.

"Ingenuity," Clem said, as if reading her mind. "Come on, we'll need to reload now that we've proved it works."

Mariah watched as the robed man continued to howl as he lay on the floor, his face burning away. Then she turned, ready to follow Clem back to the kitchen.

Another of the robed figures was running at them, and Mariah realized that apart from a couple of Cerberus people who were just being overpowered, they were the only two left.

Clem shoved Mariah back as the female assailant approached, swinging her fist at Clem's head. He protected himself, fending off the blow with the empty measuring jug. Though ovenproof, the jug shattered at the woman's blow.

"Unsociable," Clem exclaimed, as he ducked his foe's next thrust. Then, shoulder down, he charged at the woman, forcing her to give ground, albeit just two steps.

"The napalm!" Clem shouted, encouraging Mariah to toss the steaming contents of her mug.

Mariah didn't hesitate. She threw the cup, sugar solution and all, at their hooded foe's face. The woman dropped back as the contents struck her. Some of it spilled across her robe, but enough hit her skin that she began screeching in pain, sounding like a stuck pig.

Mariah felt sick at what she had done. She wasn't a soldier, nor was Clem. They didn't belong here, shouldn't be doing this. She turned, peering around the room as the lights flickered and dimmed. They may not be soldiers, but they were all that Cerberus had left here now, everyone else in this room had fallen.

"Clem," Mariah cried, turning back to him. "We're all that—" She stopped, the words freezing on her tongue.

The impressive figure of Ullikummis stood before the door to the kitchen, hefting Clem Bryant high above the floor. Clem was shouting, but Mariah couldn't make sense of what he was saying. It was like watching something in slow motion, it all seemed so inevitable.

Mariah cried out a single word: "No!"

But even as the protest left her lips, Ullikummis threw Clem across the room, until he slammed against the far wall like a discarded rag doll. Mariah turned and ran for Clem, feeling hot tears running down her cheeks even as she did so.

"Clem," she shouted. "Clem, no. Don't be…"

He was lying there, slumped against the wall, blue eyes wide as if looking at Mariah, his head at an awkward angle. The geologist knelt before him, reaching for his hair, brushing it off his forehead.

"Clem, you're not allowed to die," she told him. "It's the rule. I hadn't told you yet. I hadn't told you that I was falling in love with you. So you mustn't die until after I've told you that. You mustn't."

But Clem didn't hear. He was dead already, had been so as soon as he struck the wall. Mariah watched as a trickle of blood seeped from his nose, spreading out through his mustache and neatly trimmed beard.

She reached for his mouth, tried to push the blood away from his lips, feeling the warmth of his skin against her fingers. As she did so, she became aware of the towering shadow that fell over Clem Bryant's still body.

The voice came from behind her, sounding like two millstones being ground together. "Submit."

Mariah did not turn to face Ullikummis. Instead, she knelt at Clem's side, wiping the blood from his lips, smearing it across his face, until two figures grabbed her and pulled her from her knees, forced her to stand.

IN HER STONE CELL, Mariah Falk tried to cry again for Clem, but the tears wouldn't come any longer. She had nothing left to weep with. Why had Clem died, and she'd been allowed to live? She was just a geologist. She had no place being here, locked away in a cell, treated like something inhuman. Why was she still living?

Chapter 9

Brigid found herself alone once more in the shadowy cave with just the mirror for company, haunted by her own face peering out at her from the darkness. She tried to recall what had happened, and remembered Reba DeFore in the storeroom, distraught, sitting in a pool of blood. Thankfully, the blood had appeared to not be her own.

Brigid closed her eyes, pictured the way Reba had looked, so terrified and alone and small. But it was a picture; it wasn't a memory anymore. Brigid's eidetic memory, her ability to recall the finest details of events and the things she saw, seemed diminished. It was the lack of food and water, she knew, making her lose concentration. Her body was begging for sustenance.

Her green eyes snapped open and she peered into the mirror, saw the red rings around them where exhaustion was beginning to show. Ullikummis had told her of the way the Annunaki perceived reality, the way it was all just a surface, that what appeared to be might not truly be what was. Ullikummis was in her head, she realized. Somehow, he had done something that was changing how she thought, how she saw things. An education.

There was a gulf of time as Brigid waited uncomfortably in the chair, thinking about the things Ullikummis had told her. Her whole life had been characterized by a single trait, the total recall of her eidetic memory.

Memory was the thing that made an individual, she realized. A continuity of memory was what provided sentience. To find herself suddenly losing an aspect of that memory, however small, terrified Brigid. Whatever Ullikummis had done, he had opened her mind to the way in which the Annunaki saw the world. It was subtle, and yet Brigid Baptiste pondered upon it for a long time. She had battled with the Annunaki for years alongside the other members of the Cerberus team. She, Kane and Grant had led strikes against these terrible alien foes, and yet never once had she really stopped to consider what it was to be alien.

The Annunaki had a continuity of memory like no other, Brigid understood. They shared memories through their whole race, were gifted at birth with a knowledge of all that had gone before. It made them intelligent, learned, and gave them a perspective on life and the lives of others that was radically different to anything Brigid had experienced. And it had also done something else—it had made them arrogant and, worse, bored.

The Annunaki had the perspective of infinity, Brigid concluded, and so they played with lives, played a never-ending game where the rules must constantly change. But they were not unstoppable; she and Kane and the others had proved that, and others had found their way around the Annunaki, too. Brigid had met a group in Russia not so long ago who had hidden a doomsday weapon on a higher plane of human awareness, accessible only via transcendental meditation. It had been developed as one way to avoid an enemy who could read minds, and Brigid guessed there must be others, too. And if there were ways to avoid the Annunaki, to repel them, then there must be a way out of this chair, a way to overturn Ullikummis, to gain the upper hand. The secret must lie in memory,

Brigid told herself, for that was the only weapon that he could never take away from her. Wasn't it?

She closed her eyes once more, forced herself back to that storeroom where she stood looking at the shivering form of Reba DeFore.

Brigid remembered standing in the doorway, listening to her companion's horrified words. "He who?" she heard herself ask.

"THE STONE MAN," DeFore replied.

Crouched down before DeFore, Kane glanced up at Brigid, meeting her eyes with a significant look. They were *anam-charas,* Brigid and Kane—soul friends, destined to be together throughout time, their eternal souls reincarnated again and again, drawn together like magnets. Their shared bond was something that defied reason.

"Where is he now?" Kane probed gently, turning his attention back to the Cerberus medic. "Do you know?"

DeFore shook her head frantically, almost as though she was having a fit. "I don't… I don't…" she mumbled.

Kane reached out to her, held her gently by the shoulders to still her. "It's okay, Reba," he soothed. "We're here now. Everything's going to be fine."

"You can't stop him," DeFore spit, her eyes wide with fear. "I've never seen anything like him. He's… Nothing can stop him."

"Yeah, well," Kane said, "we'll see."

Standing beyond the door to the little storeroom, Grant turned back to his companions. "Company," he warned.

Automatically, Brigid checked the ammunition of the TP-9 semiautomatic, and Domi and Kane did the same with their own weapons.

Outside, Grant had pressed himself against the near

wall of the tunnellike corridor, the Sin Eater ready in his grip.

"What's going on?" Kane asked as he joined Brigid and Domi behind the broad-shouldered figure of Grant.

The hulking ex-Magistrate gestured down the corridor with his Sin Eater. The lights flickered and popped above them, illuminating this main artery sporadically. But as they looked, they saw a bolder rectangle of light was gradually expanding at the end of the tunnel. Someone was opening the accordion-style door that led out of the redoubt into the open air.

The Cerberus redoubt was located high in the Bitterroot Mountains in Montana. An ancient military facility, Cerberus had remained largely forgotten or ignored in the two centuries since the nukecaust. Indeed, over the years following that nuclear devastation, a curious mythology had grown up around the mountains, their dark, foreboding forests and seemingly bottomless ravines. The wilderness area surrounding the hidden redoubt was virtually unpopulated; the nearest settlement was to be found in the flatlands some miles away, and consisted of a small band of Native Americans, Sioux and Cheyenne, led by a shaman named Sky Dog.

Hidden beneath camouflage netting, tucked away within the rocky clefts of the mountains, concealed uplinks had chattered continuously with two orbiting satellites, working to provide much of the empirical data for the Cerberus staff. Gaining access to those satellites had taken long hours of intense trial-and-error work by many of the top scientists at the redoubt, but their persistence had given the Cerberus personnel a near limitless stream of feed data surveying the surface of the planet they had sworn to protect, as well as global communication links and the like. That was until the ops room had been all but destroyed under the devastating attack that Kane's team had stumbled upon less than fifteen minutes before.

Hidden away as it was, Cerberus required few active measures to discourage visitors. It was almost unheard-of for strangers to come to the main entry, a secure door located on a plateau high on the mountain. Instead, most people accessed the complex via one or other variation of the mat-trans system housed within the redoubt itself. To enter via the main door took arrogance and foolhardiness, especially with the security team that patrolled the surrounding area. Yet Brigid realized now that it was through the main access door that their mysterious enemies had entered. Impossible as it seemed, an army had walked right in.

As the distant door slowly rolled back, propelled by its whining hydraulic motor, figures became silhouetted against the sunlight beyond.

Chalk-skinned Domi muttered something to herself, slipping once more into the fractured Outland patois she used in times of stress. "Strangers at gate," she said. "Trouble."

"Stay sharp," Kane instructed, leading the way toward them on light feet.

The group followed him, hurrying along the wide corridor, keeping to the shadows as much as they were able, their movements silent. There was more blood splashed all over the floor, and several Cerberus personnel were lying dead, one of them with his skull caved in. Kane ignored them, his attention focused around him, using his fabled point man ability to stay alert to any threats. The intruders appeared to have all gathered at the end of the artery where several stairwells met. They seemed ignorant of the possibility of further resistance. Kane didn't trust that ignorance—it worried him that these interlopers were so confident in their mastery of the facility that they hadn't even bothered to post guards.

As they neared the end of the corridor, Kane and his team saw a large group of Cerberus personnel, held by the strangers in the hooded robes. They were all kneeling, hands behind their heads, now prisoners of the hooded strangers. No weapons were trained upon the prisoners, and yet it was clear that the Cerberus staff members were utterly defeated.

Kane scanned the group until he spotted Lakesh kneeling among them, a well-built man of medium height who appeared to be in his midfifties. The man's dusky face was bruised, and a trickle of dried blood could be seen below his aquiline nose. Lakesh held one hand to his head, as if in pain.

Behind him, Kane felt Domi tense, and he held his arm out like a bar, blocking her as she began to scamper ahead. "Wait, Domi," he whispered. "Let's not get crazy."

"Crazy's already here," Domi hissed, her crimson eyes flashing in the flickering illumination of the overhead lighting. "Didn't bring it, just going to fix it."

Grant stepped up behind the albino wild child, placing one immense hand on her shoulder with a gentleness that belied his strength. "Just play it cool for now, Domi," he told her.

For a moment, it seemed that she would react, unleashing the instinctive rage that simmered beneath the surface of her civilized personality. But she stopped herself, visibly relaxing, though the fierce anger was still clear in her face. Domi respected Grant, and had once harbored something of a crush on the man. Domi was different, and was never more aware of that than when she was among the Cerberus staff. But Grant had always treated her with respect, and even now she knew he was looking out for her.

"No point revealing ourselves too soon," he told her quietly.

After a moment, the albino girl nodded, dipping her head and stepping back into the shadows of the far wall, the Detonics Combat Master ready in her hand.

As Grant waited with Domi, Brigid sidled up to Kane, pressing her spine to the wall. Before them, the huge steel door was still rolling back on its hydraulic system, a slow and deliberate process. Brigid recoiled as she scanned the kneeling prisoners properly for the first time. Some had their heads bowed and several were slumped in such a way that they seemed to be barely clinging to life. Most wore the standard Cerberus white jumpsuit with a vertical blue zipper down the front, but for many the white was scuffed and dirtied now by the traumas they had evidently suffered. Several had obvious wounds, blood marring the torn material of their clothing.

Brigid recognized Donald Bry kneeling close to Lakesh, his mop of copper curls falling over his face as he bowed his head in weary defeat. There, too, was astrophysicist Brewster Philboyd, his lanky frame bent over uncomfortably as he knelt before the guardsmen. Just a few hours earlier, Brewster had been providing recon information for Brigid's field team via Commtact link; now he knelt in supplication before an enemy.

As Brigid's eyes flickered across the group, she felt a growing sense of helplessness at their plight. Here was Sela Sinclair, her face bruised and blood staining the front of her jumpsuit, her left wrist hanging limply at her side, clearly broken. Next to her was geologist Mariah Falk, tears silently streaming down her face as she knelt beside her colleagues.

But as Brigid scanned the group, she noted that there were people missing, too. She tried to ignore the awful thought nagging at her mind—that the others were dead.

Fifteen hooded guards wandered to and fro, patrolling a group made up of at least forty Cerberus personnel. Forty was two-thirds of the staff, Brigid realized. Behind them, sunlight streamed in as the main door shuddered to a standstill.

"So what do we do?" she whispered to Kane.

His steel-gray eyes shifted from the scene playing out before them to the gun in his hand, assessing their chances. He wanted to tell Brigid that they could take intruders—thanks to firepower and training and some innate ability or luck they seemed to possess—and yet he knew that the other Cerberus people had tried, and he himself had been stunned by the near invincibility that their hooded foes appeared to possess.

As Kane pondered their next move, the ground around them began to shake, and the rock walls seemed to rattle in place.

Grant stumbled away from the wall he stood by with Domi. "What th—?"

"Earthquake?" Domi suggested, though she didn't sound so sure. It would be the first time the Cerberus redoubt had been struck by such a thing.

Brigid's breath caught in her throat as she saw another figure looming just beyond the redoubt's wide entrance. It was the unmistakable figure of the would-be stone god, Ullikummis, the Annunaki prince she had met and challenged twice before.

As Ullikummis stood there, arms spread before him, pillars of stone emerged from the ground, clambering out of the soil at the redoubt's entrance like living things, twisting and spiraling upward as they stretched toward the sky. Each rough-sided pillar was four feet in diameter, and they seemed to surge out of the ground like launching missiles, kicking up dust as everything about them shook.

Brigid, Kane, Grant and Domi watched in astonishment as the pillars continued to grow, reaching higher than the top of the redoubt door, beyond where the Cerberus warriors could see. In their previous meeting in Tenth City, all four had witnessed Ullikummis's ability to somehow control stone, exhibiting a kind of psionic talent to command the rocks and stones about him. On that occasion, the stone-clad Annunaki had moved a wall into Brigid's path as she had tried to escape, drawing it from the ground like a gate.

Beyond the shaking pillars, Brigid saw the overcast skies, gray with rain-heavy clouds, and she spotted two fast-moving objects whip across the clouds, accompanied by the familiar sound of engines cutting through the air.

"They have the Mantas," Brigid stated, unable to suppress the shock in her voice.

The Mantas were sleek bronze aircraft with a wingspan of twenty yards and a body length of almost fifteen feet. They looked like the seagoing manta rays they were named for, and the beauty of their alien design was breathtaking, combining the principles of aerodynamics in a gleaming burnt-gold finish, streaking across the skies beyond the edge of the mountaintop redoubt. They appeared to be flattened wedges with graceful wings curving out from their bodies, an elongated hump in the center of the craft providing the only evidence of a cockpit. Finished in a coppery hue, the surface of each craft was decorated with curious geometric designs, elaborate cuneiform markings, swirling glyphs and cup-and-spiral symbols that covered the entire aircraft. Transatmospheric and subspace vehicles, the Mantas were used by the Cerberus team for long-range missions. They were alien vessels that had been left discarded on Earth for millennia and were discovered by Kane and Grant during one of their exploratory missions. But the twin crafts should have been safely stored in the redoubt's hangar. No one else should have been able to access and fly them. And yet here they were.

The Cerberus teammates watched as the two ships zipped through the air past the shuddering pillars, disappearing from view before looping back a few seconds later.

"They're running a surveillance pattern," Grant growled, watching the Mantas flit past the open door again.

"Keeping an eye out for stragglers, perhaps," Brigid proposed.

"No escape," Domi declared. "Stuck here."

Kane turned to the others. "Doesn't matter," he said, addressing Domi's point. "I was never one to run, and am not about to start now."

"We have to stop Ullikummis," Brigid stated, the words tumbling from her mouth in a rush. "Now. We have to do it now."

Kane's eyes were fixed on the spectacle outside as the stone pillars locked into place around the entrance, like iron bars on a prison window. "Yeah, but how?" he spit. "Answer me that, Baptiste, and I'll kiss your big, freaky memory mind."

"Stone, stone, stone," Brigid muttered as she reached for the possibilities in what Kane had just called her big, freaky memory mind. "There has to be something, some way to hurt him, put him out of commission."

"Come on, Brigid," Domi urged. It was clear she wanted to step in, to free Lakesh. She could barely stop moving, she was so keyed up.

Brigid went through a hundred options then, thinking of all the uses of stone, all the ways it could be shaped or moved. Stone masonry, hammers, heat, force… They had tried force, had even subjected the monster's body to the incredible high temperatures of a furnace. But Ullikummis had survived, had brushed off their attacks.

"Erosion," Brigid said. "If we could erode his body…"

Kane glared at the red-haired archivist. "Isn't that going to take—what?—a thousand years?!"

"Acid," Brigid said, realization dawning. "If we could get to the lab, grab some hydrochloric acid…"

Kane glanced back at her. "Would that work? Explain it to me."

"Hydrochloric acid is corrosive," Brigid told her companions. "They used to use it in oil production, making solid rock porous so that wells could be placed and drilling could begin. In theory, it could make Ullikummis's flesh porous—full of holes," she clarified as Domi looked at her with confusion, "eroding him so that we could potentially wound him somehow."

Kane turned back to the redoubt entrance. The immense figure of Ullikummis still stood there, arms outstretched as he willed the colossal pillars into place around the open doorway. Kane could sense the simmering fury from Domi as she watched her lover and his dream suffer this final indignity. Kane knew he needed to keep the albino warrior, sometimes a loose cannon, busy or she'd bring trouble down on all of them.

"See what you can find in the labs, Baptiste," Kane instructed. "Domi—go with her. Grant and I will go to the armory and grab ourselves some serious firepower."

Brigid knew better than to argue. She was already turning, sprinting down the corridor away from the redoubt entrance, heading for the nearest stairwell, with Domi at her heels. Domi's bare feet slapped in the pooling blood that washed over the floor of the tunnel like a scarlet lake.

BRIGID WAS SUDDENLY PULLED out of her reverie by a low scraping noise coming from behind her in the cave. Her eyes sprang open and she automatically turned her head, momentarily forgetting that she was trapped in her chair. In annoyance, she faced front again, gazing into the mirror, eyes frantically searching the darkness behind her in the reflection. She could see nothing there.

For a moment all was silent, and she wondered if she had imagined the noise, frightened herself the way one can when dropping off to sleep.

Then it came again, the sound of heavy dragging, of stone on stone. Brigid's heart beat quicker in her chest and she felt it thumping against her rib cage. There was nothing in the mirror, nothing but her face, her cloud of red hair obscuring the darkness beyond.

Then the voice rumbled in the darkness, from behind Brigid and all around her, its rumbling echo swirling through the enclosed space of the cavern.

"A picture," Ullikummis said, "with no more depth than the surface of a blade of grass."

Chapter 10

Alone once more in his cavern-like cell, Kane pressed himself against the place where the doorway had been, and felt for the edges that he knew must be there—but they weren't. He had seen the wall move aside with his own eyes, parting like water. There had to be a gap there, a seam, a hint of the door he had seen. There just had to be.

He peered into the darkness, struggling to make out the details of rocky surface before him. His mouth was dry, that taste of moldy food somewhere in the back of his throat.

Kane stood, running his fingers slowly across the rough surface of the rock, feeling for the tiniest seam that would prove to him where the door was located. He pressed against the wall with his fingertips, ran the edges of his nails across every tiny bump, but still there was nothing there, still the wall insisted on staying just a wall, with no evidence that a door had ever existed.

Kane continued to check systematically as he had been taught as a Magistrate. Licking his finger despite the dryness of his mouth, he ran his hand up and down, feeling for a draft. There was none. He put his palms against the wall and pushed at it, then tried with his shoulder, levering all his weight to try to achieve some kind of movement, feel the wall give just a little where he knew the door had to be. He pushed at it, gripped the rough stone and pulled at it, punched it, kicked it. Finally, he shouted and swore at it, reason finally giving way to frustration. And every single time it remained what it had always been—a solid wall.

Finally, the ex-Mag sat down on the unforgiving rock floor and leaned his back against the wall, his breathing heavy, his frustration eating at him. And after a while, he lay down on the hard floor and slept, for there was nothing else left to do.

The horror replayed itself in his dreams, and Kane relived the moment when he had come face-to-face with the stone man, whose glowing eyes bored into him through the curtain of sleep.

KANE HAD BEEN STANDING against the solid wall of the redoubt's main corridor, Grant just a few feet behind him.

"That's our stone god, all right," Grant muttered as they watched Ullikummis stride back into the redoubt through the open door, the pillars of rock sealing the great door beyond.

Kane's body yearned for action; he could feel the tension rippling through him. They had both been in a tense combat situation not five minutes before, with adrenaline pumping. Now Kane felt a wave of weariness run through him. He needed action, needed to keep going; this stop-start approach was the way that errors arose.

Kane turned, sending the Sin Eater back to its hidden holster beneath the sleeve of his jacket. "Back up," he said to Grant, "and we'll use the emergency stairs to get to the armory."

Grant didn't argue. The big man simply turned and paced back down the tunnel on silent feet. As they got farther from the activity, he ducked around the corner of a service corridor and pushed at the door that led to the stairs.

The stairwell was lit in dull red emergency lighting that drew in the edges of the stairs along thin, reflective strips. Grant turned to his partner as they hurried down the steps. "You got to figure they already know we're here, Kane," he said, keeping his voice low.

Kane cocked his head in silent query as he followed the big man.

"We've gone through eight of their number in the ops room," Grant rationalized. "They'll know they're missing."

"This is an assault force," Kane reasoned, taking the stairs two at a time and grabbing the railing. "They'll expect some losses. Domi was hidden away in the vents when we got here—they must be expecting more resistance than just one albino girl."

"Which means if they follow protocol they'll go through the redoubt with a mop-up squad pretty soon," Grant growled.

"Magistrate protocol," Kane reminded him. "And these sure as fuck aren't Magistrates."

"So what the hell are they?" Grant rumbled as he came to a stop before the door to the lower level.

Kane pushed a hand through his hair as he thought, trying to piece it all together. This wasn't something that had happened in the past few hours, he knew. It was something that had been building for months. Indeed, it had been building for centuries; what they were looking at now—the hooded warriors, or altered humans—was the culmination of some millennia-old feud between their Annunaki enemies. Ever since Ullikummis had arrived and set his claim on the Earth as his private battleground, this whole attack had been coming.

Grant pulled the heavy fire door open just a crack and peered out into the corridor beyond. The overhead lighting winked on and off erratically as Grant scanned the area. There was water pooled along one wall where a fire hose had been yanked from its housings, but other than that the corridor seemed pretty much empty. He turned back to Kane for a second, brushing his finger to his nose in the one percent salute, their personal acknowledgment that the odds were stacked heavily against them.

Then he led the way into the flickering shadows of the corridor, with Kane following a wary distance behind, checking over his shoulder to ensure they were not being followed. A few moments later, Grant had reached the security doors of the redoubt's armory. The doors were sealed and Grant tapped in the entry code on the keypad as Kane caught up to him. Together, they heard the click as the doors unlocked. But they didn't open. Grant placed his palm against the flat surface of the left door and shoved.

"Jammed," he growled, turning to Kane with a querulous look. "Something's messed up the mechanism. We could probably bust in…. Make a bit of noise, though."

Kane considered this for a few seconds, glancing down the length of the corridor to check again that no one had followed them. "It's not the noise, it's the time it will take."

Then Kane engaged his Commtact. "Baptiste?" he said quietly into the hidden receiver. "How long before you guys get back?"

For a moment there was no response, then Brigid's familiar tones came through over both their receiver units, sounding breathless as it was piped directly through their mastoid bones. "Ran into a bit of…trouble," she exclaimed. "Might be…a few minutes."

Kane could hear the determined struggle in Brigid's voice. "Everything all right?" he asked.

TWO FLOORS ABOVE, Brigid and Domi were dodging a hail of stones as they hurried through the laboratory area. All about them, glass containers were shattering, their contents spilling across the room as the stones struck them.

"Nothing we can't handle, Kane," Brigid replied over the Commtact, even as she struggled to outrun a swarm of stones that raced through the air toward her. She slid across a cluttered desk as one of the hooded intruders lobbed a flat pebble at her, the stone skimming across the neighboring desk as it hurtled toward her. A second later, she dropped over the far side, her red hair sweeping above her like a candle flame before she disappeared behind the desk. She watched as the stone clattered onward, smashing into the far wall, where its fearsome momentum was finally spent.

Kane's voice came to her again over the Commtact. "What's going on up there?" he asked, the concern clear in his tone.

"Found us a few more playmates," Brigid explained, reloading her TP-9 as she crouched behind the desk. "Hooded types, nothing new."

"Damn, it's an infestation," she heard Kane snarl before he broke radio contact.

Brigid was inclined to agree. They couldn't seem to move twenty feet without meeting another bunch of the hooded intruders.

Brigid shoved the ammunition clip home and glanced up over the edge of the desk, even as Domi drilled another of the hooded strangers in the face with a bullet from her Combat Master. The man fell, dropping a handful of stones as he crashed to the floor.

Then Domi ducked down behind a workstation beside Brigid, holding her hand over her head as a glass beaker exploded above them both. "I count two more," she said, her voice anxious.

"Me, too," Brigid said, and she glanced over to the doorway that led to a separate research room. Shadows flickered across the open doorway as figures moved beyond. "Maybe more—look."

Domi followed where Brigid indicated, saw something move in the next room. "What's in there?" she asked. "You know?" Domi wasn't an intellectual and didn't frequent the research area except when she was accompanying Lakesh, Brigid knew.

"It's a self-contained research area," Brigid explained. "Small, built for separate projects like...*shit!*"

Brigid was on her feet, hurrying across the room once more, even as a clutch of flying stones rattled against the walls.

Domi leaped up, about to follow her companion, when a stone smashed into the computer terminal at her back. The albino woman jumped aside, rolling out of its way as the monitor fell from the desk with the impact. "Brigid!" she called.

"Cover me," her teammate shouted back, not bothering to turn as she timed her run around another stone whipping past her.

Domi propped herself up on the floor, keeping low as she pumped shot after shot at the two savage intruders. She might not be able to drop them, but she sure as hell could slow them down.

"Ullikummis came back to Earth to kill his father," Kane recalled as he and Grant stood in the lower corridor of the Cerberus redoubt.

"Overlord Enlil," Grant clarified bitterly, striking his fist against the sealed door of the armory. "Remind me why we'd stand in the way of that."

"The Annunaki have always used the tools around them to wage their wars," Kane said. "Sure, they'll get their claws dirty for the endgame, but these pseudogods like to play all the pieces before that happens."

Grant looked up from the door impatiently as the strip lights flickered overhead.

"The pieces being us," Kane clarified. "Humans."

"And the stone tossers?" Grant queried.

"Somehow, Ullikummis has drafted his army from the human stock here on Earth," Kane said. "Those were people once. Normal people, with normal lives. You remember the farmers out in Saskatchewan?"

Grant nodded, recalling the strange stone construction called Tenth City by its founder, Ullikummis.

"They acted like they were possessed," Kane said. "They did their master's bidding, killed each other and themselves at his whim."

"I thought we established that that was the architecture," Grant said, "making them do shit they didn't want to. A'sigil'—isn't that what Lakesh had called the design? Some kind of magical symbol capable of influencing a person's mood and willpower."

Kane rested his back against the hard wall of the corridor, sighing loudly as the lights flickered and buzzed overhead. "The Annunaki never play just one trick," he said. "They've always kept ten plates spinning in the air at the same time, for as long as we've been in this hidden war with them."

"You're talking about Enlil, though," Grant said.

"Enlil, Marduk, Lilitu…" Kane reeled off the names of the overlords like curse words. "They've all been doing it, every last one of those snake-faces has demonstrated two backup schemes to every one that we've rumbled. And Ullikummis—the crown prince of the whole accursed line—he's inherited all those traits. He's followed in his father's footsteps, taking every devious trick of his daddy's and twisting it one turn more in an effort to ensure his victory."

"So, these people aren't being controlled by sigils?" Grant asked, starting to see Kane's point. As he spoke, he worked at the doors, pressing the heel of his hand at the seal to try to make the lock give.

Kane shrugged. "Maybe they are and maybe they're not, but I'll bet you there's more to it," he said.

Grant stepped away from the armory door and shook his head. "We need tools to get in here, Kane," he admitted gravely. "Or I can try to force it."

Kane nodded, his brow furrowed in vexation. "Dammit, everything's stacked against us today."

With a frustrated moan, Grant struck the edge of one door with his fist, denting it with a single brutal blow. "Then let's provide our people with the best backup we can," he growled.

The door had buckled just slightly, adjacent to the lock, but it was enough that Grant could get a small handhold and pull. He jammed his hand into that buckled spot and yanked hard. In a moment, the door slid back on its track, rocking along about six inches before coming to an abrupt halt.

Grant peered at the top of the door frame, where the tracks to the door were located, narrowing his eyes as the overhead lights flickered on and off. "There's some crap blocking the door," he growled, reaching up and running a finger along the inset track. "Looks like…silt?"

Kane stepped closer, peering at the track and running

his index finger along the track just as Grant had. A powdery dust dropped from the track, and Kane saw that some of it had caught under his fingernail. He cursed. "That's silt, all right," he agreed. "What the hell is happening here?"

Leaning down, Grant put both hands against the door and shoved, forcing it another four inches along its clogged track. "It's all connected," he growled. "That much is obvious."

Beyond Grant, lights flickered on in the armory as the doorway became wider. The gap was now almost a foot across, and Kane judged he could just about edge through it, even if his wide-shouldered partner might struggle.

"Stay here," Kane instructed, pushing himself through the doorway. "And keep watch," he added solemnly, as he made his way into the armory. "Lots of stuff going on here we don't have a handle on yet, and I don't want any of it sneaking the heck up on me."

Grant nodded. "Me, either," he muttered, reaching for the Sin Eater as he scanned the empty corridor beneath the flickering lights.

Two FLOORS ABOVE, Brigid vaulted over a desk and careened through the open doorway into the research room. There were four figures inside, and she raised her TP-9 instantly, choosing targets. Three of the figures were dressed in the fustian robes she recognized from the other intruders, and one had the hood down to reveal a woman's long, dark hair. Bizarrely, a midsize dog was sniffing around the room, some kind of mongrel with some coyote in it. While the dog sniffed at something spilled on the floor, the three intruders surrounded a fourth figure, a man of average build, brown hair and eyes. Right now, he was fending off the attackers with a flat-head screwdriver, wielding it like a dagger as he rolled a swivel chair across the floor before him. The action with the chair reminded Brigid a little of an old-fashioned lion tamer, holding the beasts at bay in a near comical manner.

"Keep back," the man ordered, panic in his voice. "I'm warning you."

It was Daryl Morganstern, a theoretical mathematician from Cerberus who had collaborated with Brigid on a recent project to refine the operational parameters of the interphaser. Broken instruments littered the worktops beside a deconstructed replica of the interphaser.

Brigid snapped off a burst of shots even as she ran at the hooded intruders. As one, the three strangers turned, identifying Brigid as the greater threat.

"Daryl?" Brigid shouted over the sound of her gunfire. "What's happened? Are you—?"

"Brigid? Is that you?" Daryl asked incredulously, swinging to face her.

Even as he turned, Brigid knew it was a mistake. Time seemed to slow down as the female intruder kicked out toward Morganstern, her right foot slapping against the seat of the chair, as she vaulted over it, to deliver a savage kick to the man's face. Daryl went hurtling backward, toppling over himself as he crashed into the desk behind him and smashed the replica interphaser into pieces. The dark-haired woman landed beside him, sweeping her hand out and knocking Daryl's screwdriver weapon aside.

Brigid recognized the woman, knew her for a deadly mercenary from their meeting months ago in Hope. Rosalia.

In a second, Brigid shifted her aim, spraying bullets in Rosalia's direction. Exceptionally fast, the dark-haired woman leaped aside, ducking down to the floor even as one of her hooded companions readied a slingshot and launched a stone at Brigid's face.

Brigid dodged the hurtling missile, feeling the passage of wind as it whizzed by her face. "Come on, Daryl," she instructed, "we're getting out of here."

The dog barked somewhere in the room as another stone flew at Brigid from behind, too fast for her to fully avoid. As the stone struck the back of her rib cage, she gasped and stumbled forward even though her shadow suit took the brunt of the blow. A moment later she was with Daryl, the theoretical mathematician looking woozy as she grabbed him by the wrist.

"What's…?" Daryl began.

Brigid sprayed the room with bullets, forcing her opponents to duck for cover. "Cerberus is under attack," she explained. "We just stumbled into it."

"I was w-working alone up here," Daryl stuttered. "Didn't hear any alarm or…"

Brigid glanced across the room, searching for the slender form of Rosalia, but the woman had disappeared, finding some hiding place as bullets and stones hurtled across the room.

Awkward and disoriented, Daryl Morganstern was trying to keep up with Brigid as she hurried him out the door, spraying a burst of 9 mm bullets in their wake.

"What about the interphaser?" Morganstern asked. "I'd figured a way we might circumvent the Parallax Point system by—"

Brigid gave him a no-nonsense look. "Not now."

With his tousled brown hair and sweet smile, there was something of the puppy dog to Daryl, and Brigid hated seeing him in this situation. He was a mathematician, not a soldier, and he was obviously bewildered and out of his depth. Despite the clear danger all around, the poor guy couldn't help but be enthusiastic about his latest theory. Like Brigid, he had an exceptional, near-perfect memory, and that shared trait had brought them together on recent occasions. Right now, however, Brigid knew Daryl would lose that incredible memory if he didn't—

"Get down!"

Even as she gave the order, a spinning stone came whirring at Daryl's head from the main lab, cutting the air with a whine. Brigid shoved Daryl in the shoulder as she gave her command, and he toppled just out of the path of the careening hunk of rock.

A little way across the room, the alabaster form of Domi acknowledged Brigid with a single raised hand, her Combat Master blazing.

"Brigid, let's get moving," she yelled over the ferocious sounds of gunfire and hurtling stones.

Brigid saw now that three more hooded figures had entered the lab, pinning Domi down and blocking their exit. She turned to Daryl, shoving her TP-9 semiautomatic into his hands. "We came up here to grab some hydrochloric acid," she explained. "I'm going to get a batch from that cupboard. Cover me."

"Cover you?" Daryl replied, his voice high with astonishment. "I can't… Brigid, I'm not…"

"Just do it," she told him firmly as she leaped out from cover and streaked across the lab toward a glass-fronted storage cupboard. As she ran, Daryl Morganstern did his best to cover her, blasting bursts of fire at her would-be attackers.

Domi tracked Brigid, too, and saw the red-haired archivist come to a halt at the cupboard, pulling at the door. "Come on, Brigid," she urged from her position behind one of the lab benches. The bench had a built-in basin, and the faucet pipe was spraying water into the air where one of the hurtling stone projectiles had smashed it from its housing.

Brigid pulled at the cupboard's twin handles, only to find it was locked. Behind the glass doors, she could see four tall vials of the clear liquid she was after, red rubber stoppers at their tops. *Typical,* she thought as she turned back to look around at the destruction the battle had caused. Everything else was smashed, but the glass panels of this locked cupboard had somehow remained unscathed. She needed something to break the glass, she thought, bunching her fist. She knew Kane would smash it with his hand, but some instinct stopped her from doing so.

Domi was leaping across one of the desks, spinning in midair to avoid a thrown rock, picking off another of the hooded strangers with a booming blast from her pistol. "Come on, Brigid," she urged. "I can't keep running interference!"

Brigid looked at her partner in desperation. "It's locked," she explained. "I need to find something to open the—"

Domi landed on one of the worktops as Daryl's bullets whizzed through the air, and she targeted the cupboard with her Detonics Combat Master. "Get back," she advised, unleashing a single shot at the cupboard door.

Brigid ducked as, above her, Domi's bullet drilled between the double doors of the cupboard, splitting the wood and destroying the simple brass lock. Brigid winced as she heard something shatter inside. When she looked up again, the center of the cupboard where the doors met now featured a gaping hole of splintered wood, the buckled lock hanging amid the debris. She didn't see the hooded figure edging along the wall, weaving out of the way of debris as Domi did her best to hold the other intruders at bay.

Brigid pulled at the doors as, behind her, the battle raged. Inside the cupboard, one of the four vials had shattered where Domi's bullet had cut through it, and the hydrochloric acid was smoldering, a low hiss emanating from the dripping pool that had formed on the shelf where the container had stood. The liquid looked innocuous enough, clear as water or vodka, yet this was a reminder to Brigid of just how dangerous it could be when it came into contact with any surface.

She grabbed two of the remaining containers by their tapered necks, glancing around for something to carry them with.

Across the lab, Daryl Morganstern saw Brigid struggle, in need of an extra pair of hands. Head down, he rushed as fast as he could across the lab, even as tossed stones pelted all around him. Five feet away from Brigid, he pulled himself up to his full height and smiled. "Need a hand, pretty lady?" he asked.

Relieved, Brigid began to answer just as something came flying through the air between them. In an instant, Daryl Morganstern's cheery face erupted in a wash of blood as the stone struck him, smashing a gaping hole in his left temple.

As he staggered backward and crashed to the floor, the robed figure that had been sneaking toward Brigid leaped at her, driving a brutal punch into her face.

Chapter 11

Brigid spun on her heel, turning to face the hooded figure rushing toward her and Daryl. Dressed like the others in a heavy, shapeless robe, the tall man was running at her, launching a flat stone with a graceful flip of his wrist so that it spun through the air. Brigid dodged as the missile flew at her face and felt it cut the air just inches from her hair.

In a moment, the man was upon her, driving a flat-palmed strike at Brigid's cheek. She dodged once more, taking the glancing blow and forcing her attacker to over-reach. As he did so he stumbled forward, misjudging his balance with Brigid's rapid, evasive step.

Unarmed, she drove down with both hands, powering her fists into the man's reaching arm and knocking it against the nearest worktop. The man made no noise as he struck the desk, simply turned to Brigid and fixed her with a haughty look.

"I am stone," the hooded figure stated, his other arm swinging up to slap Brigid away.

She felt the blow to her chest, grunted as she stumbled backward across the lab and crashed into the ruined door of the cupboard.

Across the room, Domi was ducking and weaving as three of the hooded figures tried to pin her down, and her Combat Master boomed repeatedly as she fought to get free.

"Get away from me," the albino girl snarled, jabbing the barrel of her pistol into her nearest attacker and unleashing a burst of bullets into his face. The assailant dropped to the floor, knocking over a display of filtration equipment as he fell.

At the cupboard, disorientation gripped Brigid for an instant and she struggled to find her bearings as her own attacker ran toward her. The man had pulled another flat stone, roughly the size of a saucer, from somewhere beneath his voluminous robes, and his hand swept in an arc as he launched it. The disk-shaped missile cleaved the air, rushing toward Brigid Baptiste.

Unable to get out of its path at such close range, she turned away, letting the flat stone strike against her back, where the remarkable weave of her shadow suit could take the brunt of the impact. Then she reached out, grabbing the remaining flask of acid from its shelf. She felt the weight of the wide-bottomed glass beaker as she turned back to face her onrushing attacker. Then she hurled it, watching as it flipped end over end at her approaching foe. Brigid turned away as the hydrochloric acid struck the man, the glass shattering as the beaker slammed into him.

The sharp stench was immediate, searing Brigid's eyes and irritating her tear ducts. Then the man began to scream, and Brigid looked up to see him dancing in place, his robe smoldering with the burning effect of the acid. She felt a wave of nausea as he clawed at his hood, pushing it backward to reveal the terrible damage that the acid was inflicting to his face.

Brigid ignored his pained cries, turning her attention instead to the figure lying on the floor at her feet—Daryl Morganstern. Another wave of stones rattled against the wall behind her as, tenderly, Brigid leaned down and stroked a hand through the man's hair.

"Daryl?" she asked. "Daryl, are you—?"

Daryl Morganstern lay there, blood seeping from the thick cut at his skull. As Brigid brushed the matted hair away from the terrible gash in his head, she saw his eyes flicker, and he looked up at her, his dimples showing as he broke into a smile.

"I think something hit me," he said, stating the obvious, "but I don't remember what."

"It's okay," Brigid murmured soothingly. "We'll get you out of here in a minute. Just relax."

Reaching over Daryl's fallen body, she grabbed the TP-9, taking the weapon from his limp grasp. Then she was crouching, looking about her at the shattered remains of equipment that littered the lab, until she found what she wanted. A glass cabinet stood on the wall by the door, firefighting equipment inside in compliance with the standard safety precautions for any U.S. government laboratory dating back to the twentieth century, when this redoubt had been constructed. Brigid hurried across to it with a swift clatter of her heeled boots, ignoring the clutch of hurtling stones that peppered the walls before her like bullets.

Then she was at the cabinet, and swiftly reversed the TP-9, using the base of the grip to break the glass. Careful to avoid cutting her hand on the shards that remained, she reached inside and snagged the fire blanket that was stored within. It was made of some heavy gray weave and was clipped to the back of the cabinet next to the familiar red cylinder of a fire extinguisher. As she snagged the blanket, one of the two remaining attackers—for Domi appeared to have dispatched the others in her own inimitable way—staggered toward Brigid, arms outstretched.

She ducked as the man grasped for her, and she threw the blanket at him. The dense cloth fell over the man's face, momentarily blinding him. Brigid didn't hesitate. Her free hand was already inside the cabinet, grabbing the fire extinguisher and half swinging, half tossing it at her opponent. The heavy extinguisher smacked against the man's head beneath the gray blanket, striking with a hollow clang.

Brigid watched as he fell backward, crashing to the floor. Then she reached down, unleashing a burst from her semiautomatic into the man's gut even as she pulled the blanket from him like some perverse mockery of the magician with the tablecloth. Beneath the blanket, the man's eyes had lost their focus, the savage blow to his head rendering him a simpleton.

Nearby, Domi had one arm hooked over a hanging light fixture, a strip lamp dangling from twin chains. From that vantage point she picked off the last of their attackers, her pistol blazing as she peppered the woman with bullets. With a flurry of her robes, the intruder finally fell, smashing to the ground with all the grace of a tranquilized rhino.

"Brigid," Domi called, "we need to get moving before they start waking up."

Brigid acknowledged that with a silent nod as she hurried back to Daryl, the fire blanket in her left hand. She skidded to a stop before him, then, leaning down, placed the blanket over his chest, turning it upward until it curled around his head like a wisp of smoke.

"Press here," she instructed, pushing one corner of the blanket against the deep gash that marred his forehead.

"Christ, that hurts," Daryl screeched as he held the blanket as he had been instructed.

Brigid fixed him with a sympathetic look. "We have

to go. Keep warm and try to get somewhere safe," she instructed.

"Like where?" Daryl asked, wincing at the pain in his head.

Brigid leaned down and kissed him tenderly on the mouth, her lips barely brushing against his. "Daryl, I always admired you because you could think for yourself," she reminded him in a whisper, feeling the stubble of his barely forming beard against her face. "Now's not the best time to lose that trait."

Then she straightened up, grasping one of the two remaining flasks of hydrochloric acid, while Domi picked up the other. In a moment, the two women were gone from the lab.

SEVERAL FLOORS BELOW, Kane was hurrying from the armory, making his way back to the door that Grant had forced open. In the light of the flickering overhead bulbs, Kane could see aisles lined with shelves, each filled with a multitude of ordnance, everything from combat knives to antitank missiles and dragon launchers. Kane had considered the heavier equipment, his hands playing over a pair of dragon launchers for a moment before he remembered Lakesh and the others being held captive close to the redoubt exit. While it was tempting to employ the most powerful weaponry against Ullikummis, the risk of a stray shot was too great, and the damage it could bring if used inside was beyond comprehension. Instead, Kane had plucked two Copperhead assault rifles from the shelves, grumbling under his breath about lousy half-baked measures.

A favored weapon of Grant, the Copperhead subgun was almost two feet in length, with its grip and trigger placed in front of the breech in the bullpup design, allowing the gun to be used single-handedly. The weapon featured an image-intensified optical scope coupled with a laser autotargeter mounted atop the frame. The Copperhead possessed a 700-round-per-minute rate of fire and was equipped with an extended magazine holding thirty-five 4.85 mm steel-jacketed rounds. Grant preferred the Copperhead as a field weapon thanks to its ease of use and the sheer amount of destruction it could create in short measure. It seemed to Kane that creating a high level of destruction was pretty much the order of the day if they were to face down the maleficent would-be god.

Taking one last regretful look back at the armory's contents, Kane turned sideways and pushed himself back out into the corridor, through the tight gap of the jammed door.

"Here," he said, handing one of the subguns to Grant, along with several cases of spare ammunition that he had picked up at the same time. "An old favorite."

Grant took the Copperhead, checking the breech with practiced ease. "Thanks," he said. "Nothing bigger in there?"

"Plenty bigger," Kane admitted, "but nothing I want to use in such close quarters to our friends. These are plenty powerful, and if they should find themselves in the wrong hands, at least it won't end with the whole redoubt falling down around our ears."

Grant nodded in agreement. "Makes sense, but don't expect me to be happy about it," he growled as Kane led the way back down the corridor.

Kane turned back to him. "Baptiste's is the main show, just now," he reminded his partner. "We're just the backup for once she's done her thing."

"Yeah, but what kind of backup are we going to provide?" Grant grumbled as he followed Kane along the tunnel toward the stairwell.

"Whatever we can," he answered. "We're all that's left now."

Striding along with Kane, Grant picked up where they had left off before his partner had disappeared into the armory. "So, you think there's more to all this? Ullikummis's attacking here, I mean. How much more?" he asked as he ducked back into the stairwell, the Copperhead ready in his hands.

"Perhaps Ullikummis is manipulating us, too," Kane said uncertainly. "I can't see why he'd break in here otherwise."

"And this is a big operation," Grant agreed with a nod. "He's here for something, all right. That armory didn't seal itself up, and you saw the shit he was bringing down outside."

"The only thing Cerberus has that this wannabe god would need is people," Kane said. "He's recruited his army, and they're…well, *invincible* is too strong a word, but they're damn tough."

"What about our satellites?" Grant suggested. "Our tech?"

"His people smashed up the control room," Kane reminded his partner. "Not the actions of a salvage crew. Even the Millennialists have the sense to leave that kind of stuff intact," he added, referring to their on-off competitors, the Millennial Consortium.

Grant nodded, feeling his gut tighten as he followed Kane's reasoning. "So, what do our people have that the big man couldn't get elsewhere?"

"Knowledge," Kane stated. "We've fought Enlil to a standstill before now and...*shit!*"

"What is it?" Grant asked as frustration crossed Kane's face.

"Ninlil," he said, realization finally dawning.

"Enlil's wife?" Grant blurted, keeping his voice low as he hurried after Kane up the stairs, the red emergency lights casting their eerie glow.

"Ullikummis's mother," Kane stated solemnly, "Ninlil."

Kane slowed as he reached the turn in the stairwell, glancing ahead to check for enemies before he continued up to the next level. "Ninlil was reborn as a hybrid child," he mused as Grant followed him up the tight service stairs. "She was taken by Balam for safekeeping, hidden where she could not be disturbed by the Annunaki."

"Or us," Grant reminded his partner.

Kane nodded slowly. "That's not quite true, though, is it?" he said. "Balam trusts us, at least more so than he does Ullikummis's father or the other overlords. So, if it came down to it, he'd hand the child over to Cerberus."

"Ullikummis is here for his reborn mother...?" Grant asked, unable to keep the surprise out of his voice.

"It's just speculation," Kane said, "but it's the only thing I can think of that we've got that he'd want."

"Hmm. What do you get for the god who has everything?" Grant muttered rhetorically as they reached the next level of the stairwell.

"Even if Ullikummis knew where she was," Kane speculated, "Balam would never hand her over, not willingly. He'd kill her before that could happen. But for Cerberus...he just might bend the rules."

"Yeah, he just might," Grant agreed as the two ex-

Magistrates eased their way out onto the ground level of the redoubt, where the rollback doors waited at the end of the corridor. "And you think that's why he's attacked us? To get to Balam?"

"To take control of the operation," Kane said, stopping in the feeder corridor, where a survival locker sat in a recess, metal door glinting beneath the flickering overhead lights. Similar lockers were dotted all about the redoubt, and they featured a simple first-aid kit, signal flares and a foghorn-style alarm that functioned via a canister of pressurized air to let out a shriek until such time as the gas ran out. It was typical military thinking, health and safety insisting the kits be uniform in their contents. The horn was ideal for attracting attention if your lost ship got lost in a storm, but useless for much else, especially in the middle of an underground redoubt. Still, some bright spark had decided all the lockers would be fitted with them, so there they were, gathering dust.

"The Annunaki," Kane continued, "control people. Their whole shtick is the subjugation of others. They never cared about material things—it's always people's emotions they want. They fight for territories just so they can brag about how many people bow down to worship them.

"Ullikummis doesn't care about the Cerberus operation," Kane continued, "that's like caring about the web when the spider's about to bite you. What he cares about is the people, the minds we have here. What he wants is us."

Grant looked at his partner beneath the flickering lighting of the corridor, and Kane saw the smile appear on his lips.

"What?" Kane asked.

"It's just ironic," Grant admitted. "After all this time,

all these millennia trying to stifle our free will, one of the Annunaki has come to us because we're not all interchangeable, after all."

"He's come to us as a means to an end," Kane growled, "and I don't think he's going to ask nicely."

"Make book on that," Grant agreed.

Across from the service tunnel where Grant and Kane were holding their hushed discussion, twin doors burst open and a hooded figure came hurtling through, followed momentarily by a second figure in similar garb. They crashed to the floor, arms sprawled beneath them. Before Kane or Grant could react, the doors crashed open a second time and the lightning-white figure of Domi came leaping through, her chrome-plated pistol blazing as she hurtled through the air. Domi's bullets peppered the floor around the fallen figures, kicking up chunks of stone and splatters of the pooled blood that lay there.

She landed in a halfcrouch before her foes, blasting another shot from her Detonics Combat Master as the first man tried to get off the floor. "Stay down!" she ordered, drilling a bullet into his face.

Then she was turning, her crimson eyes peering down the tunnel toward the far doors, searching for Kane and Grant. "Kane," Domi shouted, "we have company. Where are you?"

"Right here," he said, hurrying out from cover, with Grant just two steps behind him.

Domi shoved the muzzle of her pistol into the second hooded figure's face and snapped off a shot at point-blank range. The man's head jerked back and he sank to the ground.

"Where's Baptiste?" Kane asked as he hurried across the wide corridor, bringing the Copperhead to bear on Domi's attackers.

As if in answer, the stairwell doors burst open again and Brigid Baptiste came running through them, a wide-bottomed glass flask clutched under her arm. Her TP-9 pistol was held in her free hand, blasting a steady stream of fire behind her.

At the far end of the tunnel, shrill voices could be heard rising in alarm, and Kane turned to see what was happening. There, from the direction of the rollback doors, Ullikummis's group of hooded servants in their fustian robes were sprinting toward them, followed slowly by the great stone giant himself. Ullikummis strode with firm steps as his people ran ahead of him like dwarves.

This was it, Kane realized. Do or die.

Chapter 12

Kane stared at the container Brigid held beneath her arm. Made from clear glass, it was about the height of a family-size soft-drink bottle, with a wide bottom and straight sides tapering to a spout. The mouth was sealed with a red rubber cork. The vessel looked empty at first glance, but Kane noticed the line of distortion near the top and realized a clear liquid was swishing about within: hydrochloric acid.

"That it?" Kane asked, gesturing at the bottle.

Brigid spun back, facing the stairwell door as three more hooded figures charged through toward her. As they ran at her she unloaded a clip of bullets at them, spraying the figures and the door behind them with 9 mm slugs. Bringing his Copperhead to bear, Kane added his own blaster fire to her attack, a rapid expulsion of bullets ripping into the interlopers. Behind Kane, Grant was busy assisting Domi with the two who had preceded Brigid from the stairs, the fierce boom of his own Copperhead echoing in the confined space of the tunnel.

Breathless, Brigid turned to Kane as the robed figures crashed to the floor amid the hail of bullets. "We were ambushed, Kane," she explained. "Found four containers in the lab, but we had to use two on the attackers. Damned effective against them, too, but..." She stopped, repulsed by the memory of the damage she and Domi had been forced to inflict.

"And the third?" Kane asked, glancing across to Domi as she picked herself up from the floor to join him. Behind her, Grant drove the heel of his boot into the hooded head of one of the initial attackers, driving his jaw into the floor with finality, the Copperhead subgun booming in the struggling figure's face.

"Shattered," Brigid explained.

Kane gulped. "You okay? Is Domi…?"

"I got out the way," Brigid said, and Kane got the impression she would rather leave the comment at that.

One of the hooded figures Brigid had just felled was struggling up off the tunnel floor, pulling himself slowly erect in the manner of a wounded insect, all flailing movement with no logic. Kane saw that the man's face looked old and was bleached white where acid had been thrown at him, his skin puckered and wounded. Brigid and Domi had been busy whittling these people down, he realized with a rising sense of disgust.

Kane drew his Copperhead up and, taking a pace forward, blasted the hooded man in the head repeatedly until he finally stopped moving. "Point-blank 'em," he muttered to himself as he turned to face the next assault.

"Kane," Grant called from just a half dozen paces down the corridor.

Kane looked, already knowing what he would see. The party of a dozen hooded intruders was almost upon the Cerberus group now, with the towering form of Ullikummis bringing up the rear. The hooded ones were reaching for the cloth pouches they wore at their waists, loading up their deceptively simple slingshots and readying them as they ran.

"Baptiste," Kane instructed, "I need you to wound Ullikummis if we're to take him out. Once he falls…" Kane shrugged, leaving his sentence hanging, as if afraid that speaking the words aloud might jinx his plan.

At Kane's side, Brigid fiddled with the rubber stopper on the glass container. To her credit, Kane could sense no reservation from her body language; she was primed and determined.

"What happened up there, Baptiste?" he asked quietly.

"We had to leave someone behind," Brigid replied, not looking at him.

Nodding, Kane turned to his left, where Domi and Grant waited with their blasters poised. "Head shots only, people," he advised. "There's still a chance we can turn all this around."

Grant closed one eye as he sighted down the length of the Copperhead and snapped off his first three shots, pumping the trigger of the lengthy subgun. Despite its size, the weapon looked like a toy in Grant's huge hands. An accomplished marksman, he hit his targets, the first shot smacking dead center between the eyes of the lead attacker. The bullet struck but seemed to be deflected off his flesh, pinging away into the high rafters of the tunnel. Grant's following shots were already dispatched, and while the third did a similar ricochet, as if striking solid metal, the second drilled into the lead runner's left eye, turning it into an explosion of liquid that burst over his cheek as he fell.

Kane, Brigid and Domi performed similar bloodwork, unleashing a stream of gunfire at their onrushing attackers as the lights above flickered and dimmed. Several of the hooded figures fell under the onslaught, toppling over themselves as their robes billowed about them.

In response, the hooded strangers loosed a volley of gravel, the stone chunks whizzing through the air and

striking the surfaces all around the Cerberus teammates with bursts of sparks, sharp flecks cutting into the
shadow suits three of them wore. Domi howled in agony
as she took the brunt of the stone assault on her bare
skin.

From the corner of his eye, Kane saw her fall to the
floor, clutching at a bloody gash on her arm. Besides the
hard stone, the diminutive albino woman had been hit
with multiple grains of sand, each striking her with such
speed that it had sliced through her skin. Now her white
form was streaked with thin lines of blood, a hundred
grazed cuts peppering her body like cracks on glass as
she rolled on the floor, crying in agony.

Two more of the attackers fell under the Cerberus
team's assault, and then the first wave was upon them.

To one side of the tunnel, Grant snapped out with his
left fist, driving it into the face of the closest attacker
even as the hooded stranger tossed another stone from
his slingshot, spinning the weapon in his hand to generate the momentum needed to launch the stone. Like
a point-blank bullet, the hunk of rock struck Grant just
below the rib cage, knocking the wind out of him even as
his punch connected.

Kane saw his partner knocked from his feet by the
blow, toppling backward with a growl of agony. But there
was no time to help. Two of the hooded freaks were whipping around their own slingshots, launching a cluster of
tiny stones at Kane and Brigid as he turned his Copperhead on them. The bullets raced at the two soldiers of
Ullikummis, striking the onrushing stones and—incredibly—being deflected from their path in a blur of sparks.

Then the first of the men was upon Kane, and the ex-
Magistrate brought his arm up to deflect a savage blow
aimed at his head. An instant later he dropped to the

floor, his left leg sweeping out before him in a frantic attempt to knock his attacker off balance. The hooded figure tumbled to the ground and Kane whipped his Copperhead up at the man's face.

"I am stone," the man stated, his voice strangely emotionless.

"Well, I'm hacked off," Kane replied, snapping a quick burst of gunfire directly into his fallen foe's visage. The man's head snapped backward, sinking into the folds of the hood. But to Kane's astonishment, there was no blood.

Didn't matter. The man was out of action and that's all that counted just now, Kane realized as he whipped the subgun around to cover himself. For some reason he couldn't begin to fathom, he hadn't really paid much thought to the lack of blood from their foes until this moment. Seeing them so close up, hearing the man speak fearlessly in the face of sure death, Kane concluded there was something almost mystical in the whole situation. He had seen mystical before now; the Cerberus operation had seemed mired in combating foes with almost supernatural abilities since it was first established. Often these mystical abilities had proved to be nothing more than elaborate tricks, the employment of superior technology to disguise the true nature of the abilities on show. Kane dismissed the puzzle for the moment, turning his attention to the next of his attackers as two more rushed at him, firing heavy rocks—three inches in diameter—at his head. Whatever they really were, whatever was really going on, was something to ponder at another juncture. Right now, they were in the middle of a war zone, and Kane and his teammates were the only hope Cerberus had left. He leaped aside as the twin rocks whizzed past, striking the floor beyond him with a flurry of sparks.

A few feet away from Kane, Brigid was using her own weapon—the matte-black compact semiautomatic she favored—to fend off another of their foes as she searched for her opportunity. The hooded figure—this one a woman with long blonde hair beneath the rough weave of her cowl—used her slingshot to launch a handful of sharp stones at high velocity. The stones cut through the air toward Brigid's porcelain face as she ran forward.

Brigid sprang as the stones rushed at her, kicking out as she leaped into the air. The missiles drummed a tattoo against her leg and booted foot as she leaped, cutting into the sturdy material of the shadow suit, their sharp edges tearing slivers of black thread and pale skin from the underside of her leg. An instant later, Brigid's outstretched foot slammed into the blonde woman's breastbone, knocking her down with a gasp of expelled air. Brigid landed in a run, her weight flattening the woman even as she sprang forward and hurried onward toward the looming figure of Ullikummis. The red-haired former archivist ducked beneath another volley of flying stones as she weaved past his lackeys on her run toward the Annunaki prince himself.

Another battery of stones flew in Brigid's direction, and she brought her right arm up in front of her face, letting the ones she couldn't dodge drum against the protective weave of the shadow suit with brutal finality. Then her TP-9 whipped around again, picking off targets as she hurried on down the chasmlike corridor that ran the length of the Cerberus redoubt. Just a little way ahead, Ullikummis formed a dark shape beneath the arching roof, his magmalike eyes burning in eerie determination.

Meanwhile, Kane found himself amid a whole group of the stone throwers, dodging and weaving as they moved to surround him, cleaving the air with stones of differing sizes. Head down, Kane charged at the closest of his foes, slamming into the guy with all the force he could muster. A rain of stones slapped against his back, leaving his jacket in shreds as they sliced through the material.

The hooded figure that Kane had charged fell backward as he absorbed the force of the ex-Mag's blow. Kane blasted off a burst of fire from his Copperhead, but there was no time to follow through. Another hooded form was moving toward him, her movements masked by the flowing robe she wore.

Beside him, Kane saw Grant go down amid three more of their foes, a curtain of tattered robes sweeping across his partner like the black wings of a crow.

With a growl born of sheer frustration, Kane drove the muzzle of his Copperhead into the gut of the woman before him. Her hood fell back as he squeezed the trigger, and Kane felt his blood turn cold as he saw her face properly for the first time. It was Helen.

Helen Foster was a member of Cerberus's engineering division, an attractive woman with medium length, dark hair. Kane had spent almost three days sharing a Manta craft's cramped cockpit with her as they performed repairs on Cerberus's Vela-class satellite. He had developed a friendly rapport with the woman, and his friends had teased him that he and Helen had a little something going on. That had been just three months ago.

The sound of the Copperhead's blasts became muffled as the subgun drilled a relentless stream of bullets into the woman's gut, forcing her to bend double like a hinge over the extended muzzle of the weapon.

Kane felt her body shudder as his bullets drilled into

it. "Helen?" he spit, releasing the trigger and grabbing her as she sagged in place.

The engineer stared into his eyes with only the slightest hint of recognition, and she bared her teeth in a snarl. "I am stone," she growled, a foaming streak of saliva oozing over her clenched teeth.

Kane stepped back, stymied by this sudden turn of events. From behind him, another hooded figure reached around and grabbed Kane by his throat.

He struggled in his new assailant's grip, trying to dislodge him. Before his eyes, Helen Foster brushed at the foamy smear at her mouth, then reached for the hood of her robe and pulled it back in place, hiding her features in its dark shadow once more. As she did so, Kane spied what appeared to be a scuff of dirt on her forehead, like a little blister. His heart sank as the woman stumbled backward, weaving in place before sinking to the ground, wounded but somehow clinging to life.

From either side of the fallen Cerberus engineer, two more robed figures approached Kane, reloading their slingshots with stones. He watched as they began to twirl their weapons, whipping them around in arcs until they picked up the momentum required to launch the bullet-like missiles. And then the stones left the slingshots, cutting the air at incredible speed. Kane timed everything in his head, keeping track of the variables with practiced surety.

With a powerful twist of his shoulders, he jerked the man trying to strangle him just as the stones were launched, tossing him over his back and straight into the path of the hurtling objects. They drummed against the man as he flew through the air, slicing gaping trails through his robes as he crashed to the ground.

Kane brushed at his shoulder, where one of the stones

had nipped his shadow suit. The thrown man's figure had blocked the majority of the assault, but the attackers were reloading, and Kane saw no obvious shield for the next barrage. Instead, he ran at the three of them, Helen's fallen form included, holding down the trigger of the Copperhead to unleash a continuous stream of fire.

A LITTLE WAY AHEAD down the corridor, Brigid Baptiste was the first to meet with the hulking stone-clad Annunaki called Ullikummis. Eight feet tall, he loomed before her like some primitive statue, an impressive presence in the wide, rock-walled tunnel.

"Submit," he ordered, his voice as brutal as a blacksmith's hammer striking an anvil.

Swiftly, Brigid fingered the rubber stopper of the glass flask she held, pulling it loose and tossing the contents— and then the jar—in the monster's face. Automatically, Ullikummis lifted his arms, turning his head as the colorless hydrochloric acid splashed him.

For a moment—the impossible. Ullikummis, stone prince and furious sire of the Annunaki gods, stopped in his tracks, a shrill curse of pain emanating from his flamelike mouth.

In over three millennia, the sound of Ullikummis in pain had never been heard. The scream seemed to rock the mountainous redoubt, its noise piercing through Brigid's body and making her bones vibrate beneath her skin.

Then the wide-bottomed glass container shattered as it struck the monster's towering form, its shards twinkling as they soared away beneath the flickering overhead lights. A plume of thick smoke erupted from Ullikummis's face and the top third of his rocklike body.

The pluming smoke was accompanied by a loud fizzing sound, like bacon sizzling on a griddle.

Then the stone overlord staggered back, wiping at his face as the acid ate away at his rocky hide, that thick stream of white smoke pluming from his face and arms like some kind of living fog.

Brigid did not hesitate. Her TP-9 pistol was in her hand, pumping bullet after bullet into the stone god's face as he staggered before her. "Go back to the hell you came from, you evil son of a snake," she growled as the TP-9 spit bullets at her stumbling adversary.

FURTHER ALONG THE TUNNEL, behind Brigid and Kane, Grant tossed one of his attackers aside, throwing the man into the nearest wall with bone-breaking finality. The other two were still gripping him, one pulling at his left arm while the other had her arms around his waist, trying to yank him down from behind.

Grant skipped backward, slamming into the wall there, forcing the woman behind him to loosen her grip. The other one was tossed aside when Grant flipped his left arm out, and tumbled across the floor before the huge ex-Magistrate. After taking a step forward, Grant fell back again, slamming against the wall a second time, forcing the hooded woman to take the brunt of the assault. With a third maneuver, she finally let go, sagging to the floor.

"Third time's the charm," Grant muttered as he turned his attention to the last of his assailants.

The hooded man grabbed for him, pulling him forward by his right forearm. Trying to hold Grant was like trying to hold down an angry grizzly bear. The ex-Mag raised his right arm, the robed figure still clutching on to it, and shook. The figure there clung on, teeth bared in determination.

"Suit yourself, then," Grant growled, and squeezed down on the trigger of the Copperhead he still held.

A stream of bullets blasted from the nose of the weapon, slamming into the figure that gripped him until the man was forced to let go. Grant watched as he flew through the air, his robes fluttering about him as bullets drilled into his chest and face. When his foe crashed to the ground, Grant leaped away, hurrying to assist Kane and Brigid in their assault on Ullikummis. Grant owed that stone monstrosity, and right here, right now, he intended to deliver.

Kane was just finishing off the last of his own combatants, flipping the robed figure to the floor with a leg sweep. The would-be attacker slammed against the hard flooring, his head striking with a loud crack.

Kane stepped away, bouncing on the balls of his feet to keep himself moving, all agitation and adrenaline. Helen Foster, his strangely affected Cerberus colleague, remained slumped against one wall, the hood of her robe bunched around her face.

Grant caught up with Kane, silently gesturing down the corridor to where Brigid was battling with the terrifying figure of Ullikummis. Kane brushed his finger to his nose, that superstitious acknowledgment of the long odds once again. It felt somehow more appropriate now than it ever had before; Helen had been turned somehow, and that probably meant others had been, too. And now they faced a monster they'd struggled to overcome twice before.

Together, Grant and Kane charged down the corridor, sweeping aside the last of their hooded assailants with violent booms from their Copperhead assault weapons, even as the angry form of Ullikummis swayed in place beneath Brigid Baptiste's brutal attack. Far behind them, Domi lay on the floor, her pale form twitching in semi-consciousness; they would worry about her later, when all this was over.

Ahead of them, they saw Ullikummis rear up, the glowing magma of his screaming mouth a fiery circle in the stuttering lighting. The rock lord's face and torso were still smoldering, the hydrochloric acid eating into his flesh. Then, as if in slow motion, Kane saw the stone creature's smoldering right arm reach out, the bullets from Brigid's blaster glancing off its dark surface. Ullikummis's stony hand grabbed the blocky black square of Brigid's semiautomatic, seizing it even with Brigid's finger locked on the trigger. With a burst of sparks, the gun ceased firing as Ullikummis crushed the barrel in a show of incredible strength.

Brigid fell backward, letting go of the weapon even as it seized up, and Ullikummis tossed it aside.

Then the stone giant was standing over Brigid, looming over her like some ugly, primitive statue brought to life.

Running beside Kane, Grant was firing shots from his Copperhead at the hulking stone figure. They had no great plan, Kane knew—it came down to this, a show of force against a wounded enemy.

"Get Brigid!" Grant instructed as he crouched low and charged at Ullikummis.

Kane obeyed, leaping over the prone form of a fallen hooded warrior in his path. Then he was just five paces from Brigid, calling out to her, his own Copperhead drilling shot after shot into the towering form of the would-be god. Ullikummis halted in place, his head rearing back as the bullets from Kane's and Grant's weapons slammed into his ruined flesh. The hydrochloric acid was eating at his hard covering, and their shots were causing the great Annunaki lord pain.

Grant's Copperhead spit as he charged at Ullikummis from the other flank, the bullets slapping against the Annunaki's monstrous hide where it remained undamaged by the corrosive acid. Ullikummis looked up as he made to grab Brigid, and when he saw Grant's charging figure, a look of recognition crossed his fearsome features.

"The man bull?" Ullikummis queried, even as Grant's powerful form slammed into him with all his might.

In a blur of movement, Kane snagged Brigid, yanking her aside even as Ullikummis grasped the air where she had been just a fraction of a second before.

Grant's incredible charge pushed the stone god back a stumbling step, just out of reach of Brigid Baptiste as Kane dragged her from the floor. However, it was like slamming into a brick wall. Grant bounced backward, the Copperhead clattering from his grip as he landed hard on the floor.

Across from Grant, without even looking, Kane stepped on the Copperhead as it skittered across the floor. His mind was focused on Ullikummis as the stone giant turned on him with fury in his burning eyes. Standing ready, Kane blasted bullets from his own weapon, using the bullpup grip to create a wide spraying pattern, locking the monster in place as the blaster spit titanium steel. There was something remarkable about Kane in that moment. The fabled point man utilized his special gift in the tensest of situations, and Grant recognized he was employing it now. Despite the noise and fury all around, Kane was one with his surroundings, his attention utterly devoted to the task at hand.

A little way down the corridor, a handful of hooded

strangers were righting themselves after the initial affray, while down by the rollback door, more guards were making their way toward the scuffle, leaving their defeated prisoners—remarkably—unguarded.

Grant righted himself, clambering off the floor, his breathing heavy. With a practiced flinch of his wrist tendons, he called the Sin Eater into his grip from its wrist holster, his eyes fixed on the looming figure in the center of the corridor.

Kane stood eight paces to Grant's right, feet widely spaced, his Copperhead spurting furious bursts of bullets at the smoldering stone monstrosity as gouts of white mist puffed from the Annunaki's ruined face.

And a half dozen paces from Kane, Brigid Baptiste was readying herself, after retrieving Grant's Copperhead from the floor by Kane's foot.

As one, the oft-fabled triumvirate of Cerberus warriors unleashed a storm of bullets at the wanna-be overlord, the fizzing of the acid that ate at his body filling the air like a snake's hissing as the overhead lights shimmered. The sounds of gunfire filled the air as streams of bullets pelted the monstrous figure, some locking in his ruined flesh while others struck the hard rock skin and zipped away to the air, where they slammed against the walls, floor and high ceiling. Ullikummis ignored them, his fierce eyes glowing a hellish orange as the lights above them flickered and dimmed, flickered and dimmed.

Then the stone overlord took a mighty step forward, despite the bullets blasting against his incredible flesh. Ullikummis began his final assault, his stone feet stamping against the plates of the floor as he trudged toward the trio of Cerberus warriors, a handful of his hooded warriors at his back.

This is it, Kane thought.

Chapter 13

Kane's bullets cleaved the air, 4.85 mm slugs whipping across the space between himself and Ullikummis as the stone god trudged toward him. To Kane's right, Brigid Baptiste was using the recovered Copperhead subgun to drill the monstrous figure with more slugs, even as it stormed at them. Meanwhile Grant stood eight feet to Kane's left, his Sin Eater belching 9 mm bullets in a lethal stream.

Ullikummis's tree-trunk-like feet slammed against the floor as he stomped toward them, and Kane watched as the stone creature's right arm lashed out, knocking Grant off his feet with an almighty slap. His fellow ex-Mag hurtled backward, slamming into the far wall.

To Kane's right, Brigid Baptiste's Copperhead clicked on empty, its ammunition spent. Grant had the spare ammo, Kane knew, although he himself had several cartridges stuffed in his pockets for his own use.

"Get out of here, Baptiste," Kane shouted. "Go free our colleagues."

She shook her head. "No, Kane," she said, "he's wounded now. We have to find some way…"

"I'll find the way," Kane promised. "You free Lakesh and the others."

Brigid glanced past Ullikummis, saw that her defeated Cerberus colleagues were unguarded now. And yet, despite that, they did nothing to fight back or make a bid to escape. Even the security personnel seemed to be beyond caring, just kneeling there with their hands entwined behind their heads, the fight gone out of them.

While Kane and Brigid continued their hurried exchange, Grant forced himself back to his feet, and he reached for Ullikummis, grabbing one of his thick wrists, as the stone monstrosity passed. Ullikummis pulled his arm close to his body, dragging Grant nearer, the ex-Mag's booted feet scraping across the floor. And then Ullikummis's misshapen face split in what passed for a smile as the corrosive continued to billow smoke around him like a halo. "You make fine sport, Enkidu," Ullikummis growled. "It almost saddens me that I must end this now."

Before Grant could guess what the stone creature was referring to, Ullikummis flipped his mighty arm and pulled him from the ground. Suddenly Grant was hurtling vertically, and the high metal girders that held the rock ceiling in place came rushing toward him. Grant twisted his body, bracing for impact. Then he slammed into the ceiling, his left arm and shoulder striking first with bone-jarring finality. Mercifully, perhaps, Grant blacked out for a moment before he began the twenty-foot fall back to the floor of the tunnel.

The hard impact of his landing brought him back to full consciousness, and he struggled to right himself and bring the Sin Eater pistol to bear once more. Ullikummis batted the stream of bullets aside, while behind him Kane contributed his own lethal salvo to Grant's frenzied attack, drilling slugs into the monster's back where it continued to billow white mist.

Then Ullikummis's arm swung and he slapped the supine Grant across the face with the back of his rocky hand. Grant rolled over, feeling as if his head would tear from his neck. His vision swam, the flickering of the lights doubling and tripling as he hurtled into the wall to his left. He struck the rock with the force of a battering ram, howling in agony as he slumped to the floor. Ullikummis stood there a moment, looking at the ebony-skinned ex-Mag as he struggled to stay conscious.

"A worthy foe," Ullikummis growled when Grant's head finally tipped backward and he sank into the quagmire of unconsciousness.

BRIGID WEAVED BETWEEN the hooded figures as Ullikummis shoved her partner aside, and sprinted down the tunnel toward the rollback door. She ducked the assault of one guard, leaped to avoid a low kick from another.

Ullikummis turned and, with a seemingly casual flick of his hand, commanded the floor to part beneath Brigid's feet. She stumbled as a ridge of rock appeared, burrowing up from the floor plating, splitting the tiles apart.

Brigid leaped over the next hump as, behind her, Kane drilled shot after shot into Ullikummis, drawing the stone god's attention. Then another of the guards reached out as Brigid ran past, and he snagged her red-gold hair, yanking it with such force that she felt a strand tear from her scalp. She screeched in agony, stumbling and righting herself in the same movement.

But Brigid's momentary pause was enough. The guards had her now, leaping upon her and brutally forcing her to the ground.

Brigid Baptiste was slammed facefirst into the floor, and the sounds around her seemed to become distant. Her vision swirled and blurred, and she felt the weight upon her back as someone drove her head into the tiles a second time. If there was a third time, Brigid didn't know.

TWENTY FEET AWAY, Kane's Copperhead clicked on empty, finally out of ammunition. With a weary shake of his head, he clawed for the spare ammo he had stored at his belt, his eyes fixed on the hulking monstrosity of stone that stood before him, the figure's face and upper body still smoldering from the acid attack.

Kane already knew how this had to end. Grant was down; Baptiste was down. It was just him now, and he'd tried this twice before with the stone god, had tried to defeat him in combat, and both times had failed. Still, what was it Grant had said? Third time's the charm.

As Kane grasped for the spare ammunition, his hand brushed against the equipment he stored at his belt, and a desperate plan formed in his mind. He reached into the clip-down pouch there, pulling out three of the tiny explosive charges he carried as protocol. Small, spherical items about an inch in diameter, the charges were called flash-bangs, and were primarily used by Cerberus field teams to shock or divert an enemy. Now, with the stone giant still reeling from the hydrochloric acid, they might give Kane a further—and much needed—advantage.

With a sweep of his arm, he tossed the spheres at the stone figure looming toward him, a half dozen of his hooded subjects hurrying in his wake. The flash-bangs hurtled through the air for two seconds, and Kane saw Ullikummis reach up to swat them aside. On short timers, the flash-bangs detonated, still flying through the air within arm's reach of the stone monster, and the shadowy tunnel of the redoubt was suddenly lit up like a sunburst. The flash of light was accompanied by a colossal bang, the noise echoing loudly in the enclosed space.

Flash-bangs were not designed to cause damage, just to startle and confuse an opponent, their unexpected brilliance stunning an attacker.

Prepared for the explosion, Kane turned away as they went off, bathing the redoubt's main tunnel in light. There was no time to place protective eyewear over his face; he just closed his eyes and turned away from the savage burst of brilliance. There was no defense from the cacophony the triple explosion brought, however, and Kane gritted his teeth against the ringing pain in his ears as he reloaded the Copperhead subgun with practiced surety.

When he turned, the flash-bangs were fizzling out, drifting in the air like the trails left by spent fireworks. Screaming was coming from the far end of the tunnel, where Ullikummis's people had looked straight into the spasmodic bursts of light, and Kane could hear several of the hooded intruders behind him cursing and groaning, as well. Twelve feet away, just past the dwindling lights of the spent flash-bangs fluttering back to the floor, Ullikummis was reeling in place, shaking his head and grumbling in irritation. One thing about light, Kane thought—no matter how big or nasty a foe, five will get you ten he'd be affected the same way as anyone else.

As Ullikummis struggled to make sense of what had happened, Kane charged toward him, the Copperhead spewing bullets from his outstretched arm. The projectiles slapped against Ullikummis's stone shell, batting against his skin and hurtling off in all directions. Kane smiled grimly as he saw Ullikummis stagger backward, and he reassured himself that several of the bullets had driven through the monster's acid-damaged skin, embedding themselves in the stone overlord's flesh, where the corrosive was still eating at it.

"So you can be hurt, you son of a bitch," Kane muttered to himself as he continued drilling the stone figure with 4.85 mm bullets, running an evasive pattern around Ullikummis's towering form.

With a savage growl, the monster lunged forward, blindly grasping for Kane with one of his stone hands. Despite his bulk, Ullikummis moved with astonishing speed and his reach was far greater than a normal man's. Kane leaped as he ran, averting the stone claw by just a few inches, the Copperhead booming once more into that monstrous stone face.

Like some crazed jack-in-the-box, Kane kept moving, circling Ullikummis and blasting shots at him from all sides, never more than six feet away from that monstrous stone form. All the while, Ullikummis was reaching out, smoke billowing from his misshapen features, his long arms grabbing at the air where Kane had been just a second before.

Then, with an animal-like snarl, Ullikummis powered forward, his hulking legs kicking off the ground and sending him blasting at Kane like a stony missile as the Cerberus warrior neared one of the tunnel walls. With nowhere to run, Kane ducked, bending so low that his empty palm slapped the floor to keep him upright. Above him, the bulky shadow passed by, and then Ullikummis's tree-stump feet crashed against the wall behind Kane, sending a shock wave down the length of the tunnel as he sprang from it like some deranged stone monkey.

Ullikummis landed on the floor with his back to Kane, but already he was turning, his movements so fast they were a blur in the winking overhead lights.

Kane ran backward, the shock-resistant soles of his

boots slamming against the floor as he dodged away
from the attacking god. Kane had fought with the Annunaki before; he had even battled the dark goddess Lilitu
to a standstill in a brutal fistfight aboard the living moth-
ership *Tiamat*. But even that could not prepare him for
the speed and savagery with which Ullikummis attacked
within the confines of the Cerberus sanctuary, his face
billowing with smoke as the acid ate away at his strange
rock flesh.

Once more Kane's Copperhead clicked on empty, and
he tossed it aside without a second thought. There was
no time left to reload, he knew. He had to finish this as
quickly as he could, no matter how messy that might be.

The useless Copperhead subgun clattered against the
floor, skittering away. Even as it did so, Kane retrieved
his Sin Eater from its wrist sheath, standing his ground
as the fearsome figure of Ullikummis began to run at
him.

Steadying himself, Kane raised the Sin Eater and targeted the hulking figure between his glowing eyes. Ullikummis was charging now, his feet thumping against
the floor with mighty drumbeats, his arms outstretched
to encompass the vast width of the corridor that ran the
length of the Cerberus redoubt. Kane's Sin Eater spit,
bullet after bullet rushing through the air and slapping
against the brute's face. Some shots zipped away in rico-
chets, but one in three seemed to find purchase, embedding itself in the monster's fearsome face as he charged
at Kane.

With a mighty howl of defiance, Ullikummis bore
down on the Cerberus warrior, the shots smashing against
his rocky hide with bursts of fiery sparks. At the last
second, Kane started running at the mighty stone giant,
then dropped to his knees, dipping below the monster's

reaching arms and sliding between his hurtling legs. Still on his knees, Kane spun, his finger never easing the pressure on the Sin Eater's trigger, and a line of bullets sprayed across the wall to his right as he located his gruesome target once more.

The bullets smacked against Ullikummis's broad back, and Kane watched in awe as his monstrous foe stumbled and fell, crashing against the floor with the force of an avalanche.

FARTHER ALONG THE CORRIDOR, lying on the cold floor, Domi struggled to regain consciousness, the flickering lights making her eyes ache. She saw Kane's muscular figure whipping his Sin Eater around, firing shot after shot at the powerful form of Ullikummis, a lone man fighting a god. Kane's denim jacket was shredded, just a tattered rag clinging to his back now. Beneath it, Domi saw, the black weave of the shadow suit was torn, and red streaks lined Kane's skin where the thrown rocks of their enemies had cut into him. Then—incredibly—Ullikummis dropped, stumbling to the ground.

Domi struggled, trying to pull herself out of her daze. "Kane..." she muttered, his name tumbling from lips made thick from the assault she had suffered.

Her hand reached for the Combat Master handgun that lay beneath her, and she brought it around, her hands shaking as she forced herself to move.

But it was impossible. She was so tired. Domi's eyed closed once more as she drifted in and out of consciousness.

ONLY NOW WAS KANE's hearing coming back properly, the ringing effect of the flash-bangs subsiding. He peered behind him as he got to his feet, checked that the hooded attackers were still down. They seemed to be; it was just him and the Annunaki god-prince now.

Lying on his back beneath the flickering lights, the colossal form of Ullikummis stretched his arms out and pushed himself up into a crouching position before easing up off the floor. He was moving slower than before. He was wounded, Kane realized. Kane snapped off another burst of bullets at the creature's back, targeting the spot at the top of his armored spine where acid still bubbled. Ullikummis seemed oblivious, ignoring the bullets as they embedded themselves into his skin.

Then he inclined his head, peering over his antlerlike shoulder ridge at Kane with those glowing magma pools of light that formed his eyes. "You're impressive," the beast intoned, his voice like grinding millstones, "for an ape."

"Yeah," Kane snarled. "Impress this, you son of a bitch!" And with that, the ex-Magistrate's Sin Eater spit a continuous stream of bullets as Ullikummis padded toward him, his trunklike feet crashing against the floor of the redoubt's tunnellike jackhammers, picking up speed as he ran for his opponent.

FARTHER BACK ALONG THE TUNNEL, unseen by either of the combatants, Rosalia emerged from the stairwell, her face half-hidden within the folds of her hooded robe. The noise of the battle drew her, and she hunkered in the open doorway, her hand on the dog's neck, both of them peering out at the incredible fight that raged forty feet away.

"Kane," Rosalia said, the word barely louder than her breath. "Magistrate man Kane."

She knew Kane from before, from back when they had encountered one another in the coastal village of Hope. For all his irritating morality, Kane was an adept fighter, she knew, and he would stand up to protect others. When they first met, he had even recruited her into helping save the victims of a tidal wave that had crashed into the fishing village from the Pacific. Yes, Kane could be annoying, but he would stop at nothing to achieve the things he believed in. And if she played him right, one of those things might just be her freedom.

Beneath the shadows of her hood, Rosalia smiled. "Things have just taken a turn for the *very* interesting," she murmured to herself.

BULLETS SLAMMED AGAINST Ullikummis's smoldering features as he rocketed toward Kane like an enraged bull. Kane saw the giant's stone arm sweep through the air at him, and he leaped aside, springing high and kicking out, his feet slamming against the stone monster's chest and flipping him over Ullikummis's shoulder, drilling bullets into his face from just inches away.

Then Kane was landing on the far side of the monstrous would-be god, rolling over to disperse the momentum he had built up in those brief instants of furious movement.

Ullikummis turned, sweeping a hand across his face where the bullets had struck. Kane watched as the monstrous, malformed figure used his rugged fingers to pluck a bullet from his acid-damaged cheek, flicking it to the floor. Five more followed, a tinkling of misshapen titanium shells smattering against the tiles.

Kane stood his ground, the Sin Eater poised before him. The weapon was having some effect, he could see, but would it be enough?

Kane turned, looking around him for something else to hit the monster with, something more powerful. Ullikummis's troops seemed to have stopped in place, stunned spectators to this battle between man and god.

Frantically, Kane scanned the scene as the great stone figure took another stride toward him, his rough, rocky hide lit in staccato bursts by the flickering lights. In that instant, Kane shifted his aim, pointing the Sin Eater directly above his head and unleashing a triple burst of bullets as Ullikummis gathered his pace. Twenty feet above the combatants' heads, Kane's bullets smacked into the lighting rig that flickered there, bursting one of the cylindrical tube bulbs before catching the chains that secured it in place, riveted to a scaffold that spanned the width of the tunnel. The long metal light fixture swung free, dangling for a moment from its remaining chain link before its own weight, coupled with one of Kane's perfectly placed bullets, broke that fragile link and it plummeted to the floor.

Kane dived backward as Ullikummis charged at him, just as the fixture dropped from the high ceiling. The light crashed down onto the stone colossus in a shower of sparks, and Ullikummis dropped to his knees, bellowing in pain.

In the wake of that explosion, the tunnel-like corridor seemed to go silent. Kane crouched, his breathing heavy as he watched the motionless figure of Ullikummis sprawled on the floor, like the wake of an avalanche.

Kane stared for a long moment, feeling slightly unreal. His breathing chugged from his open mouth like a steam engine, and he struggled to bring it back under control, feeling the cooling beads of sweat on his brow.

It was over.

Reluctantly, Kane turned, bringing his Sin Eater up to cover the handful of hooded figures who stood in stunned silence barely two dozen feet from the wreckage of the battle. Brigid Baptiste lay among the debris there, the floor ripped apart beside her in what looked like an open fault line in the mountain itself.

With effort, Kane stood, feeling his strained muscles threatening to rebel. Using his left hand to steady the Sin Eater, which shook in his exhausted grip, Kane drew the silent pistol across each of the stunned hooded figures in turn.

"Your god is dead," he snarled. "You can either stand down or I'll make sure you follow him into the pits of Hades."

For a moment, no one spoke, and the only noise in the wide artery that spanned the redoubt came from the tinkling overhead bulbs as they flickered and sparked. Then a voice shouted from behind Kane, calling out his name. It was Domi, issuing a desperate warning.

Kane half turned even as he heard heavy footsteps behind him, and Ullikummis rushed toward him once again. Then the stone monster swept out one of his long arms, striking Kane in the back of his neck. It was like being hit with a boulder.

Kane was shoved forward, his boots skidding across the floor. At the same time, Domi's blaster boomed, drilling a bullet into Ullikummis's flesh. Then he was falling down, striking the tiled floor with his chin as he skidded across it toward the robed figures.

Whatever happened next, Kane couldn't recall.

KANE OPENED HIS EYES, looking around the now familiar rock-walled, eight-by-six cell. The faintest glow of orange lava came from a tiny circular rent where the rough wall met the ceiling. His breathing was labored and he released a sigh through gritted teeth as he tried to calm himself down.

Kane didn't remember it all even now. But he remembered enough, and he had pieced the rest together in his mind. He had taken on a god and had come up wanting.

As he lay there in the semidarkness, his back resting against the rough stone floor, he muttered to the ceiling above him, "Baptiste, where the hell are you when I need you?"

For the moment at least, the ceiling chose not to respond.

Chapter 14

"Stupid dog, take your shit already," Rosalia muttered, watching Belly-on-legs running around the windy little rock ridge outside the prison.

Not a prison, she reminded herself. A life camp. That's how they referred to it. A place where people came to be reeducated, to open their eyes to the joy of the future. How had Ullikummis explained it to his supposedly loyal troops?

"A death camp is a place people are brought to die, but a life camp is where they come to be born."

"Ptah," Rosalia muttered. Mumbo jumbo, that's all it was. Semantics and bullshit, that's all this Ullikummis creature fed them, a steady stream of lies dressed up as philosophy.

She had met with him out in the old province of Mandeville, heard him speak briefly as he addressed a thousand of his followers, every last one called Stone. Some idiot rally, like the others that First Priest Dylan had hosted, where he had told people all about heaven and utopia and some fairy-tale future where he was a big man and Ullikummis would be their benevolent god. A baron by any other name, Rosalia recognized. Bullshit, all of it.

"Bullshit-flavored bullshit," she muttered as she thought back, brushing the loose strands of hair from her windswept face.

Before her, the dog was hurrying down the slope as the wind blew through the leaves around him. It was May, and spring was turning to summer, the blossoms giving way to green leaves, berries and cones. Rosalia wasn't supposed to be out here, not officially. But the dog needed to run, and she wasn't going to hurry behind it inside the prison caverns, picking up after it as it urinated and defecated when it felt the need. Nature didn't like being caged.

The main entrance was well guarded, of course. Despite the security of the sealed cells, there was always the risk of their guests escaping—indeed, rumor was that one of them had tried, the Magistrate man called Grant, and that Dylan was sore as hell about it, concerned that this lapse would be fed back to Ullikummis and that his priesthood might be stripped away.

Turned away by the guards at the main entrance, Rosalia had explored the facility on her first day here, mutt in tow, until she'd located an area set aside for vehicles. The vehicle bay featured a huge rollback door, and a smaller side entrance presumably used for scouts or sentries. The door was sealed with rock, but Rosalia's obedience stone had opened it, the same way it could open the cells. With Belly-on-legs running back and forth at her heels, she had led the way out the door, onto a steep slope where the forest grew thick. The tree cover was cleared only around the rollback door itself, enough to allow vehicles free passage should the hangar bay be used. Beyond that, the area was given over to trees, a perfect place for her dog to exhaust itself with its silly dog games.

She had smiled when she had found it, this little secret area that no one else visited, remembering a childhood story that the nuns had told her. A secret garden, right here in the shadow of the life camp.

On the rocky slope now, Rosalia's dog was scampering around, hurrying between the trees, sniffing at a burrow it had found among the foliage. It was a mongrel, Rosalia figured, half coyote, half something more soppy, all stupid. The beast had no common sense, got scared at the silliest things, and had the palest eyes she had ever seen in a dog, so pale they looked almost white. She had found the hound in the desert, or maybe it had found her—she wasn't sure. It had been following her ever since, keeping watch sometimes when she slept, sharing her food without greed. Calling it a good dog was being too generous, she thought, but it was a companion in a harsh world where everyone else was geared to screwing their fellow man over, or indoctrinating him into this growing cult religion of Ullikummis the savior.

Savior? What kind of savior was he, to come and terrify people, brainwash them, break their necks? Rosalia thought back to her schooling, out in the nunnery at the Mexican border. Less than two centuries ago, the whole of this country had been devastated, a so-called deathland, its people eking out a meager subsistence amid the radioactive debris of nuclear apocalypse. In that context, Ullikummis as savior made sense, Rosalia thought. In his harsh way, he had vowed to change the world for the better. Their world now was the product of the Deathlands, a struggling emergence from the end of the world, where civilization sat side by side with the pioneer spirit, where survival still came at a price.

There was a bark then, and Rosalia looked up as the mountainous wind whipped around her. Twenty feet ahead, the dog was gazing into the dense branches of a tree, yapping at something it could smell there, running back and forth trying to see what it was. Squirrel probably, Rosalia knew; there were no people living close to

Life Camp Zero. The camp was high in the mountains, surrounded by trees and seemingly bottomless ravines, but the forest that surrounded it held plenty of wildlife, groundhogs and timberwolves and the like. All these things fascinated Belly-on-legs; the stupid mutt would chase after anything once it got the scent. Rosalia had heard that the nearest settlement was to be found in the flatlands some miles away, leaving this rocky prison facility utterly undisturbed. Even so, Life Camp Zero remained well guarded. People could live without fresh air, perhaps, but dogs—got stir-crazy quicker than human prisoners. However stupid the mutt might seem, Rosalia knew it packed a savage bite if it was roused. She had seen it defend her back when they had been sleeping in the fishing ville of Hope.

The dog barked again, turned its head briskly as something scampered across the branches above and leaped to a nearby tree. The dog scurried after it, running farther down the slope.

"No," Rosalia called, stepping sideways down the steep slope to stop the canine. Its yapping could be mistaken for a wild animal, but if the guards above her spotted the dog it might draw attention; and neither of them should be out here, anyway.

Stupid men and their stupid rules. The guards were as much prisoners as the prisoners.

Rosalia caught up to the dog, speaking softly to keep it from panicking so she could grab it by the scruff of its neck.

"You do your business," she encouraged, "and then we go inside. Won't do for either of us to be missed. They put another one of those stones in me and I'll forget to feed you."

The dog pulled back its lips from big teeth, yipped once in delight, tail wagging.

"Come on, stupid mutt," Rosalia urged. "We're getting out of here soon enough. You just play along for now, okay? For me?"

The dog opened its mouth, made to bark again, and Rosalia stroked it, tickling it behind the ears. As if understanding her, the dog pulled away and headed back up the slope toward the hidden door, stopping once to urinate on the side of a tree.

Back at the doorway, Rosalia pushed her dark hair behind her and brought the hood of her robe up to cover it once more. She took one last look at the mountainous vista as the wind shook the branches of the trees. Soon she would be out of here. Things had turned so hostile that she might not last out there on her own, but with the Magistrate man at her side…? She would have to convince him, and convince him it was his idea.

Chapter 15

To Mariah Falk, it seemed that she had been crying forever. For the past several hours she knew she had been lying in this sealed cavern, neither asleep nor truly awake, just dwelling on what had happened to Clem in some twilight dream state. How long, Mariah couldn't be certain. But ultimately, something within her seemed to snap to attention, and she rolled off the hard, unforgiving floor and sat up, opening her tear-hot eyes for the first time in what seemed a lifetime.

She had paid scant attention to the cell when she had been placed inside, but now she looked at it, *really* looked at it, for the first time. It was rock; the whole cell was rock. The walls, the floor beneath her, the ceiling above.

In her day, Mariah had been a renowned geologist; her area of expertise was rock. When she had been assigned to the Manitius Moon Base along with numerous other valuable military and scientific personnel, and cryogenically frozen as some kind of gift to the future, Mariah had never really thought much of her specific role. She had volunteered, feeling that it was her patriotic duty, her personal responsibility, one of those nebulous concepts that speak of morality and selflessness. But in all honesty Mariah knew she had mostly taken up the opportunity because it promised adventure. How many people got the chance to see the world two hundred years after their birth? Even if it wasn't the plan, Mariah felt like—who was that guy?—Buck Rogers, zipping off to the future and finding out how wonderful everything had turned out.

Except the future hadn't turned out to be very wonderful at all. In fact, she had woken to a society just barely storing the concept of civilization, the memory of the brutal era known as the Deathlands still fresh in people's minds. The establishment of the Program of Unification was a threshold in the recent past that spoke of withdrawing from the brink of apocalypse, and it had come at a terrible price: the subtle subjugation of humankind under the all-powerful alien race called the Annunaki, then disguised as allies.

Like her fellow Manitius refugees, Mariah had been adopted into the Cerberus operation, which was led by another man from the twentieth century—Dr. Mohandas Lakesh Singh. But while her fellows had been doctors, physicists, cybernetics engineers and other explorers at the very edge of scientific discovery, Mariah had never felt her contribution matched up. She was a geologist, an expert on rocks. Rocks weren't at the cutting edge of scientific invention. Rocks were those things people stood on while they invented, and then they got carved into statues to celebrate the discoveries.

Now, sitting alone in the tight little cave, its walls seemingly sealed all around her, Mariah Falk peered into the gloom and laughed. Ullikummis's troops had sacked Cerberus, killed some of her friends, imprisoned the majority. And they had imprisoned them in rock.

Stretching her weary limbs, Mariah ran her fingers across the floor, feeling the thin bed of sand there. She pawed at the sand, burrowing beneath it with her fingertips. Less than one knuckle's depth below the surface she found the solid floor. She scraped at the sand, leaning close to peer at the exposed rock. It was the same kind as the walls. The cocoon of the cell reminded her of a honeycomb.

Beneath the dim light that glowed from a small panel above her, Mariah studied the rock for a moment, checking it and comparing it to the wall before her. It was igneous rock, she suspected, formed by magma flow. Very little natural porosity, which meant it would be very solid—solid and heavy. But a corrosive could damage this, she knew.

More importantly, the suggestion that this had once been magma gave Mariah some clues about its origin. She had seen Ullikummis up close, had seen the rivers of lava that seemed to flow through his veins. Igneous rocks—the rocks around her—were formed of lava, and it didn't strain credulity to suggest there might be a link between the two.

When placed in a cave, it was only natural to assume that the cave had always been there, and not to question its structure. But what if this cave was some kind of manipulation? Mariah wondered. What if Ullikummis had created this cell, had utilized his seemingly mystical power to draw caves in place the way an artist might paint them onto a canvas?

She had seen him do it before. Ullikummis had moved rocks, drawing them from the surface of the Earth using some kind of sympathetic telekinesis. He had created a whole settlement, the stone construction called Tenth City. The number had been important, Mariah recalled. Clem Bryant had explained it to her.

The Annunaki had hidden in nine villes set across America. Nine barons, nine villes. Nine was the number of the universe, Clem had said. Nine was both creation and destruction; nine was the all.

"It is an ouroboros number," Clem had said one day as they sat together. "It feeds upon itself. In Hindu belief, four is destruction, while five is creation. Add them together and you represent all the energy in the universe."

Clem had been trying to explain to her why Ullikummis had chosen to call his settlement Tenth City, after Mariah had expressed her recurring nightmare of being forced to return.

"It's entirely understandable that you're worried about returning to the scene of the crime," Clem said, indicating Mariah's wounded ankle, where she had been shot while in Ullikummis's ghost city. "But if you understand it, you can conquer your fear."

Mariah wasn't so sure, but she listened to Clem's soothing voice, admiring the man's fortitude and his passion for reducing everything to logic and emotion. "So if nine is the number of everything," she'd asked, "why would Ullikummis choose ten?"

"In the simplest terms," Clem said, "to suggest superiority over the other Annunaki overlords, perhaps."

"But…?" Mariah had pressed. She knew Clem, knew how he would be working through the problem on several different levels at the same time.

"To be greater than nine," Clem said, "to be more powerful than creation and destruction, to be more powerful than the all—that's one ambitious godling. I daresay our godling has a god complex!"

Mariah looked at Clem for a long moment as he sipped his steeping tea. "You think there's more, though, don't you?" she asked.

"Human history," he mused, "has been subtly dictated by the Annunaki. Their symbols underpin every development, every human endeavor. We have things, concepts, that show themselves in different ways across different cultures, but all seem to be in tune, as if they all came from the same source. In the Kabbalah, ten is the number of kingship. Known as Malkuth, it is unlike the other nine sephirot. The tenth is considered an attribute of God that does not emanate from God directly, but rather from his creation. God's creation reflects God's glory from within itself.

"In naming his creation Tenth City," Clem continued, "Ullikummis was building a structure to reflect his own magnificence. That city design was a sigil, a powerful magical sign that can influence the course of events, and even the rational thinking of humans. You yourself were caught in its thrall."

Mariah blushed, her acute embarrassment at recalling the event clearly written across her face.

Clem shook his head as if to chastize her. "Few people could resist that for very long, Mariah," he explained. "There's no shame in being trapped by its power. We— which is to say, civilized man—have these symbols indoctrinated into our thinking from a very young age. The cities of man, the great ones like Paris and New York and London—these all follow the sigil design, the same design Ullikummis used to create Tenth City. The Annunaki have been playing a very long game with mankind, one far more insidious than we first suspected."

"So it's possible that Tenth City is calling me back," Mariah reasoned.

"You told me that the city was destroyed," Clem said, "leveled to the ground by explosives. I doubt even a city can call to people from beyond the grave."

In the cavelike cell now, Mariah wondered if perhaps this place was the city calling from beyond the grave, or at least clawing from it. Cerberus had been chasing after Ullikummis, bumbling into him since he had first arrived on the planet several months ago, but they had never considered what this monster could do. Typically, Cerberus had involved itself in engagements with the rogue Annunaki as they had with his father and family before him, but if they had considered what he could be capable of, they might have stayed one step ahead of him and prevented his successful attack on their home base.

Mariah eyed the wall under the dim, flickering glow of the recessed magma light, searching for a jutting piece. There, a little to her left, she spotted just what she was looking for—a piece of the rough stone, no bigger than her thumbnail, poking out on a tiny bridge of rock, barely connected to the wall.

Mariah reached across and pulled at it, worked it for a moment, pushing against the thin splinter that joined it to the wall. Given time and a little effort, it would break away, she knew.

The stone god had made a mistake in letting Mariah live. He had pushed her about in Tenth City, tried to kill her and failed. But killing Clem—that had been something new. A line had been crossed.

Mariah ran her hand along the rocky wall, then prodded the little jutting piece again, feeling it move just a little as she put pressure on it. "I know you, don't I?" she muttered.

Sure, Mariah wasn't an ex-Magistrate fighting machine like Kane, or a hyperintelligent warrior woman like Brigid Baptiste. All Mariah Falk was—all she had ever been—was a geologist. But a geologist knows rocks.

Using the heel of her hand, she gave a final push against the little jutting piece, felt it snap away. It skittered across the floor before bouncing off the far wall and coming to rest in the sand.

"Watch out, stone face," Mariah whispered as she picked up the tiny shard. "I've got your number now."

SELA SINCLAIR THOUGHT she could hear a marching band. The muscular, dark-skinned woman was ex-air force, and she had seen her fair share of parades and marching bands.

This music was coming from nearby, she was sure. She could hear it distinctly enough, although it seemed to be muffled, like voices from another room or music from the apartment above her own. It was at its loudest when First Priest Dylan visited her. Did she like him?

She was lying down, she realized, lying on something hard and cold, her eyes closed. She had been sleeping through the parade.

Sela opened her eyes and looked out on darkness. No, not darkness—not quite. As her eyes adjusted she became aware of a faint red glow above her, a red like blood seeping into her vision.

She rolled a little, struggling to make her muscles move. Her arms had gone numb thanks to the cold surface she had been sleeping on, and what little warmth she generated seemed to be lost in the cold place she found herself.

It was a cave, she realized, looking about her. A cave deep underground. At least, she assumed it was underground, though there was no real way of telling.

Sela pushed herself up from the cold rock, bringing her knees close and hugging them as she sat up, feeling the freezing cold of the chamber bite at her as she moved. "Where's the band?" she muttered, peering around.

The music was still coming to her, as if from close by, perhaps from another room within her old frat house.

"They don't have frat houses in caves," Sela whispered to herself as the band played on.

She pushed herself up, finding it was a struggle, given the way her body seemed so heavy just now. It was as if she had been drugged, she felt so weary.

They don't have bands in caves, either, Sela reminded herself as she looked around the space, still trying to fathom where the music was emanating from.

Slowly, her movements appreciably strained as if she had aged forty years in a day, Sela Sinclair walked around the little cave, searching for a doorway. There was none.

"What the hell?" she asked, rubbing her palm against her head as the music played on. She stopped suddenly, pulling her hand away. There was something there, in her head.

Tentatively this time, Sela brought her hand up and placed her fingertips on her forehead at her hairline, running them slowly down toward her eyes. On the second try she found the bump, a small calluslike thing located almost dead center of her forehead, where the mythical third eye was shown in those old trippy hippie paintings she'd seen years ago. Still standing, she bent over and ran her fingers around her forehead, reassuring herself that this was the only lump she was carrying. There were bruises and cuts on her face, and she winced once or twice as she probed at them, but the thing on her forehead was different. It seemed to sit there, a hard lump beneath the skin, moving slightly to her touch as if floating on a bed of Jell-O.

Sela pushed at the bump for a moment, using finger and thumb to trace its edges. It was quite large, about the size of her thumb joint, and it was entirely beneath her skin. She felt her head but could find no wound, no cut where it might had entered. Yet it didn't feel like a swelling—it felt like a stone.

Sela couldn't imagine what the thing was as she ran her hands over it again and again, worrying at it with the blunt edges of her short nails.

And somewhere, distant but not *too* distant, the music played on.

Chapter 16

"Wake up, Magistrate man." It was a woman's voice, throaty, with the lilt of an accent.

Kane's eyes opened, the hard crust of sleep caught between the lashes of his left. He reached up, brushed the sleep away, trying to focus his mind.

"Are you awake?"

It was the woman's voice again. Kane recognized it now as belonging to Rosalia, the street thief cum bodyguard who had accompanied First Priest Dylan into his cell.

Kane sprang like a jungle cat, grappling her legs and dragging her to the floor. He heard her head thump against the wall behind her, and she spit out a curse as she collapsed before him.

To his right, something barked, and Kane felt a furry lump of muscle barrel into his side—Rosalia's dog, an ugly, pale-eyed mongrel. Kane kicked out, booting the animal away. It slammed against the wall, whined as it fell down.

Kane turned back to the woman as she struggled to get up, and his hand snapped out, thrusting her back to the floor of the cavern. He was on top of her in an instant, drawing his fist back, ready to pound her as she squirmed beneath him.

"Let me out of here!" Kane snarled.

With her hood and long hair splayed around her,

Rosalia looked back at Kane through the semidarkness. "Don't b—" she began.

But Kane didn't let her finish. His hand snapped out, striking her across the face. When he pulled it back there was blood on it, and the woman's lip was split, and bloody.

"Let me out of here!" Kane snarled again, his eyes fixed on the woman's.

"Just wai—"

He struck her again, his open hand slapping across her jaw. "Let me out of here!" he repeated. Beside him, the dog was barking, baring its teeth but not quite brave enough to approach the ex-Mag.

Rosalia's dark eyes fixed on Kane's, and he was impressed to see they betrayed no fear. She waited, saying nothing for an extended moment while he crouched atop her, his hand poised to strike her again.

He waited but she said nothing, just holding his gaze with her own. The cavern was still sealed closed, with no sign of the door through which the woman must have entered.

Finally, Rosalia spoke. "Listen to me," she said. "Just listen for a moment and stop thinking with your fists. Can you do that?"

Kane looked at her, relaxing his hand but still holding it above her like a threat.

She turned then, hushing the dog with a few calming words, the way a mother would address an irritating child. The dog whined momentarily, then fell silent, its tail brushing the wall of the cave as it skulked away. Then the beautiful dark-haired woman turned back to Kane, the trace of a smile on her cut lips.

"You're a fool, Magistrate man," she hissed. "We're both trapped here. Don't you realize that?"

"You were with him," Kane growled. "Dylan. The first priest of the New Order."

"Do you think I chose to be there?" Rosalia challenged.

"I dunno," Kane snapped back. "The last time we met you were in the employ of street scum. I'm not seeing much difference, except this guy's dressing up what he's peddling as religion."

"They tell you to submit, Kane," Rosalia told him, and he realized she was using his name for the first time, "and you have to."

"That's not true," he retorted.

"Yes, it is," she said. "They don't give you a choice. They ask and then they tell and then they force you."

"They force *you?*" Kane asked.

"I don't know how much you've seen," Rosalia told him as she lay sprawled on the rock floor, "so if this sounds like lunacy then you'll just have to trust me, okay?"

"You must be thinking of a different Magistrate man," Kane said mockingly, turning her curse against her.

Rosalia ignored him. "They have things called obedience stones," she said. "They plant them inside you. They block your thoughts, sap your willpower."

Kane knew she was telling the truth. He had watched one of the stones the intruders had thrown as it tried to bury itself in his flesh. The Annunaki, for whom these people worked, were masters of organic technology. What she was saying sounded like madness, but it had the ring of truth.

"Go on," Kane instructed.

"You think maybe you can get off me first?" Rosalia asked.

"Don't push your luck, princess," he growled. "So, these obedience stones. You have one?"

"Yes," Rosalia said. "It's in my arm. It's how I got in here."

"Say that again?"

"The doors are operated by a pulse from the stones," Rosalia explained. "Only the faithful can come and go as they please in the new world."

Kane could worry about that later. "But this thing— this stone—it makes you obey the big cheese? Is that right?"

"It works better on the weak-minded," Rosalia said, "and needs a broadcast unit to have the desired effect."

"Broadcast unit," Kane mused. "So, if you're in the gang, how come you're telling me this?"

"It works on the weak-minded," Rosalia repeated, and Kane noticed there was a degree of arrogance to the set of her jaw now.

"And you're telling me," Kane said slowly, "that you're not."

"I figured out a way to vent it," Rosalia said. "Catch it quick enough and it can't take proper hold."

Something occurred to Kane then, and his hand tightened, ready to hit the woman beneath him again. "This a trick to get me to accept one of these things? To submit?"

"Oh, Magistrate man, you are so naive," Rosalia mocked. "You've lived in a world of blacks and whites for so long that you've forgotten what it is to have color. Look at you. Look around you. You're one man, stuck in a cell with no door, suffering from dehydration and slowly being starved to death. And you think I'd come here and trick you into giving up when they know you're so close to doing so."

"I'm not close," Kane growled. But he could feel the light-headedness, feel the empty chasm of his gut.

"What, you think Dylan will say 'We tried keeping him three days in a cell. Might as well give up and let him go'?" Rosalia challenged.

Kane thought about that, let the woman's argument sink in. Finally he nodded, and then he climbed from Rosalia's form, stepped away. As he did so, the dog snarled again, but Kane just glared at it, his tolerance exhausted.

Before him, Rosalia reached into her robe and produced a handkerchief, which she used to wipe the blood from her lip. The cut had dried now, and she spit on the handkerchief to moisten it and clean the blood that had dried against her skin. Standing, she brought her face close to Kane's beneath the flicking magma light, gesturing to the cut. "All gone?" she asked.

"Why?"

"They see I'm hurt and they'll know something happened," Rosalia explained. "Not good."

There was a thin line of blood still on her chin, and Kane wet his finger to clean it. His saliva was thick and gunky, as if he'd dipped his finger in sauce. "Stay still," he instructed.

Once he'd finished cleaning her face, Rosalia continued her explanation. "You're stuck here, Magistrate man," she said. "It's just a matter of time now, and they know it."

"Dylan?" Kane asked.

"Others, too."

"We saw fifteen, maybe twenty when they attacked Cerberus," Kane recalled.

"More than that," Rosalia told him with irritating

vagueness. "They want you to submit because you're a leader."

"What about Lakesh?" Kane asked.

Rosalia looked at him blankly. "The name means nothing to me," she admitted.

Kane pondered how much he should tell this woman, this potential enemy. But she was right—he was stuck here and she was all he had for now. "Lakesh Singh," he told her. "He runs the Cerberus operation."

Rosalia shrugged. "There are others being kept here, in this facility. So—maybe?"

Others, Kane heard, and his thoughts automatically went to his *anam-chara,* his soul friend. "What about Baptiste? And Grant," he added.

"Kane," Rosalia urged, "I don't have much time here. You're out of the game right now, you understand me?"

He nodded.

"I'm offering to deal you back in if you'll trust me," she continued. "You in?"

Kane held out his hand to her and she took it. "I'm in," he assured her.

"Then this is what we're going to do," Rosalia began.

Chapter 17

Domi lay in the semidarkness of her cell, the light above her fluttering like the feathers of a crow taking wing. She held one bone-white arm over her head, using it to cover both her ears, with hand and upper arm respectively. She was naked through choice, having stripped off the slight garments she had worn when she had entered this now-sealed cavern. Beneath the fluttering magma glow of the light, her goose-white skin looked orange, like an evening ray of sunlight snapped off and thrust into the cavern. Hidden by her right ear, her wrist bore the jagged scarring of a hideous wound, its blush of red looking horribly out of place against her pure white flesh. Domi cried in silence, thick tears drooling down her face from her eerie red eyes. She ached.

Domi was especially sensitive to changes in the atmosphere around her, some curious byproduct of her upbringing in the savage Outlands, and the albinism that defined her. Now she lay crying beneath the dim light of the magma pod. Its flickering was faint, and others less sensitive than her might not have even noticed the changing frequency. But she saw it, *felt* it deep within her brain. It was giving her tangle-brain, the same way that the towers of the villes gave her tangle-brain when she was cooped up within them for too long.

Domi glanced up from the stony floor, scanning the rocky ceiling seven feet above her, where the single indentation of light glowed with all the intensity of a cooking ring, a little blister of orange in the blackness of the cave. It wasn't just a light, Domi realized, it was a broadcaster. It sent out a signal that could dull a man's thoughts, could make him placid. But the broadcast beacon did not work on its own. A broadcast unit needs a receiver.

Instinctive and emotional, Domi was considered by many of her peers to be a barbarian. And they were right to an extent, but it was folly to confuse a barbarian with a simpleton. Domi was smarter than many gave her credit for; her smarts just worked in different ways from the likes of Lakesh and Brigid and all the other scientists and doctors and big brains that inhabited the halls of the Cerberus redoubt.

Domi had figured out that the broadcast signal required a receiver to do its work. Sure, the lights could affect the brain in a dull sort of a way, but to really work to their fullest extent, they needed a pickup unit to feed the transmission to their victims.

They had tried to give Domi a receiver before they'd locked her in this cell. A tiny stone no larger than her thumb joint had been placed at the hollow of her wrist. She had been in the main corridor of the Cerberus redoubt at the time, close to the now-sealed rollback doors where the gaudy painting of Cerberus, the hound of hell, watched over everything with six fearsome eyes. She had gazed in horror as Kane had fallen to the might of the stone god, where Brigid and Grant had already been dispatched by this inhuman monstrosity. Domi had tried to help Kane, but her energy was spent, used up by crawling in the ventilation system of the redoubt, too much running, too long a fight against superior might. Half-giddy and light-headed, she had been dragged by the hooded figures to join her colleagues at the end of the corridor, where Lakesh, Falk, Bry and the others waited, hands knitted behind their heads like good little prisoners. Grant's unconscious form had been dragged along, too, but Kane had been left where he lay, the bloody wounds on his grazed face glistening, the shadow suit torn where it had taken unimaginable punishment at the hands of Ullikummis and his men. Domi peered at Kane through narrowed eyes as she was dragged past his motionless body, and she silently hoped he was still alive.

Farther down the corridor that ran the length of the redoubt, Brigid Baptiste lay on her back, her hair spread about her head like a fiery halo. She twitched and moaned as she lay there, unconscious but restless, and Domi struggled to reach for her, shrugging away from the grip of the hooded figures who held her.

"Let me go," she'd snarled. "I have to see if Brigid's okay."

One of the hooded figures reached for Domi, grabbing her wrist and pulling her back like an errant child. She had hissed at the contact, baring her teeth at her attacker.

Then another of the hooded intruders grabbed Domi's other hand and, as she tried to kick out, two more grabbed her by the legs, carrying her between them like a splayed star. After a moment, Domi stopped struggling, realizing it was hopeless, that she was expending energy for no purpose other than to indulge her own temper. A short while later, she was tossed in among the other captured personnel, the robed guards watching her with contempt, the way one would watch a rabid animal.

Daryl Morganstern, the theoretical mathematician Domi and Brigid had been defending in the upstairs lab, had also been dragged down to join the others, and he looked close to death, his face bruised and bloody, his eyes wandering and unfocused. Domi wanted to ask how he was, but the rumbling voice of the stone god burst into her thoughts like a hurricane smashing into an old barn.

"Obedience," Ullikummis stated, his burning eyes flicking across the group, "is your key. Obedience will open up the new world for each of you. And through obedience you will learn progression, such as it ever was writ."

Domi tried to make sense of the stone monster's words, studying where his face and chest had been burned by the acid, a blackened charring, black on black. He was talking about conformity, she realized, and that was something Domi had little tolerance for. Until she had reached her teens, she had avoided ville life for that very reason, only arriving in Cobaltville as a sex slave in the Tartarus Pits. Domi was no scholar of history, but she had picked up things from Brigid and Lakesh, and she recognized that history was often built on agreements and obedience. What Ullikummis was bringing them was an old, old story, a scenario that had been with man since the dawn of civilization. It was a scenario that seemed ingrained within the very genetic makeup of humankind.

Ullikummis strode along the group of wary prisoners, studying each in turn the way a sergeant major might study his troops.

"Submit," he explained, "and the future will be yours. We shall build utopia together. Embrace the future. Submit."

And then the great stone god had touched his upper thigh, brushing the rough, lumpy stonework there until he came away with a dozen flecks of stone, snapped from his body like scabs. A moment passed as Ullikummis scanned the group sitting before him. Domi could feel the irritation emanating from this stone creature as he looked them over. The people of Cerberus had caused him trouble, more so than he had expected when his troops had infiltrated the mountain redoubt. Kane had dropped him, hurt him, almost defeated him in one-on-one combat. Perhaps this Annunaki prince held himself above the simple apekin that cowered before him, but Domi sensed he was angry, that he wanted to conclude this swiftly so he might move on, wash the burning acid from his body, pluck the bullets from his flesh.

Ullikummis paced for a moment, his footsteps echoing loudly in the tunnel, looking at each of the exhausted figures resting there on the cold floor of the redoubt—Lakesh, Philboyd, Sinclair, Falk. His stonelike flesh still bubbled and misted with the corrosive effects of the acid, although it had dulled to a whisper of smoldering trails now when he walked. Finally, the stone giant stopped, standing before Daryl Morganstern, the most recent addition to the prisoner group. Kane was being dragged to join them now, along with Brigid, but both remained unconscious. Morganstern, at least, was awake.

Ullikummis reached for Morganstern where he knelt, plucking him from the floor with an easy show of his phenomenal strength, lifting the mathematician into the air with one hand. In his other hand, Ullikummis rattled the clutch of stones he held, shaking them like dice. Then, still holding Morganstern's trembling body three feet off the floor, Ullikummis reached out with his other hand and brought one of those strange stone growths toward the man's forehead, rubbing it against the bloody skin of his head with a misplaced sense of gentleness.

Delirious from his earlier beating, Morganstern struggled to maintain eye contact, burbling something at the monster who held him, the scabbing blood streaking down the side of his face in red and black.

"Submit," Ullikummis instructed, his voice eerily calm. Then he pressed the fleck of stone he held to Morganstern's forehead with his thumb, forcing it into the skin in the space between the man's eyes.

Morganstern began to scream, and several of the Cerberus prisoners gasped or turned away. Mariah Falk muttered a prayer she remembered from high school, turning away from the vision before her as the man struggled in Ullikummis's grip, his legs kicking out and his voice hoarse with screaming. The bloody gash at the side of his head was oozing blood once more where the scab had broken.

"Please stop," Lakesh pleaded from the group of captives. "Please don't do this terrible thing. The man is doing you no harm now. No one is."

Ullikummis ignored him.

Domi just watched, saying nothing. She had grown up in the Outlands and had seen worse sights than this.

Ullikummis pushed the stone into Daryl Morganstern's head, exerting incredible pressure with just his thumb, forcing the small stone against the man's skin until it ruptured, embedding the stone there like a tack.

Then, with a casual brutality that surprised Domi, Ullikummis dropped Morganstern like a rag doll, letting the slender mathematician tumble to the floor. The man was still gasping, tears running down his cheeks, his fists clenched and his limbs twitching in agony. He cried out in pain as he landed on the floor of the tunnel.

Domi and the others watched in amazement as the stone at Morganstern's forehead began to sink beneath the skin, like a pebble dropped in milk, disappearing under the surface with just a circling ripple of skin marking its passage. Where the skin rippled, the scab at the side of Morganstern's head tore open wider, and a rich line of red spilled down the side of his face. Daryl Morganstern cried out in agony, slapping his palms against the floor as the alien thing drilled into him. "Make it stop," he cried. "Make it stop."

Ullikummis looked down at the writhing figure and breathed a single word: "No."

Rolling on the floor, his limbs twitching, Morganstern looked at the stone god with pleading eyes. "Please," he cried, "make it stop."

"Submit," Ullikummis instructed, "and the pain will pass."

"N-no," Morganstern muttered, but it wasn't clear anymore if he was talking to Ullikummis or the agony that was gripping him inside his head. Then he shuddered, and a bloody rent opened on his forehead, oozing another thick ribbon of blood down his face. "No," he screamed as his head literally tore apart.

Domi watched, keeping a tight rein on her emotions as Daryl Morganstern's head was ripped apart by the thing that Ullikummis had placed there. The theoretical mathematician lay twitching in a scarlet puddle of his own blood as his head disintegrated before Domi's eyes. His hair fell away, clumps of it dropping to the floor, matted with blood. Suddenly the brain was visible, brain stem glistening as the man's skull fractured, parting as though cut with a blade. And still he cried out, seemingly longer than he should have the conscious will to do so. But finally his struggles ended, and his body stopped twitching, its horrifying dance of death ceasing at last.

Ullikummis turned back to the remaining Cerberus exiles, who knelt before him and his people on the floor of the redoubt tunnel. "Submit," he instructed.

Then Ullikummis held out the other stones he had plucked from his body, passing them to the hooded figures, who began to move among the crowd, choosing who would suffer the intrusion of the strange stones. To Domi's relief, her lover, Lakesh, was passed over, described as "too old" for what these people had in mind. It was understandable. It was evident that the procedure was physically traumatic, and Lakesh had been getting more and more infirm over the past few months. Although Domi did not know why, he was suffering from accelerated aging, his body leaping years in the space of weeks. The man had been plagued with bouts of exhaustion for the past several months now, and he seemed only to be getting worse. For once, Lakesh's ill health might prove his unlikely savior.

However, where Ullikummis had placed the stone in his victim's head, the hooded figures instead used people's arms as the insertion points for the stones, pressing them into the soft flesh of the inside wrist, holding them there until they burrowed beneath the skin and attached themselves to their unwilling hosts. Some people screamed as the stones drilled into their bodies, while others wept quietly. Several of the stronger members of the facility remained stoically silent, letting the stones infiltrate their bodies without complaint. Perhaps these last had already submitted mentally, resigning themselves to their fate, as Ullikummis had urged.

Domi watched warily as several of the robed figures turned toward her, and to her surprise she recognized one of them with a start—it was Edwards, the ex-Mag turned Cerberus rebel whom she had accompanied on field missions time and again. The broad-shouldered ex-Mag was doing Ullikummis's bidding, doing it willingly. As he stepped closer, Domi saw that Edwards had a scuff mark on his forehead like some dark pimple, and she concluded that the man had one of these terrible stones buried there, hidden at the front of his brain. How long had he had that? Could Edwards have been carrying this evil seed ever since he first encountered Ullikummis—perhaps three months ago? Had Edwards been in the Annunaki's thrall all along?

Domi recalled how Edwards's Commtact unit had ceased working while they were out in the field recently. The radio unit was inserted in his mastoid bone, but its contacts had failed somehow, some kind of blockage to the sensors rendering it inoperative. Could that have had anything to do with this whole affair? Could the buried stone have somehow disrupted the comm device?

But if Edwards was a sleeper agent, then it was obvious how Ullikummis's troops had gained access to the redoubt. Edwards had let them in.

Domi felt fear rise within her, more so than it had when these beastly attackers had arrived, more so even than when she had seen the looming form of Ullikummis striding through the Cerberus redoubt—through *her home*. She realized for the first time in a long, long time that they had been caught napping. The whole of Ullikummis's deadly plan had been put in motion months ago, when he had first fallen to Earth in a meteor shower, and he had had the foresight to recruit operatives like Edwards into his band of followers, had merely waited for the right moment to call on them, and so to strike.

Cerberus had spent years defending humanity, uncovering conspiracies and facing deadly foes. But somehow they had become lazy, had trusted things to stay as they were because that's how they always had been. Now, Ullikummis was the catalyst for a change that would fundamentally alter their world. And they had let him come, had done nothing to stop him, had failed to understand the bigger change that his appearance would bring. With all the tools and expertise at Cerberus's disposal, they had entirely failed to look beneath the surface of Ulli-kummis's plan until it was too late, and the Annunaki and his followers were among them, wearing the faces of their colleagues.

Led by Edwards, the hooded figures held Domi down while Ullikummis watched. They placed one of the dark stones, this one the size of Domi's thumb joint, against her wrist and held her down, held her as the stone bur-rowed into her body and disappeared beneath the pale flesh like a grub burrowing into a corpse. Once the stone had disappeared, the skin of Domi's arm went smooth, no cut visible. There was a lump there, like a blind boil forming, but no cut, no clear demarcation point where the stone infiltrator had entered.

Domi cursed and screamed as the stone tried to bond with her, and then she had done something remarkable, something that Ullikummis's troops had not seen before. The second they let go of her, Domi had grasped at the disappearing stone with her right hand, snagged it with her busy fingers the way one might find a splinter hidden in the skin, and she had plucked it from her flesh in one hideous tearing movement. Blood spurted from the wound she'd created with her nails, red runnels pouring down her arm like spilled paint. The stone thing seemed to pulse in her hand as if alive, and Domi tossed it to the floor of the redoubt tunnel. It writhed there a moment, a hideous mockery of life as Domi felt the warm blood pouring from her torn wrist and out across the planes of her small white hand.

Then Edwards stepped forward and, with a smile on his lips, struck her across the face. Still in shock from the terrible surgery she had just performed on herself, Domi staggered back, glaring at Edwards with bloodred eyes.

"Temper down, freak girl," Edwards snarled, drawing his fist back to strike her again. "Always had you figured for a waste of time."

Then he'd pumped his fist at her head, and she saw something dark and shiny glistening between his knuckles. It was a flat stone, used like a blackjack to cuff a disruptive foe. Domi stepped aside, crying out as the blow struck her right shoulder instead of her face. Her shoulder burned with pain and her arm went numb instantaneously, but she was determined not to go down without a fight. She jabbed the flat of her left hand at Edwards's hooded face, bringing the heel up to meet his nose as droplets of blood flew from the open wound at her wrist. Edwards avoided the blow by the smallest margin, then brought his hand up once again to strike Domi with the blackjack.

Already weary, Domi stepped back, avoiding the arc of Edwards's savage punch by the merest fraction of an inch. He stumbled, misjudging his balance as his swinging punch glided past the albino girl.

"Hah," Domi taunted. "Too slow."

Edwards glared at her as he brought himself back up to his full height, the monstrous form of Ullikummis watching from behind him, volcanic veins glowing across his stone body like magma rivers.

Despite her exhaustion, Domi remained light on her feet, bare skin slapping against the tunnel flooring as she stepped out of Edwards's reach. But as she did so, she found herself surrounded by four more of the hooded figures, each of them reaching for her with grasping hands.

"Hold her down," Edwards snarled, drawing his fist back once again.

Suddenly, Domi was being yanked off her feet, drawn backward until she tumbled over and slammed against the floor with a blurt of breath from her lungs. She reached up, tried to push the intruders away from her as Edwards's dark shadow loomed above her, but her right arm still felt numb and it wouldn't react, while her left wrist poured with blood.

"Dammit Edwards, don't—"

IN HER CELL, Domi lay huddled into herself, crying with despair. What Edwards had done then had been mercifully brief, and when she had awoken she had found herself in this eerie, doorless cavern.

Her left wrist felt heavy where the blood had dried and scabbed over, the scab itself restricting her movement like a hard shell. They had not replaced the stone, as far as she could tell. Domi was sure she would know, for she was sensitive, very conscious of things done on or in her body. She disliked clothes, habitually wore only those deemed most necessary to cover her modesty, and shed them when the opportunity arose. The stone was no different. These were alien things, and drew Domi away from the purity of herself.

She lay in the swirling glow of the magma light, listening to its flickering inside her head. The stone had been in her wrist for less than a minute, but she had felt the way it responded to Ullikummis, felt the way it was drawn by his hot blood, his presence. The lights and the stones were a form of control, something Ullikummis craved.

Domi lay nude in the cell, the thin carpet of sand pressing against her legs, knees up and coiled into her chest. She had not eaten in over two days.

Chapter 18

Brigid peered over the mirror, left and right, trying to find where he was. What she could see of the cavern appeared empty, except for herself, the chair and the mirror. "Where are you?" she asked, her tone demanding. "Show yourself." She was angry with herself for being fearful, angry with herself for being scared.

But there was no response, just that infernal scraping of stone against stone. It was *him*. The movements, the noise he made as he walked, she realized, were as distinctive as the movements of a shackled prisoner bound in irons.

"Show yourself," Brigid demanded again. "Show yourself, Annunaki. Show yourself, you damn coward. You damn, damn coward." She was crying when she said the last, her voice cracking as she mumbled the words.

Immediately, Ullikummis's voice rumbled back from the gloom of the cave. "You should not attribute to others the qualities you fear in yourself," he said.

Suddenly, he was standing right before her, striding from the shadows of the rock wall, the fiery lava flow sparking to life in orange traceries across his body, like a light switch being flicked. "You feel fear, Brigid," Ullikummis told her, "and so you think yourself a coward and thus tell me I must be one also."

Brigid glared at the stone-clad Annunaki prince defiantly, her lips pressed tightly together, the hot tears streaming down her cheeks.

"Fear does not make one a coward," Ullikummis told her calmly. "Fear is the mechanism for survival, the facet that keeps all things alive."

Brigid continued to glare at him, this monstrosity, as the tears dried on her face.

Ullikummis took another pace closer, stepping in front of the mirror, placing himself so close to Brigid that they almost touched. "We are not different, Annunaki and humans," he told her. "We just see the world in different ways."

"Set me free," Brigid said. "If we're not so different then set me free from this chair, this cave. I read up on you, learned how you spent millennia inside a prison of rock. You know what it is to be trapped."

"You're not trapped," Ullikummis said. "Not physically."

Brigid pulled at her bonds, assuring herself that she was.

"I chose you because our minds have touched before," Ullikummis said.

Brigid recollected when she had sent her consciousness into the sentient data stream of the Ontic Library to repel Ullikummis, of how they had conversed in a world made of knowledge. She had been guided then by perception and desire, had seen things change at her whim. Temptation had called to her, and she had struggled to resist it.

"You have the capacity to see the world as it is," Ullikummis continued. "You need only cast aside all that you have learned up to now."

Brigid glared at him. "How can…? Why would I?" she corrected herself, stumbling over her own words.

"Did it never strike you as strange that the moon appears exactly the same size as the sun from the surface of the Earth?" Ullikummis asked. "Didn't the nature of an eclipse seem somehow too convenient, like some great cosmic joke?"

Brigid listened to the words, trying to make sense of them.

"When we are finished," Ullikummis told her, "you will see the eclipse as it truly is."

"YOU ARE THE MOTHER," Ullikummis stated, as if from nowhere.

Brigid had been sleeping in the chair. Well, perhaps not truly sleeping, just dozing, catnaps brought on by exhaustion. She had been in the cave a long time now, so long that her time sense had faded, lost to the darkness of the gloomy shadows all around her. She looked up and saw that the mirror had gone, been taken and placed to one side of the orange-lit cave.

"I'm no one's mother," Brigid replied. "I have no children."

Ullikummis looked into her eyes, the fiery orange of his own swirling with the certainty of his words. "You have one."

"I have no children," Brigid assured him. "I don't understand why you'd think—"

"Tell me her name," Ullikummis said, interrupting Brigid's denial.

Her name, Brigid thought. *Her. The girl. Abigail.*

"You still fear me," Ullikummis stated.

"No, I don't," Brigid began, but she knew as she said it that it was a lie. Of course she feared him, this towering monstrosity that stood before her, held her captive in a cave painted with thick shadows.

"Your world has been black and white of necessity," Ullikummis observed. "You and your companions understand the Annunaki only in terms of good and evil. You fear us because we are different, and you attribute that difference as an indicator of malefaction, of evil.

"You apekin are so fragile," Ullikummis continued. "If I wanted to hurt you, I could simply twist your neck where you sit, turn it until the bones snap, leave you there to suffer. You have seen my strength. You know that this is something I could do."

It was, Brigid knew.

"I am not going to kill you," Ullikummis stated, "nor hurt you. I will set you free."

Brigid Baptiste looked at Ullikummis, feeling strangely that she could trust him as he uttered those words. There was a perverse kind of logic to what he said; had he wanted to hurt her he would have done so already.

"Then what...?" Brigid asked.

"Your child," Ullikummis said, his feet kicking up sand as he paced the cavern before Brigid. "She has a name."

Brigid drew a long, steadying breath and slowly let it out. "I had an imaginary child, a niece. It was a trick, nothing more." The trick Brigid referred to had been played while she was trapped in a virtual reality, and her fictitious niece had been a way to hold her there, to distract her. When she had traveled to the Ontic Library and fought with and ultimately repelled Ullikummis, she had been tempted to use the vast resources there—the tools that shape reality—to make Abigail, her niece, real. It had been a momentary whim, an effect of the incredible data stream on her mind.

"Tell me her name," Ullikummis requested, repeating his earlier statement.

Brigid looked at the monster before her, fixed his glowing eyes with her own. "Abigail," she said. "That was her name."

"Can you see her?" Ullikummis asked. "If you think of her, can you see her?"

Brigid nodded slowly, just once. "Yes."

Ullikummis strode away for a moment, his head bowed in thought. "I am to give you a gift, Brigid," he said finally, turning back to her. "The Annunaki are powerful, but your comprehension of that power remains tiny."

Brigid watched this strange being of stone and wondered what he meant. What was he? The stonework that covered his body was like nothing she had seen before, like no other Annunaki before him. He seemed barely like a living being at all.

Ullikummis kicked at the thin layer of sand that carpeted the cavern floor, watched as it clouded and floated away on the slight breeze that spun through the cave. "Do you wish for your freedom, Brigid?" he asked.

She nodded. "Yes."

"Then you will do something for me in order for me to grant that freedom," Ullikummis said. "There is a story, a myth from your race's past, about a queen who so desired a daughter that she implored the gods themselves. And the gods heard her and granted her wish, having the queen shape her daughter of clay."

Closing her eyes, Brigid tried to place the story. But she was exhausted and hungry, and all Ullikummis's talk had left her feeling strangely empty and dizzy and not at all there, as if she was constantly about to awaken from a dream.

When Brigid opened her eyes once more, Ullikummis was crouching beside her, his hand stroking along the arm of the chair where her wrist was tied. Suddenly, there was a click and the wrist bond retracted into the chair, sliding away with the uncomfortable scraping sound of rough-edged rock on rock. Dumbstruck, Brigid stared at her freed hand for a moment, not even moving.

"Wha—?" she began, the word stumbling out of her lips half-formed.

Ullikummis reached across, brushed his misshapen, rocky fingers against the other restraint, the one that held her right hand in place. Like one of those touch-responsive plants that so fascinate children, the rock bond twitched and split, the two halves sinking away into the arm of the chair.

Warily, Brigid raised her hand, rolling her wrist this way and that. It felt tired, aching with stiffness. Then she glanced down, and her eyes scanned the arms of the stone chair where the bonds had been. They appeared—well, not smooth, but flat, giving no indication that they had featured clasps just a handful of seconds before. There was something about Ullikummis, Brigid realized. His psionic link with rock changed its properties, made it into a malleable thing.

"Impossible," Brigid breathed. And yet she had seen it with her own eyes. The evidence was before her right now, even as the stone god leaned down and commanded the bonds at her ankles to disappear, to return to their hidden housings, just a part of the chair.

Ullikummis looked up at Brigid, and she fancied that the expression he wore was whatever passed for a smile on that malformed, rough stone face. "Few things are truly impossible," he told her.

"For the Annunaki?" Brigid finished, her response a query.

"A male and female creature meet," Ullikummis said, as Brigid swung her legs free for the first time in two days, "and they feel desire. Perhaps the female feels the desire and she woos the male, or perhaps the male has need and he simply takes the female in a show of strength."

"Or perhaps they fall in love," Brigid said. "That's how humans would phrase it."

Ullikummis shrugged, the great spiked ridges that towered over his shoulders moving up and down like lancing flames in the air. "The female is fertile, becomes heavy with child. An egg grows to become a new being.

"That is your history and mine, is it not, Brigid?"

Still sitting in the chair, she nodded slowly. "To an extent."

"The odds of those souls meeting," Ullikummis said, "of the egg being fertile, of the fertilization taking place—these are impossible things. Yet they happen. We are proof of that. Our very existence here proves that the impossible happens, and there is a whole world beyond these walls that is full of these impossible meetings, the birth of impossible things."

Brigid shook her head and, underfed and dehydrated, felt light-headed as she did so. She stopped herself, unsure if she was swaying in the seat or if it just felt that way. "No," she said. "Those are just the rules of life. They happen every day. Theory makes them sound unlikely, but we know—"

"The universe is very big," Ullikummis said, "and you are very small. The things that appear impossible appear so because your perspective is too limited. Every occurrence may be considered impossible until you witness it."

He stood before her then, a towering, misshapen thing, veins of fiery magma lining his body between dark rock plates of skin, and his hand reached out for Brigid, like a dance partner, offering to help her from the chair.

"Show me your daughter," Ullikummis intoned, his glowing eyes fixed on Brigid's. "Describe her face."

Taking the proffered hand, Brigid eased herself from the chair on unsteady legs. She had been locked in the same position for so long that her muscles had become locked, and they burned like fire when she moved. She took a tentative step forward, using Ullikummis for support, shuffling forward like an elderly woman.

Three shuffling steps, then Brigid stopped, her hand still pressed in Ullikummis's gentle grip. Over to one side, propped against the wall, she saw the mirror, its tall, oblong reflection angled to show the wall to its side. Automatically, Brigid turned, peering behind her with her own eyes for the first time, looking at the gloomy cavern she had only seen cast in the mirror's reflection. She suspected a trick, expected to see an open door, a flat surface, a curtain made to look like rock. But no, the cavern was as she had seen it in the mirror. Ullikummis had played no trick there, had let her see the place she was in for what it was, bleak and lifeless, just a shadow-filled cave with rock walls and a smattering of sand littering its floor. She could see no exit, no obvious gap where sunlight might poke through. The solid wall reached all around, and the cave stretched a long way back, with just the lone chair placed somewhere off center, closer to the near wall.

It was possible there was an entrance hidden in the far shadows, Brigid knew, tucked there within the darkness. Was that her escape? To use it she would need to trick Ullikummis, fool him somehow into trusting her, leaving her alone, leaving her free to run. That was, of course, assuming there was an exit. The overlord had moved whole chunks of rock in the same way as he'd moved the shackles that had bound her to the chair, Brigid recalled. The reason this place appeared to have no door might be simply that it did not, that it contained a door only Ullikummis could perceive.

There were other ways to escape an impossible room, too, Brigid knew. Out in old Russia, she had been party to an experiment in opening up the higher levels of human consciousness. In that adventure, she had used a mandala—a pattern designed to induce a state of meditation—to exit her body and let her mind roam within a place dubbed Krylograd, the Astral Factory. Employing a similar trick here might grant her freedom, at least from her physical self. But to what purpose? Brigid had an eidetic memory, so she could picture things she had seen as if she were flicking through a photo album. Even now she could picture the mandala design that she had been tasked to memorize, to enter the state of transcendental meditation required to depart her body. The Astral Factory had been specifically designed by the Russian military as a place that the Annunaki could not enter, a place hidden deep within the shared experience of mankind. If this monster wanted the impossible…

"Describe her face," Ullikummis said, his words coming back to Brigid as if from far away.

She was swaying in place, the lack of sustenance making her half-asleep. It was like a waking dream, and Brigid realized then that her mind was subject to drifting, was prone to lose focus unless she disciplined herself.

"Abigail was beautiful," she said, turning back to face the stone thing. She remembered the girl's cherubic face, not yet six years old, a girl programmed to exist in a reality that did not. "She had hair the color of honey, round apple cheeks, and her eyes were like mine—the green of emeralds."

"No, Brigid," Ullikummis said, stepping back and gently letting go of her. "Describe her face. Here. With your hands." Ullikummis was gesturing to the rough floor at their feet, where the sand played in little eddies of wind.

"I don't understand," Brigid admitted, swaying a little in the gloomy cave.

"Make her for me," Ullikummis instructed. "A child of clay, of sand, of dust."

Poupée de son, Brigid remembered. Doll of dust.

"In the story, the queen was tasked to make her child from the earth," Ullikummis reminded his companion. "And you shall do the same. Once this is done, I will grant you your freedom."

Brigid stood there looking at Ullikummis, wondering why he would ask such a thing. Abigail was a figment of her imagination, nothing more than a trick that she had learned to see past, to escape the Janus trap she had been placed within by Cerberus's enemies, the Original Tribe. Whatever emotional bonds Brigid had felt, she had got over them, had left the child behind in her unreal world. The child had no power over her, did she? Or would Ullikummis somehow bring the sand to life, as he had the stone of the walls, the chair? Could he be making her create something with her hands that would come to life? Could hurt her? No. If he did that, she would turn Abigail, would make her her own again.

Kneeling, Brigid clenched her teeth and ran her fingers through the sand. "It's dry," she said.

"I will bring you water," Ullikummis told her, his

shadow looming over the floor where she knelt, "that you may make the child grow."

And then he turned, striding across the cavern and leaving Brigid in the echoing cave. Alone, she began to picture Abigail in her mind, running her hands through the thin grains of sand.

Chapter 19

Kane waited on the far side of the cavelike cell, listening for the noises of movement. It was so well sealed that he could hear nothing other than his own breathing and, if he stood very close to it, the swirling of the magma energies in the overhead light pool. Rosalia had offered to deal him back into the game and, despite his distrust of the mercenary woman, he was reaching the seemingly inevitable conclusion that it was the only option he had left. Kane had been in bad situations before, had suffered defeat at the hands of his enemies, had placed his life in the utmost danger. But those had been temporary things, situations where one option still remained if he looked hard enough.

Here, in this completely sealed cell, he was utterly without hope. He could be left to die here and no one would even know.

And what of Grant, his partner? What of Brigid Baptiste, his *anam-chara*? Were they in this situation, too? Had each of them been placed in solitary confinement in a cell with no door? Kane would risk everything to free them; he would sacrifice himself to save his friends if that was what fate demanded of him.

So he waited in the silent cell until eventually the strange stone door oozed back on its hidden housings, flowing like a thing of liquid, and two figures appeared in the doorway, lit by the bubbling lava that flowed in the walls beyond.

Dylan stepped forward, his face half-hidden beneath the shadows of the hood he wore. "This is your future, Kane," he told him. "The world changed while you weren't looking, and you've woken up to the new reality. Rejoice."

Sitting on the floor, his back against the wall farthest from the doorway, Kane looked up and smiled. "Didn't we do this already?" he chided.

Behind Dylan, Kane recognized the slender figure of Rosalia, her mongrel dog following languorously in her footsteps.

Dylan nodded. "You will rejoice when you embrace the new reality, Kane," the first priest of the New Order said. "It's only a matter of time."

"Why does it matter to you so much?" Kane asked, his voice rough from dehydration.

"To me?" Dylan replied. "I serve only Overlord Ullikummis, and it matters to him. He has seen the things you are capable of, and he requires your service in the upcoming God War."

"God War," Kane muttered, forming the words with his dry, cracked lips. "That's what this is all heading to?"

Dylan nodded. "The sides have been chosen already, Kane," he said. "You need to submit so that things can progress. You will lead a great army into battle against the forces of the devil Enlil. And in return you will live like a baron."

Kane bowed his head, rubbing his hand over his face as if giving this some thought. A rough beard was forming on his chin, sharp stubble bristling against his touch. "What would this process entail?" he asked finally.

"What do I have to do to pledge my allegiance to your master?"

First Priest Dylan eased himself down on his haunches until he was crouching just a few feet away, roughly at eye level with the broken ex-Magistrate. To Kane, the man's eyes seemed alight—with madness. "There are things in this brave new world that need to be embraced if you are to become a part of it," he explained. "These things hurt at first, but you will learn to accept them, and they in turn will become a part of you."

The obedience stones, Kane thought. That was what the dark-haired man was referring to.

"And what about my friends?" he asked.

Behind Dylan, Kane saw Rosalia subtly shake her head, warning him not to pursue this course, but he ignored her. He had agreed to accept her wisdom on this matter, on how to get out of this diabolical prison, but he still had to play it as himself—otherwise this jumped-up sod buster would get suspicious.

"My friends," Kane repeated. "Grant, Baptiste, Domi, Lakesh—"

Dylan held up a hand to halt the list he was reeling off, and that insane smile crossed his features once more, teeth twinkling orange in the faint overhead glow of the magma pod light. "You won't need them," he assured Kane levelly.

"Won't need…?" Kane repeated as if offended. Then he reached for Dylan, grabbing the front of the man's robe and bringing his face closer. Kane's movement was so swift that the priest didn't have time to defend himself. "These are my friends, you jumped-up little toad," Kane snarled. "If I'm going to embrace this fucking utopia of yours I'll do it with my friends at my side."

In the back of the cell, Rosalia leaped forward,

stamping down with her foot on Kane's outstretched forearm. The blow was enough to force Kane to break his hold on the first priest, and Dylan toppled over as he was let free.

Then Rosalia was astride Kane, a leg to either side of his slumped body, her hands stretched out to form flat edges like knives. "Careful, prisoner," she snarled. "The future looks a whole lot bleaker when you're dead."

Kane glared at her, seeing the flash of warning in her own eyes as the dog yipped behind her. He had to play this right, though, had to convince Dylan that he wasn't an easy mark, that this decision was something he was making as Kane, not as part of an act.

Dylan was standing once more, backing away from the scuffle and brushing down the rough material of the robe where he had fallen into the sand. "Rose," he instructed, "let him go."

Rosalia issued a hiss between clenched teeth before backing away from Kane, her eyes never leaving his.

Resting against the wall, Kane watched his two captors warily, before he spoke once again. "I want to see my friends," he said, his voice grim with determination.

Dylan nodded. "You will," he promised. "In time."

"When?" Kane asked.

"When Lord Ullikummis deems it," Dylan replied. Then the self-proclaimed first priest of the New Order reached into his robes, fidgeting with a hidden pouch. A moment later his hand reappeared clutching a smooth pebble no larger than a silver dollar. "Once you embrace the future, you'll see how foolish you've been. These trivialities will melt away and you'll reach a new comprehension. This I promise you, Kane."

Kane watched as Dylan turned the stone over in his hand. Its polished surface glimmered as the orange glow of magma played across it, faintly reflected from the lights of the corridor and the lone pod above Kane's head.

"What does it do?" Kane asked.

"It brings peace," Dylan told him, his voice reassuring.

Kane's eyes were fixed on the stone, and he felt the fear rising inside him. Rosalia had explained how it worked, what had to happen now for Kane to be accepted into the new regime and so be given the opportunity of escape. He was to bond with the stone, which relied on organic technology the way of all things Annunaki—something grown and almost alive, yet not sentient until it was joined to something else, such as a human's nervous system. Kane would submit to this bonding so that he might free his friends. This was the plan; this was how Rosalia had proposed he be dealt back into the game, as she had put it.

"What do I have to do?" Kane asked, his voice low, fearful.

"Hold out your arm," Dylan instructed.

He did so, and then Dylan told him to roll back the torn sleeve of his shadow suit to fully expose his flesh. Kane pushed his sleeve back so that it bunched just beneath his elbow, then held his arm horizontally as if waiting for an injection.

Dylan's robes fell around him like a blooming lotus in the flickering volcanic light of the room as he crouched down by Kane, holding the pebble between thumb and forefinger like a precious egg. Kane waited, his arm outstretched, as Dylan brought the stone seed closer to him, the light glinting off its polished surface in the gloom.

"Will it hurt?" Kane asked then, and his question was genuine, no longer a part of his innocent act.

Dylan nodded. "The future has to be born, Kane," he said, "and birth is traumatic. But it will be brief, and the new world awaits you once it's done. You need never look back, never regret. God will be with you."

Kane gritted his teeth as he watched Dylan bring the stone closer. Then he felt it brush against his skin, its surface cool, and for a moment the ex-Mag tensed.

"Relax into it," Dylan advised. "Don't fight it."

Dylan pulled his hand back slowly, leaving the stone balanced on Kane's outstretched arm. The stone was resting against his wrist now, in the groove at the heel of his hand. Kane watched as the stone sat there, doing nothing out of the ordinary. And then he felt it move, like an insect's tiny feet tickling his wrist, and he almost laughed. The movement was so slight that, in the gloom, he could not really see it. All the same, he felt it, felt as it rolled and turned, inching around in a slow turn at the base of his palm.

Suddenly, Kane felt a strange kind of pain, his skin splitting at his wrist with a burning sensation. It reminded him of the way chapped lips feel in cold weather, a hotness around the wound. He watched as the stone seemed to become slightly smaller. It was sinking, he realized, sinking into his flesh, burrowing there like an insect.

Kane grunted, the noise coming from the back of his throat as he felt the discomfort at his wrist. It looked as though the stone was sinking, pushing against his flesh and parting it, to disappear within his body. It was a form of osmosis, an absorption of one thing into another, something the human body, Kane felt sure, had never been prepared to do. Yet here it was, the stone burrowing into him, being absorbed by him.

Despite the sensation of pressure on his flesh, despite the feel of ripping skin, Kane could see no blood in the poor lighting of the room, could not feel that familiar warm trickle that would alert him to the wound. Instead, it seemed that the pebble just disappeared into his flesh, its dark round shape becoming smaller as less and less of it was left exposed.

Kane's lips pulled back and he grunted again, holding back a scream as he felt the stone scrape against the bone beneath the flesh. It was a cold, empty scraping, like the dentist's drill against a rotten tooth, a strange kind of discomfort for which Kane had no name or frame of reference.

And then, as he watched, the pebble was gone, the whole of its polished surface disappearing beneath his skin, digging into his flesh and burrowing into his body. All that remained was a lump in his skin, like a forming boil, its whitehead not yet emerged. The skin itself was pristine; there was no suggestion that it had been cut, no hint of a wound. Just the bump in his wrist, a protrusion about as big as an eyeball on his otherwise smooth arm.

Beneath his skin, Kane could feel the thing moving, securing itself, exploring the inside of his arm, his body. He reached for that bump, wanting to run his fingers over it, to feel it as it floated beneath his flesh, but Dylan grabbed his hand. Kane looked up at him, remembering for the first time in over a minute that he was not alone in the room, that this alien thing had been placed on his flesh by someone else, like a leech to suck his blood. Dylan shook his head, advising Kane with a single word of instruction: "No."

Kane relaxed his right hand, watched as the lump began to sink into his left wrist, slowly disappearing into his flesh. Ripples appeared around that bump, concentric circles running across his skin as the stone dived deeper and deeper into his body. Kane could feel it pressing there, nosing at the inside of his being, moving about as it sought refuge.

Suddenly, the stone was pushing inside his arm, and Kane growled in pain.

"Embrace it," Rosalia advised from her standing position close to the open door to the cell.

Could he really trust her? Kane wondered. He had put his faith in this woman, this mercenary who had tried to kill him on more than one occasion when they had previously met. She had come at him with knives and a sword, turned a gun on him and his teammates. Yet here he was, taking her advice when she told him to submit to the will of Ullikummis's first priest, to allow himself to be joined with an obedience stone.

"I must be crazy," Kane muttered, the words forced painfully through his clenched teeth, sweat pouring from his brow, dampening his hair. Even as he said it, he sank back, crashing against the wall as the pressure of the stone inside him built, an infectious kind of pain that spread into his muscles there, reaching across his whole body in a pattern that emanated from his left wrist.

"You'll be fine," Dylan assured him as he heard the muttered words. "It will all be over soon enough. Wonders await."

Then First Priest Dylan pushed himself up from the floor and stood looking down at Kane as the ex-Magistrate writhed on the floor like a beached fish, his legs kicking out as the pain gripped him.

"Don't fight it," Dylan advised. "It will be much easier if you embrace it."

Kane felt a coldness then, sweeping across his brow, and he realized he had broken into a sweat at some point during the procedure, while his attention had been focused on his wrist. His whole body was taut, and a strange kind of pain ran through his muscles now, as if he were being stretched on a rack. The pressures seemed to come from everywhere, but centered on his arm.

Vaguely Kane was aware that Dylan and Rosalia had left, with the dog in tow. The cell wall closed behind them, a facade of solid rock once more, the darkness becoming deeper, more absolute.

Alone in the cave, Kane writhed against the floor, his body racked with pain. "Don't fight it," he told himself, remembering Dylan's advice. Whatever it was, it was in him and it could fight harder, keep pushing into him until he submitted to its will.

Kane sank back, his breathing coming fast and shallow as he tried to work through the pain. He tried to relax as best he could, embrace the pain and let it play itself out in his body, let the stone attach itself howsoever it must.

He felt something changing in him as he let the stone reside there, felt a kind of inner peace come over him, the fight leaving him. Despite the pain, he felt tranquil somehow, as if he had trust in the world about him. Faith, that's what it was. He was discovering faith.

As he lay there on the rocky floor in the sealed cave, Kane remembered something that Rosalia had said. She had told him how the stones only work on the weakminded, that she had found a way to break its grip by acting quickly enough. Even if that was true, even if its hold could be broken, what if he wasn't strong enough? Did a man truly know if he was strongminded or weak? Or did he delude himself about being strong, delude himself that his will couldn't be broken? Even if Rosalia came back, did all she had promised when they had agreed to the plan in the tiny cell, would it be in time? Could Kane shake the grip of this terrible thing that had plunged into his body and taken hold?

Waves of blind faith coursed through his mind as he lay there, his body twitching as though jolted by electricity. And the thought of it all, the *horror* of what he had embraced, came to him in a single blinding flash of recognition.

What if there was a sickness, and the sickness was called God? he asked himself.

But the empty cavern offered no answers.

Chapter 20

Alone in the cavern, Brigid explored the limits of her strange cell. It was roughly circular, stretched almost thirty feet across, and was lit by a smattering of wide-spaced pods that glowed with the fiery blur of swirling magma. These pods were recessed into the rock walls and ceiling, and one was in the floor near what Brigid thought of as the back of the cave, for it lay some distance behind the chair in whose embrace she had spent the past two days. As she had suspected, there was no visible exit from the cavern; it seemed to be absolutely sealed. But when she ran her hands along the floor, she found a light breeze blowing through the room. The breeze captured particles of the sand that dusted the floor, picking them up and toying with them until they finally fell back to earth in a swirling dance.

Ullikummis had brought a clay container filled with clear water, the liquid held in place by a stopper also made of clay. Brigid recognized it as an ancient design of water bottle, dating from before the days of strengthened glass, when pottery was the most practical manner for carrying precious fluids. Brigid had poured a little of the water onto her hand and sniffed at it. It looked clear in the dull light, smelled of nothing. She dipped her head and jabbed her tongue at the water that swilled in the cup of her hand, lapping at its coolness and letting it relieve her parched lips. Though it had no discernible taste, it felt wonderful swishing through her mouth, washing over her tongue. It had been so long since she had drunk that Brigid wanted to cry at the feel of it now.

"The water is to help you shape the sand," Ullikummis reminded Brigid, his voice cool and emotionless.

She nodded, placing the stopper back on the clay bottle.

At Brigid's request, Ullikummis had left her. "I need to gather my thoughts to create the face," she had explained. "I've never done anything like this before." Ullikummis had assented, assuring her he would return in a few hours.

Thus alone, Brigid had begun exploring the limits of the cavern, finding nothing that might direct her to freedom. She took careful swigs from the clay bottle, letting the cool water wash over her teeth and quench her dry throat, urging herself not to be greedy, knowing that that would only bloat her stomach and slow her down now when she could least afford it, a step nearer freedom as she was.

Finally, she turned back to the chair that had held her, ran her hands across it. It, too, appeared normal, carved from rock, rough and supremely durable, like something nature had created, ugly and thus beautiful. Aware of the irony, Brigid returned to the chair and sat down in it, resting her aching muscles.

She was alone.

Ullikummis had told her he would grant her her freedom if she showed him the child's face. It seemed like something from a nightmare, a vague and indefinable horror that Brigid could not put her finger upon, unsettling yet innocent all at once. She had to assume it was a trick. Ullikummis was an Annunaki, one of that race of self-styled overlords who had come to Earth to relieve their boredom, toying with and extinguishing humans simply to pass the days. And yet this great beast thing, this Annunaki prince, expressed himself with nobility. He drew things to Brigid's attention that she had not considered before. In short, he seemed strangely honest in his dealings with her.

"This is crazy," Brigid murmured under her breath. "I'm the bird trying to second-guess the cat as if it hasn't already caught me."

There was nothing else to do. Climbing out of the chair, she dragged her foot sideways across the floor of the cave, shoveling a little of the sand together in a mound. Then she leaned down, scooping up more sand with her hands. It sifted through her fingers, its fine grains running away with all the properties of liquid.

Kneeling on the rock floor, Brigid reached for the clay flask, wedged it firmly between her thighs and yanked the stopper from its neck. Carefully, she tipped the flask, dribbled a little of the precious water into the sand between her legs, rationing herself because she was aware she might not get more for a long time. The liquid sprinkled over the sand, darkening it from pale yellow to a color closer to brown. Dampening the sand made it firmer, and Brigid scooped up a handful, squeezing it so that it oozed between her fingers like paste.

A smile crossed her lips as she placed the glob of sand on the ground, scooping more around it to create a little shaped mound. She looked at the sand and thought of what it was she was trying to create—a representation of the girl in her mind, a human fetish made of dust. Brigid moved, her slender fingers working, gathering more and adding drops of water, two or three at a time, to alter the texture of the sand, forcing it to bond.

The waters had broken between her legs and now

Brigid was giving birth to the child of her mind. Was this how it would feel to have a child, to bring life into the world? Was this what they fought for? Of course it was—wasn't this all that humankind had always fought for? A place to bring new life into the world.

Brigid pictured Abigail in her mind's eye, the girl with her round face and innocent smile, her little nose and her eyes that twinkled like jewels. But before her, all there was was sand. Brigid needed to form it into a shape first—a head and shoulders, like a bust. Scooping more sand, she tipped the flask once again from where it rested between her thighs, added just a few drops of cool water to the mixture, making it firm so that she could shape it. A ridge on which would sit an elongated sphere, a head atop the shoulders. It would take time, she knew.

One byproduct of Brigid's eidetic memory was that she was a good artist, at least in that she could re-create things she saw with pens, paper and other tools. Focusing her mind, she willed the image in her head to her hands, gradually forming the features of the girl. At first, she had balked at the thought of showing this child to Ullikummis, feeling it was somehow wrong, a perversion that she wanted no part of. But how could a fictitious child hurt her? How could something that had never existed possibly be used against Brigid? She had made her peace with losing Abigail in the Janus trap; the girl's shape could not hurt her now.

And so, as the hours passed, Brigid continued to work at the sand, dripping water into the grains to make them firm, to hold a shape. There were no tools in the cave other than the pebbles that littered the floor here and there. Crawling around on hands and knees, Brigid found one that was flat with a sharp point, used this to help add detail to the thing that was forming before her on the floor of the cavern.

The fictitious girl, Abigail, had been like a daughter to Brigid Baptiste. Stuck in a false reality, she had become attached to the girl, had lived with her, provided for her, taken care of her. It had seemed that they had been together forever. When Brigid had left the trap, had awoken and returned to the conscious world, she had still wondered at Abigail's fate. The girl's existence, however one chose to interpret it, had ignited something deep inside Brigid Baptiste.

Brigid's hands worked at the sand for a long time, her fingers gathering and shaping the mound of sand until it had the rudimentary appearance of a child's shoulders and head. The shoulders were almost life-size, ten inches across and sloped downward until they disappeared into the floor of the cave. Brigid played her hands across them like a potter, adding water and smoothing them until they seemed to be something almost human.

Then she turned her attention to the neck, piling sand to form its thin trunk, adding weight to ensure it could support the head. Brigid was no sculptress, had never really done something like this before. It was a feat of engineering, she realized, as much as it was a work of art, creating a bust that could stand under its own weight, not topple or—more likely, given the suppleness of the medium—slip away.

She sat on the floor of the cave, working at the sand, piling more on and brushing it smooth, shaping the girl's neck. If this was what it would take to buy her freedom, then it was an inconsequential price to pay, building a little tribute to her child who never was.

Several more hours passed, and Brigid felt the aching in her own neck and shoulders. She had been crouched here a long time, working at the sand sculpture, and she needed to stretch, to work out the kinks in her muscles. Brigid pushed herself off the floor with a groan, stretched her legs out before her, one at a time like a ballerina going through her warm-up routine, then clenched and unclenched her hands, wiggling the fingers. She was stiffening up, and exhaustion was creeping in.

She looked down, staring at the little mound of sand in the orange glow of the magma pods. The shadows cast by the gloomy light seemed to give the sand character, made it somehow more real. It was unsettling, looking at this girl child bursting from the ground, her head just a blank, faceless bump of sand.

Brigid took a deep breath, let it out with a slow ten count, calming her nerves. She thought back, picturing the girl who had existed only in the faux reality. Her memory of Abigail—of her little munchkin—was just as real to her as anything else she had experienced in her life, Brigid acknowledged. This was the reality of having an eidetic memory; even the most valueless recollections had resonance, stayed with her as if crucial. The others—Kane and Grant—had left the false reality with her, but they had been unaffected, had given little more than a second thought to everything that had gone on in that dreamlike trap with its narrow logic and emotional landmines. But Brigid would wake now and then thinking of Abi, of her child.

"Damn you," Brigid muttered, her hands clenching unconsciously into fists. She saw something of what Ullikummis was doing. He was using her memory of a false reality to show her how little she truly perceived. Angrily, she turned to the mound of sand and kicked it, knocking the sand across the stone floor of the cave.

The sand tumbled in on itself where the water held it

together, crumbling and breaking like a cliff breaking apart and crashing into the sea. Clumps of sand spilled across the floor, hunks of shoulder and neck sprawling across the rock at Brigid's feet. She stood there, breathing hard, angry with what she had done. This was her chance at freedom, this one simple task, and she was failing it. She was so determined to work out the mind game that Ullikummis was playing that she was creating an enemy not of him but of herself.

Brigid stumbled backward until she met the edge of the rock chair, slumped into it without looking. "You're better than this, Brigid," she whispered to herself. "You can get past this, defeat this monster."

Her voice seemed to crack on the last word, and she wondered if she truly considered Ullikummis a monster anymore, or if she thought of him as—what?—a man? No. An Annunaki, then, but not in the way she had seen them before. He had opened her eyes somehow, made her realize how flawed her perception of the Annunaki had been. People in masks and rubber suits pretending to be aliens for a story, a play to fool children, nothing more. That's what he had told her; that's how they had seemed.

Slumped against the back of the chair, her breathing still coming hard, Brigid tightened her fists, pressing her sharp fingernails into the palms of her hands. "You're better than this," she told herself. "You're better than he is."

After a while, when she had finally calmed her swirling thoughts, Brigid went back to work. Kneeling on the floor of the cave, she gathered up the sand and began reshaping the figure before her, head and shoulders as she saw them projected in her mind. "Come on, munchkin," she muttered, dribbling water into the sand to make it bond. "Show your face."

Chapter 21

They had dragged Grant's unconscious form back to his cell, tossed him inside and sealed the hatch using the command stones that were buried in their flesh.

Grant had awoken hours later, sprawled on the cold rock floor and feeling the pressing need to vomit. He rolled, retching up a watery drool that looked little different from the meals he had been fed over the previous forty-eight hours. He lay there, leaning on his elbow, head bowed low as he spluttered up the measly contents of his stomach. It struck Grant that he had eaten hardly anything in the past three days, and so he was vomiting nothing more than the yellowish lining of his stomach now, thick chunks of his own secretions slapping against the floor, his nose and eyes streaming thick water tainted with mucus. Ultimately, he drew a breath, felt his stomach finally stop complaining. He still felt sick, and his body trembled as he rested there on the sand carpet, but the initial need to vomit had passed, quelled by nothing more than a lack of any content left to bring up.

Grant cursed as he sank back to the cold rock floor, the acrid stench of his stomach's contents assaulting his nostrils in the closeness of the cave. He had tried to escape while he still had the strength to do so, and he had failed. This was his reward—a beating and sickness.

For a long while he lay there, trying to fathom a way out of the cave-like cell, out of the complex of tunnels he had seen. They had a mat-trans. That was the key. Despite what Edwards had said, how this place was hell, Grant knew that the mat-trans could be used to take him somewhere else. The nature of the mat-trans system was such that, if used, the unit would send him to a receiver unit, from which he could program another journey and disappear into the ether before anyone could stop him. While his hooded jailers might endeavor to follow him, the boot-up and wind-down sequence would be enough to allow him a second jump before anyone could catch up. And once he'd performed the second jump, that would be it—he would be free. The rest was simply a case of backtracking via the Cerberus monitoring system, which he knew could be utilized to learn the location of this cavernous prison.

Grant belched, tasting the bile in his throat. The thought of mat-trans travel was making him nauseous all over again. He had never been a fan.

He lay there a long time, the ceiling seemingly spinning just a little overhead, until he finally heard something from off to his right, a shuffling, scraping noise. Grant recognized it immediately: it was the sound the walls made when they prepared to move, to shift like water to create a doorway through which one of his hooded captors could enter.

He turned, watching the wall move as he lay on his side, his stomach still feeling like some echoing chasm within him. The wall parted, the magma lights of the corridor beyond becoming visible through the widening slit. Three people stood there, dressed in the shapeless robes, hoods up.

"Can I help you?" Grant asked sarcastically, his voice weak.

One of the hooded figures strode into the room, while

the others remained in guard position by the door. The leader pushed his hood back and looked down at the weary figure of Grant. Despite the man's beard, Grant recognized Dylan, the farmer he had met in Tenth City.

"You tried to escape," Dylan intoned.

"Yeah," Grant agreed, seeing little point in denying it now. "What did you expect…. Dylan, is it?"

"First Priest Dylan of the New Order," Dylan barked, glaring fiercely at Grant's lounging form.

"Nice promotion," Grant observed, stretching his arms out as he lay there, pain running through his body. "Last time I saw you, you were getting ready to return to digging up the earth."

"I was introduced to something better," Dylan said, "found a better harvest to reap. The future."

"Oh, yeah," Grant muttered as his arm reached just a little farther, "that's one heck of a harvest you've planned for yourself."

"You disappointed me, Grant," Dylan said. "Lord Ullikummis said you were worthless, a rebellious blot on the future, made of muscle but with no sense. He said that at the first opportunity you would try to run."

"What, you lose a little wager here?" Grant asked.

"The future will be a utopia," Dylan said as he looked down at him, "built upon the bones of the past. You could have been a part of that, Grant. Instead, the best you can hope for is to be a slave, if you live that long."

"I ain't real keen on building on bones," he said, "nor being a slave to a council of idiocy." Grant's hand snagged Dylan's ankle as he spoke, and he yanked with all his might. In an instant, Dylan fell to his knees, his arms reeling as he struggled, but failed to keep his balance. Grant was on him in a second, clambering up the man's fallen body, fist drawn back to hit him. "You have any other positions opening up?"

Then Grant drove his fist into the man's smiling face, even as the guards at the door rushed over to pull the ex-Magistrate from their leader's body. Grant felt the blackjack crack against the back of his skull with a hard impact, stopped struggling as he was pulled off the hooded man's body. As Grant was dragged away, Dylan continued smiling, a trickle of blood forming in the gaps between the ex-farmer's teeth.

Grant was manhandled, tossed against the wall with brutality. He was too weak to fight back, simply reveled in what little satisfaction he had gained from surprising the leader and striking him.

"We don't need to feed this one anymore," Grant heard Dylan say as he lay there against the wall, the back of his head throbbing from its savage meeting with the blackjack. "Kane has agreed to lead the armies. We won't need this one again."

What? Grant asked himself. They had Kane? But how?

Grant felt the nausea rise within him once more as, behind him, the door to the cell slid shut on its invisible tracks. If they had Kane, he realized, then he would need to work out a way around the prison, locate Kane before he could leave. And if they had Kane, then it stood to reason they might have Brigid, too. But why would Kane agree to lead their armies unless he was playing some bluff? Impossible—these people wouldn't fall for a bluff like that, would they? There had to be more to it than that.

Slowly, Grant drifted into a pained sleep, pressed up against the hard, unforgiving wall of his cavelike cell.

Chapter 22

Those whom the gods would destroy they first turn mad.

Brigid's stomach rumbled, reminding her of her need to eat. She had toiled over the sand sculpture for a long time, shaping it to look like the cherubic little girl in her mind's eye. Abigail had been a part of her life for a short period of time, and yet Brigid felt that she knew her. Not in the way she remembered other things, the way her perfect memory would retain the tiniest detail, but in a way that exists only within a person, when love is felt for another. Abigail was the daughter she had never had, Brigid knew, a horrible trick to mess with her mind. In constructing her image from the sand, perhaps this would be a cathartic experience, to finally make solid the dream she had buried deep within her, and so see it for the fallacy it was.

The girl looked like her, like Brigid, with her flowing hair and her soft face. Brigid's face was harder, the planes a little sharper, but the girl looked similar enough that their family resemblance was clear. The shoulders appeared to slope down into the cave's floor now, the neck springing above them in a slender line. Above that, the head, the face, the hair behind. Brigid had spent a long time working at the hair, carving its intricacies, adding detail to create the illusion of substance and depth. She had used the sharp, flat-edged pebble to draw more detail

there, marveling in the twisting, tangled lines she was
carving from the sand. Abi had always had twisted hair,
never sitting still long enough to let Brigid run a brush
through it. By keeping the sand wet, Brigid found she
could make it hold a shape, and could carve into it with
miraculous detail and extravagance.

The Annunaki were masters of genetic engineering,
and it dawned on Brigid as she worked at the little sculpture that Ullikummis might use it as a template, bringing
the child to life somehow, crafting her from clay just like
the myth he had spoken of. Could he do that? Would he
do it simply to spite Brigid, or perhaps appease her?

It seemed unlikely. Ullikummis was many things,
willful and brutal, perhaps, but he was not spiteful, had
demonstrated no capacity for spite.

On the front of the sculpture, the face remained a
blank thing. It had features, Abigail's lines of jaw and
cheek, her little nose. But the mouth had yet to be added,
and the eyes were just hollows in the sand created by the
heel of Brigid's hand pressing lightly against the moist
surface. Still on her hands and knees, Brigid gathered
more sand from the far wall of the cave, scooping it up in
her hands and adding water to make it cling. The water
bottle was almost empty now; she had to tip it almost entirely upside down to get just a few drops out of it.

"I should drink this," Brigid whispered to herself,
as if afraid the sand child would hear. But Brigid didn't
drink.

She made her way back to the sculpture that rested
close to the chair, the little head and shoulders protrud-
ing from the ground, and she brushed gently at the face,
smoothing the forehead the way one holds a sickly child.
Carefully Brigid took the damp sand from her hand and
worked it into the forehead, low across the ridges above

the hollow, empty eyes. Then she plucked the sharp pebble from the floor once more and began shaping the eyebrows with it, chipping carefully away at the ridges of sand until they formed the delicate lines of Abigail's brows.

She had patiently worked at the sand representation of Abigail for a long time when Ullikummis made his presence known. Brigid turned, peering behind her and seeing the great stone figure standing amid the deep shadows of the cavern, the magma traceries running like fire over his huge body. He had not spoken, but there had been a scraping noise, his foot against the cave floor, perhaps, or his hand brushing the wall. He may well have been there for minutes before Brigid had noticed, hours even. It was in that moment that she appreciated how quiet Ullikummis's movements could be. Here he was, a grand thing covered with stone, yet when he chose to he could move in silence, giving no hint of his presence to the unwary.

Brigid fixed him with a stare. "You don't look like the other Annunaki," she said.

Ullikummis smiled as he stepped from the shadows to reveal himself fully to her. At eight feet tall, he towered over her as she knelt on the floor, working at the sand sculpture she had made.

"My father changed me," Ullikummis explained, "before I was born. The Annunaki have ways to change things—they understand genetics in a way your humans have yet to comprehend. I was changed while still growing in the egg, prepared for what I was to become for my father."

"And what was that?" Brigid asked.

"The Annunaki are gods," Ullikummis stated, "and

the gods fight. My father brought me into the world to act as his hand in the darkness. To kill for him."

"You were an assassin," Brigid stated.

Ullikummis nodded. "The first one I killed was called Enia. I still recall how she pleaded with me, tried to reason me out of killing her and her unborn." He trailed off, the glowing lines burbling and fizzing across his stone body.

Brigid looked at the blank-faced sand figurine before her and then spoke without looking at Ullikummis. "Can you still see her face?"

If Ullikummis answered, he did so in silence. Brigid turned her attention back to the sand thing on the floor, working at it with her fingers, forming the features that would define the face.

"My father brought me into this world in violence," Ullikummis told Brigid after a while. "He created me not out of love but in an act of hate. It was appropriate then that I became his tool of hate, delivering his ruthless ambition at the end of my blade, Godkiller, or with a twist of an enemy's neck. I was not born as you see me. Things were placed inside me, and I was remade as I grew older, changed into the thing my father needed—a living personification of his hatred."

"But he sent you away," Brigid said, piecing together what she knew of Ullikummis's story. "He banished you."

"My father made me a living tool of hatred," Ullikummis continued. "In turning on me he unwittingly turned that hatred upon himself."

Brigid was using the flat-edged stone once more, smoothing over the cheeks of the girl's face before her, molding the bright eyes. It looked like Abigail now, the curve of her smiling lips, the eyes wide open with a child's interest.

Brigid turned as she heard Ullikummis stride toward her, his feet beating the lightest tattoo upon the hard rock floor of the cave. He stood at her shoulder, peering down at the finished representation of the child. It looked almost human, formed of the tan shingle of sand that layered the floor. Brigid was satisfied with it.

"Is that her?" Ullikummis asked, wonder in his voice.

"Yes." Brigid nodded.

"It looks quite real," he observed. "Does it look like her? Truthfully?"

"Yes," Brigid replied. She reached for the clay bottle then, loosened the stopper and brought it to her lips, only to find it was empty.

"You used the last of your water on the girl," Ullikummis stated, a simple observation.

"You said you would free me," Brigid reminded him, "once I was done." Slowly she stood, bringing her head level with Ullikummis's chest and staring defiantly up at him. "I'm done."

Ullikummis looked down at her, the whisper of a thin smile on his misshapen mouth. "You are done," he agreed, "and I said I would set you free."

Brigid looked at Ullikummis, waiting for him to act, to do as he had promised. Instead, all he did was talk.

"Are you thirsty?" he asked, his voice a great rumbling like approaching thunder.

"You said you'd free me," Brigid reminded him insistently.

"Are you thirsty?" Ullikummis repeated.

Brigid's mouth was dry. Ullikummis had seen her tip

the water bottle, had known that it was empty. "Yes," she said.

"There is moisture in the sand," Ullikummis told her. "You put it there, and it retains it for a long time now that you've packed it the way you have."

Brigid glared at him, wondering what his trick was.

"Until it dries out entirely, you can eat it," Ullikummis told her. "Like fruit or cake. The sand has no nutrition, but it would serve to slake your thirst."

"I'm not going to eat…sand," she said, looking back down at the representation of the girl's head and shoulders. It seemed to stare back at her.

Ullikummis reached out then, his hand flicking in the most casual of gestures. Beneath her feet, Brigid felt rumbling. The floor of the cave was shaking, rocking as something tunneled up from below.

Suddenly the sand representation of the girl split apart, crumbling away as a spear of stone emerged from the ground, its point drilling up through it. Brigid watched as the sand fell away, as all of her hard work disappeared into nothingness. All that was left of the sculpture was sand—shapeless, formless sand.

"Your world," Ullikummis said, "is a thing of impermanence. No matter how long you work at something, it crumbles, disappears, turns to dust."

Brigid heard the words as she watched the particles of sand sink away, drifting across the floor of the cave, no more a part of the face than they had been before she had begun her sculpture.

"The Annunaki are capable of single thoughts that last longer than the whole of your lives," Ullikummis said. "And you wonder why you struggle to understand us."

Brigid turned, but Ullikummis was already striding

away, leaving the cave. She found herself alone once more, just the empty clay flask, the mirror and the chair for company. He had promised to set her free....

Chapter 23

It was like going through withdrawal.

It was like dying.

Kane lay there, his face pressed against the rock floor of his cell, the sand rough on his skin as the stone forced itself upon his nervous system like some swooping bird of prey, impressed its will upon his own. He could feel it there, this physical lump within his flesh, like a tumor under the skin. And in a way it was a tumor—a cancer, an infiltrator inside his body, changing him and making him less himself and more the infection.

He scrunched his eyes tight, lying in a ball, reverting to the fetal position as all mammals do when in real pain. It was only right that he adopt such a position, Kane realized, for he was being born, or at least reborn—that was what Dylan of the New Order had said.

He was being expelled from the old world, ejected from the world of Cerberus and outlanders and Magistrates. That world was redundant now, a distant memory or a dream. The new world was one of gods who would stride the Earth as they wished, who would control its people as was their right. Kane felt all of this in his mind, words whispered to him from the obedience stone burrowing beneath his flesh.

He reached for it then, the nails of his right hand clawing at his smooth skin where the stone had been absorbed, plucking at the diminishing lump that was hiding in his own body. He scratched with his nails, tearing until a sliver of skin was pried free. A tiny trace of blood blossomed along his wrist then, a thin line of red in the faint dawn glow of the swirling magma light. In that glow, Kane saw how his fingernails were dark—black crescents like negative moons topping each of his fingers where the sweaty skin and blood was congealed beneath his nails.

He tore at his flesh again, actions born of desperation, revealing more lines of blood. The blood intermingled, and the three thin lines became one blotch as blood filled in the space between them, flowing across his skin. But the stone would not be freed. Kane could feel it and yet he could not reach it. It was buried too deep already, clinging to him deep down beneath the flesh.

The cool air of the cave played around his arm where he had cut himself, making the blood there tingle as it dried against his skin. Reluctantly Kane drew his right hand away, the dried blood and slivers of skin still darkening his nails. He could not remove the stone.

"No," Kane spit, the word coming from his mouth like vomit.

He didn't want this to happen; he didn't want to be changed, to be altered. Rosalia, the dancing girl, had promised to help him, had told him this was the only way to fool them, the only chance at freedom. But as he lay in the dark cave, the six-by-eight cell that was his world, he wondered if she had tricked him. If, after all his protestations, his refusal to submit, his insistence that First Priest Dylan and his master, Ullikummis, surrender, they had found a way to make him join them, after all. Perhaps this whole thing had been a trick.

Kane was shaking as he lay on the cave floor, rocking back and forth as he curled in a ball, with spasms jolting the muscles of his arms and legs. His body was trying to reject the stone that had been placed inside it, antibodies rushing to battle the thing that had been inserted within him, hopeless in the face of such an obstruction.

"Damn you, Rosie," Kane gasped, sweat beading on his top lip like human rain. "What did you make me do?"

He lay there, shaking, shuddering, a newborn infant feeling the sheer alienness of the world about him, and he cursed himself for falling for it. He had always had a blind spot for a pretty face, no matter what way he couched it. So these Annunaki-devoted bastards had sent a pretty face, knowing that he would cave, that he would believe her, despite his doubts. That he would want to because he believed in some inherent nobility within people.

The stone was moving now, he could tell. Clawing its way under his skin, branching out with tendrils, with feelers, reaching through his flesh and his nervous system, plucking at parts of him until there was no real way to know where the stone thing ended and Kane began. The stone was Kane now and he was the stone. At the back of his neck, something seared, fizzing and molding itself into his spine, his brain stem. Kane lay there in the gloom, shuddering beneath that internal assault, and felt the streams of water on his face—not sweat but thick, salty tears running down his cheeks, dripping into the thin carpet of sand that covered the rock floor.

"It works better on the weak-minded," Rosalia had told him.

"Dammit," Kane muttered to himself, "I'm not weak. I can't be."

He tried to dismiss the pain, to feel past it, but it burned brighter in his spine, a supernova bursting beneath his flesh. This mindscape wasn't his forte; this was Baptiste's world, this battleground of the soul. Kane thought of her, of Brigid Baptiste, his *anam-chara,* his soul friend, a treasured companion throughout eternity. He tried to picture her, emerald eyes in a porcelain face, her swirls of red hair billowing about her head like a sunset halo. What would she do?

Kane shook, trying to visualize Brigid, how she would trick this attacker of her mind and of herself. How would she run some clever interference and so block its infiltration, stop it as it tried to claw at her brain?

Is that what it was to be strong-willed? Kane wondered. Did it take a sense of self so strong that it could overcome any obstacle? Perhaps.

Kane, however, needed a physical thing, something he could strike, could shoot, could kick. And this invader beneath his flesh had none of those attributes; this thing was hidden from any possible attack.

Rosalia had said something else, he remembered. She had said that the stone needed a broadcast unit to be effective. What was the broadcast unit? This place? This tiny cave with its flickering light? Kane's muscles tensed, his toes scrunching up in his boots, his fingers turning in on themselves, not in fists but so that the fingernails dug into the flesh.

"Stop," he breathed. "Stop. Leave me. Leave me alone."

The stone continued to burrow and to expand, making new synaptic connections beneath his skin. Kane cried out, an animal noise now as he began to lose himself to the stone's will. The Annunaki were their masters; the Annunaki were their gods. And man? What was man other than a worthless thing, a thing of dirt next to the gods of gold?

Kane wailed and cried and jabbed his fist at the wall

before him, or maybe it was the floor. And all he knew was the pain of metamorphosis, of change.

The pain racked his firm body for a long time, and lying there in the cold cave, in his underfed and dehydrated state, Kane was unable to do anything other than suffer the pain, feel it as it coursed through his system like some melancholy sickness, meandering through his bones and muscle fiber, jabbing and taunting him. His mind raced on, thinking of devotion, of obedience. He had been indoctrinated from birth to accept orders, had been trained as a Magistrate in the golden city of Cobaltville, and it had taken a supreme effort of will to break that indoctrination, to dig beneath the surface and turn away from the commands that had ruled his ordered life. That decision had led Kane to Cerberus, and he had been questioning ever since, as if frightened that accepting anything was to step back into his former role of unquestioning enforcer. And now he felt that call again, that need within him to be given instructions, to be told how to live and whom to obey. A Magistrate was taught to judge everyone, and yet he never judged himself.

"What if I judged myself?" Kane asked the darkness, trying to keep his reason intact. If he chose to judge now, if he found something to judge, perhaps he could shirk off the commands of the stone and stay focused on the things that made him. Perhaps merely by remaining strong he could rid himself of this mind worm that coursed through his system.

But no.

It attacked him, slithering around inside him, reaching for the core of him, the center of his being. Kane was its victim now, a willing participant in his own demise. It had seduced his insides, and already it was feeding him instructions. No, not instructions—suggestions. It was telling him he was okay, that this would be good, that the new dawn was coming, that the new age was arriving, that the world was better than he had ever seen it.

Hunkered in upon himself, his body locked in that familiar fetal position, Kane cried. Eyes closed, he sobbed quietly in the darkness, knowing that he was disappearing, that he was lost. For a long while, the sound of Kane's tears were all that could be heard in the little cave, until finally he cried himself to sleep.

AND THEN, AS IT HAD BEFORE, a woman's voice came. "Wake up, Magistrate man," she said, her voice throaty, with the lilt of an accent.

Kane's eyes opened, and he was immediately aware of the pain in his wrist where the stone had burrowed. His right hand reached there immediately, felt the ridge where he had scratched open the wound and the congealed blood had scabbed over into a bumpy line like the segmented shell of an insect.

"Are you awake?" Rosalia asked, her voice hard and urgent.

Kane turned his head to look at her beneath the faint glow of the roiling magma, and his head felt as if it was full of cotton candy, sticky and sweet and weightless. She was crouching at his side, and behind her Kane saw the familiar form of the mongrel dog, which seemed to follow her with little enthusiasm.

"What did you do to me?" he asked, the words plunging from his thick tongue as though he was drunk. "What did you make me do?"

"Stay still," Rosalia commanded, and she grasped his left forearm, exposing the place where the stone had burrowed. Kane saw something flash in her hand then, smaller than a knife, just a little spike, like a toothpick.

"What are you—" he began, pulling away.

But Rosalia shoved his hand back down, pressing his arm against the floor with surprising strength. "Don't squirm," she ordered, sounding as if she was dealing with a tempestuous child.

Kane lay there, his strength already ebbed away under the strange assault of the stone and of everything that had led to this moment. He watched as the beautiful, dark-haired woman pushed the little sliver of metal against his wrist, plucking at his flesh just next to the scab he had created with his nails. The thing in her hand was a sewing needle, Kane saw now, no longer than his pinkie finger.

"You made a mess of yourself," Rosalia told him, but it was just an observation; there seemed to be no emotional resonance to what she said.

Automatically, Kane tried to pull his wrist away, flinching as he saw the needle breaking into his flesh.

Rosalia shot him a look. "Stay still," she snarled, and behind her the dog whined. "Look away if it helps you. And you, stupid mutt—be quiet."

The dog's whine died in its throat and it lay down on its belly, pale eyes fixed on Kane. Kane looked at the dog for a moment, wondering what breed it was. Its sharp features looked a little like a coyote's, but that wasn't all that had come to make the ugly thing, he was sure.

Kane winced as he felt the needle pluck at his flesh, and he resisted the urge to pull his arm back from where Rosalia worked at it. "This going to help me?" he asked, fearing it was another trick.

"I told you I would," Rosalia said.

"Yeah," Kane recalled, "but I'm not so sure I believe you."

She looked at him, and he saw the anger on her

features. "You stop that shit right now, Magistrate man," she told him. "You and me are getting out, but if you start questioning me now, then we'll be getting out only as corpses."

"You want me to trust you," Kane responded, "but I haven't seen anything to make me believe I should."

"See this, then," Rosalia spit, and she jabbed the little sewing needle deep into Kane's wrist, twisting it as she rooted around beneath the skin.

Kane drew a sharp breath, not really feeling pain so much as thinking he should. It was so unnatural—so unreal—having this woman prod at his flesh with a needle. Then he felt something almost tickling against his bone there, buried deep beneath the flesh. Something hibernating that was waking up, pulling into itself, dragging its parts back to its body as it took up a defense. The stone, Kane realized.

He lay on his back and brought his other arm up to cover his eyes, to block the dull flickering of the dim orange light. Kane concentrated on regulating his breathing as Rosalia probed beneath his flesh with the needle.

Then her voice came to him, husky and enticing. "It's made itself right at home," she said. "Good."

Kane turned to her, anger and fear rising. "Good?" he snarled. "Good? Is that all you can say?"

"Keep your voice down," Rosalia spit.

"He put that thing in me and all you can say is 'good'?" Kane continued, ignoring her instruction. "You made me do this. You told me it was the only way."

"And it is," Rosalia assured him, drawing the sewing needle carefully from his wrist. A single drop of blood clung to its point. "We'll remove it soon enough, Magistrate man. You just keep calm."

Kane gritted his teeth as another surge of pain vibrated

through his arm. "I thought you were going to take it out," he growled.

"Do you even listen?" Rosalia retorted contemptuously. "For now, you will need the obedience stone. It is your key, you understand? Pish—Magistrates."

"Hey, you listen, sweetheart—" Kane began angrily.

"No, *you* listen," Rosalia snarled, waving her finger in his face. "You have such fucking trust issues you're going to get us both killed. Put your head in the game, Magistrate man. I'm relying on you now."

Lying there, with the alien thing implanted beneath his skin, Kane let out a long, slow breath. "It's Kane," he said finally. "My name is Kane. Not Magistrate man."

"You think I care?"

"Look, Rosie," Kane said. "I'm trying to trust you, but you have got to meet me halfway here. Otherwise, we're both going to get ourselves killed so fast it'll make our heads spin. Right?"

Rosalia let out an irritated sigh, glaring at the man who lay before her with rage still burning in her eyes. For a moment, she turned her attention to the little sewing kit she carried, replacing the needle and hiding the kit beneath her robe. "You make it so difficult," she told him. "You're so self-righteous. Where do you get off telling Dylan to surrender? What did you think that would prove? I could have got you out of here two days ago if you'd been smart, but instead you go looking for fights, the same way you got yourself put in here in the first place."

"Ullikummis, your lord and master, attacked my people," Kane pointed out. "I was defending them. Well, trying to, anyway."

"I saw," Rosalia acknowledged. "You fought well.

Lost, but you fought well. And he's not my lord and master. He's nothing to me."

"You have one of these things in you?" Kane asked. "These obedience stones?"

"I do and I don't," Rosalia said with a cunning smile. "You can control it, if you know how."

"And you'll show me?" Kane asked.

She nodded. "Yes. But you need it right now, or you'll stand out to the others. They'll sense if you don't have one, and they'll know something is wrong."

"Okay," Kane agreed solemnly. "How long before it starts messing with my thoughts? I mean, properly messin'—I felt a little of it once it embedded itself."

"I've retarded its passage," Rosalia said. "You'll be yourself for a little while yet."

"How long?" Kane pressed. "Rosalia?"

"I found that if you pierce the stones, they cease to take hold," she replied. "But you have to time it right—too early and they break apart, fail to register in your system, and the other firewalkers see you don't have one and try to place another inside you."

"Firewalkers?" Kane asked, surprised.

"They're not in their right minds," Rosalia explained. "They remind me of firewalkers—you know? Meditating so they can walk through fire, yet not feel pain."

Kane laughed, a warm sound in the barren cell.

"What's so funny?" she demanded.

"My friend Brigid Baptiste said the same thing," he explained, "when we first saw people under the control of Ullikummis. It's just—I don't know—an odd coincidence the way you settled on the same term."

Rosalia leaned close to him, holding her beautiful face barely an inch away, her hazel eyes peering into his. "Maybe it's a good omen for us," she suggested.

"So how long do I have?" Kane asked, closing his eyes.

"In three hours it will bond with you permanently and you'll never be free," Rosalia said, leaning back once more. Beside her, the dog snuffled as it napped, and she ran her hand through its matted fur.

"Three hours," Kane mused. "That's pretty specific."

"It's a guess, Magistrate man," Rosalia said, the old contempt for him back in her voice. "What, you think I set up a little laboratory, a control group, rats in mazes? Use your head—there's probably a hundred factors contributing to how these things affect people—your constitution, your weight, your age. Who knows what else? I dug these things out of me and I watched how they affected others. I figure I don't want to be part of this mind cult, not ever."

"You value your freedom," Kane muttered.

"The only rats running through the maze are us," Rosalia said, "and Ullikummis knows it."

"What about Dylan?" Kane asked. "First Priest of the New Order, yada-yada. He not in on this?"

"He has a stone buried in him," Rosalia said, "just like all the rest of them. Susceptible and happy to join up for the latest promise."

"While you value your freedom," Kane mused, almost repeating what he had said just moments before.

"Why do you keep saying that, Magistrate man?" Rosalia asked. "Are you slow?"

"I left the Magistrates to search for true freedom," Kane told her. "I joined Cerberus to secure it, not just for me but for all mankind."

She stifled a laugh at his words, and when Kane glared at her she did her best to look contrite.

"When we get out of here, I'm not doing it for you," Kane told her. "I'm doing it for everyone. Freedom for all."

Slowly, Rosalia nodded in understanding, letting his words sink in. "You said 'when' and not 'if'," she murmured after a moment's thought.

"Never go into a battle saying 'if,'" Kane told her. "Do that and you've already lost."

Rosalia nodded once again, considering his words. "Okay, Kane," she said, for the first time using his name without contempt, "we'll get everyone out."

Kane allowed himself just the whisper of a smile at that. For the first time in over two days, he had a good feeling about where things were leading.

Chapter 24

Lakesh sat in his own cavelike cell, his thoughts running wild in his head. He was the director of the Cerberus operation—indeed, it had been established at his insistence and he knew every inch of the hidden redoubt base. Lakesh might be little more than a nominal head at times, and he was well aware that the members of his team didn't always understand—or trust—his motives, but he still felt responsibility for all his personnel, in much the way a ship's captain would take responsibility not only for his crew but for any passengers his vessel carried. While the Cerberus staff might not have always appreciated Lakesh's interference, he still held their safety and well-being paramount.

The attack had come with the swiftness of lightning. He had been overseeing a field mission from the operations room when Edwards had excused himself from his sentry post at the doors. Edwards had exited, complaining of a headache, muttering something about needing fresh air. Lakesh sympathized—located in the heart of a mountain, the Cerberus redoubt could become a little claustrophobic at times. Automatically, Lakesh had waited until a light on his control desk winked on, alerting him to the fact that Edwards had used the redoubt's main exit—the rollback door that led out onto the mountain plateau, a barren spit of rock and dust.

Perhaps thirty minutes had passed before Lakesh

noticed Edwards return to the ops room. By then, the elderly cyberneticist had been working with Donald Bry on a remote command to fire up the sprinkler system in a far distant redoubt, a plan that would aid the field team led by Kane. Edwards had returned to his post in silence, joining Domi where she crouched close to the doors.

Domi had looked up, acknowledging Edwards with a brusque nod. To her surprise, Edwards had been accompanied by someone else—a figure dressed in what appeared to be a monk's habit, its hood drawn low over his face. Even as Domi watched, a second robed figure entered the ops room, then a third.

Lakesh turned at Domi's shout. "What is it, dearest?" he asked, as he tried to locate her in the busy ops hub.

Over by the entrance, Domi was pushing herself up from her haunches. Beside her, Lakesh spotted Edwards and three hooded figures he did not recognize. The high doors to the room were still open, and another of the monklike figures entered as Lakesh watched.

"Now, see here," he began, striding across the ops center. "Just who the devil do you think—?"

The closest of the hooded figures brought his hand up in a rapid flipping motion, and Lakesh saw the blur of something roughly the size of a man's fist being thrown at him.

"Grenade!" Lakesh shouted, lunging to one side as the projectile hurtled through the air toward him.

Considered levelheaded by his friends, Lakesh was not a man prone to panic. When he shouted his warning, the personnel in the ops room responded immediately, diving for cover even as the thrown object flew across the room. The fist-size missile bounced off one of the computer terminals before dropping to the floor and skittering across its tiled surface, eight feet from where Lakesh lay. He turned away, covering his head with both hands. But to Lakesh's surprise the thing did not explode.

Voices were coming from all around the room now as people gave vent to their confusion. Lakesh turned back to look at the thing he had taken to be a grenade, and saw it was just a rock, smooth and circular, a little smaller than his bunched hand.

"Curiouser and curiouser," Lakesh muttered as he turned back to study the hooded figures at the door. There were seven of them now, and he saw them draw back their arms and launch a barrage of similarly sized rocks across the room, smashing terminals and striking unwary personnel as they peered from their hiding places.

Domi was pulling the Detonics Combat Master pistol from the waistband of her short shorts, bringing it up toward the nearest of the hooded strangers as Lakesh watched. Then Edwards struck out with his right palm, powering it into her outstretched arm even as she prepared to take her shot. Surprised as she was, her shot went wild, the great boom of the blaster loud in the enclosed operations center.

Lakesh watched helplessly as Edwards backhanded Domi across the face, knocking her to the ground, even as a second barrage of stones came hurtling across the room from the group of hooded intruders.

A leader's job was to lead, Lakesh reminded himself as he reached for the microphone of the public address system where it lay on his desk. An unobtrusive green light winked on.

"We are under attack," he began, speaking into the microphone as a rock hurtled past him. But before he could even finish those words, the PA system went dead, a burst of sparks exploding from the pickup unit at the side of his desk.

On the other levels of the redoubt, all that the personnel heard was Lakesh saying "We are—". Many of them took this to be a simple error, the wrong switch being flicked during some tedious moment in the ops room. When no further words were issued, everyone ignored the announcement.

Lakesh's heart sank as the PA mic fizzled and died. There was a second microphone set in the body of the desk itself, but it was already too dangerous to sit down, he knew, to lean over and talk into that. Ahead of him, he saw one of the hooded figures spinning something in his outstretched hand, and Lakesh recognized it as a whirling leather slingshot. As the slingshot reached the apex of its arc, the hooded stranger flicked his wrist and a stone was launched from the simple weapon, rocketing across the room at incredible speed.

Lakesh dived out of the path of the hurtling stone, heard it whiz past him less than a foot away. Around him, the hooded group was fanning out, corralling the personnel in the room and attacking them with stones and savage blows from their fists. Although all the Cerberus staff had some military training, the majority of people working the ops room were scientists and clerical personnel; they had little stomach for the harsh reality of combat.

Lakesh weaved among the desks, feeling disheartened as one of the terminals to his left exploded in a shower of sparks as another of the thrown stones tore into it. Across the room, Domi was engaged in a brutal hand-to-hand fight with Edwards and one of the hooded figures, bringing her gun to bear, only to have it slapped away before she could unleash a shot from its chrome-plated muzzle.

A moment later, Lakesh found himself at the arma-glass walls of the mat-trans, as far from the figures at the entry doors as he could manage. The mat-trans unit dominated one corner of the operations room, the unit itself hidden behind brown-tinted glass walls. From here, Lakesh could survey the damage already being inflicted on his operations room, and his mind raced, wondering if this scene was being repeated everywhere, or if the attack was just here at the heart of the Cerberus facility.

"This is Lakesh," the elderly scientist shouted, raising his voice to be heard over the sounds of combat. "Clearly, we are under attack. Defend the equipment if you can, but not at the expense of your own safety."

A rock hurtled toward his head, missing him by inches before it crashed against the reinforced glass of the mat-trans.

"Protect yourselves," Lakesh shouted. "Run if you can."

He needed to alert the security personnel, but with Edwards apparently working with these mysterious strangers, Lakesh wasn't sure who he could trust.

At the far side of the room, Domi was surrounded by Edwards and two of the robed figures. Like a jack-in-the-box, she flipped, kicking one of them in the face with her left heel even as her other leg stretched above her in a graceful arc until the pointed toes connected with Edwards's front teeth. The man fell backward, growling in pain as his lip split open. Domi ignored him, using her impetus to vault the nearest desk and leap high into the air.

Lakesh watched as she made a grab for the metallic grille high above her. Fifteen inches by twelve, the grille was a part of the air-conditioning system, a vent used to distribute air to the room. Small but sinewy, Domi pulled at it with both hands, lifting herself up until her bare feet were pressed against the ceiling tiles, her body poised like an upside-down crab.

With a grunt, she pulled the grille from its housing, and screws snapped from the wall like bullets fired from a gun. She was falling then, the grille still in her hands as she tumbled back to the floor. She landed hard, taking the impact with bended knees, then rolling automatically into a crouch.

One of the hooded attackers was running at her, and Domi turned and threw the rectangular grate at him, tossing it like a discus so that it flew through the air in a spinning, horizontal arc. The heavy grate slammed into the man's stomach, making him double over and fell backward.

Domi turned, spying her lover at the far end of the room. "Lakesh," she shouted, pointing to the hole above her. "Quickly, I'll help you up."

"Dearest, I don't know if—" he began. Then one of the slingshot-thrown rocks smashed into his head and he was out cold.

As Lakesh's still form collapsed to the floor, taking the contents of the nearest desk with him as he fell, Domi leaped up and disappeared into the ventilation pipe. The time to mourn was later, she knew—right now survival was her priority.

Lakesh had seen his people ambushed, overwhelmed, their equipment destroyed. When he had awoken he had been in the redoubt's main corridor along with his colleagues, their ankles restrained, more of the robed and hooded figures patrolling around them. The sounds of combat echoed through the tunnel.

Groggy, Lakesh turned, peering around him at his

fellow prisoners. There was no sign of Domi, and so he had to trust that she had escaped somehow.

Beside him, Brewster Philboyd noticed that Lakesh was moving, and he offered a wary smile. "How's your head, Doctor?" Philboyd asked gently, his voice little more than a whisper.

"It's—" Lakesh winced "—more painful than I expected. I was hit?"

"Someone threw a rock at you," Brewster explained. "Knocked you out cold."

Lakesh thought back, the faint feeling of nausea threatening to bring the contents of his stomach up into his mouth for a moment. "What did I miss?" he asked.

"Trouble and lots of it," Philboyd began, explaining everything that had happened since Lakesh had been struck. It amounted to the same thing, really—the Cerberus redoubt had been overwhelmed by these mysterious enemies armed with stones and slingshots. "They're damn strong, too," Philboyd continued. He and Lakesh looked up then as security specialist Sela Sinclair, beaten and bloody, was dragged in to join the group, along with several others, including geologist Mariah Falk.

Lakesh waited, watching in silence until their hooded guards moved away once more.

"How many of them are there?" he asked Philboyd.

"Don't know for sure, but there's got to be at least thirty," the man replied. "My guess is if they don't outnumber us then they at least come close."

Lakesh nodded gravely. An army then, an organized squad come to take control of Cerberus. He felt tired in that moment, tired and old.

Now LAKESH SAT on the floor, his back propped against the cold, unforgiving wall of rock. A shallow bowl of something rested beside him. Food, he knew, but other than that he couldn't find a word to describe it. It was liquid with lumps in it, cold and viscous. It tasted like a texture rather than a flavor.

He and his people had been captured. It stood to reason that if he had been imprisoned like this, then his fellows had been likewise incarcerated, those that hadn't died like Morganstern, at least. Lakesh estimated that it had been two days, perhaps three, since he had been placed in this tiny, entranceless cave. He had had almost no human contact in that time, and it was becoming harder to judge time's passage now, with his wrist chron removed.

The food was unappetizing; it smelled of nothing and tasted of phlegm. He had eaten it because it was there, and because he wanted to survive, but it had taken all his willpower to stomach it. And it had gone through him rapidly, expelling as watery diarrhea—with no toilet facilities.

No one had spoken to him. No one had questioned him, threatened him. No one had even told him why he was here, wherever here was. The blow to his head had left a wound that scabbed over, and the edges of the scab felt hot when he touched them. He had slept for two days as his body recovered from the punishment it had received. He had woken sporadically during that period, but by the time he could finally organize his thoughts properly he had lost his sense of time.

"They have locked me away and yet they feed me," Lakesh mused to himself, "so they do not want me to die. They are keeping me alive for a reason. They have asked me nothing, so either they are wearing me down first or they have it in mind that they may need me in the future.

"So—why?

"My primary field of knowledge is of the mat-trans procedure, but the system itself is easy enough to operate. But the Cerberus operation…perhaps they need me for that?"

He coughed then, feeling the muscle ache of age as his lungs went into spasm. "If that is the case," he mused aloud, "then an old fool like me must be very low on the list of available candidates, surely." He laughed a little in spite of himself. He had been getting older these past few months—noticeably older, aging far faster than a normal man. It was Sam the Imperator's blessing of youth finally backfiring, turning the young-old Lakesh back into the old-old Lakesh he had been before Sam's magical touch had metamorphosed his cells. He had kept this fact from his peers, hidden the details of his curse from the others. Some had noted he was acting out of character, that he seemed more lethargic, more prone to rash decisions than he had been. Age could do strange things to a man.

But Lakesh still had his brain, his fearsome intellect. If he was to be locked in this impossible cell, then he needed to work out everything he possibly could about his situation. "If I am here, then I am not the only one," he said to the empty air around him. "But where would you trap sixty trained personnel once you had overwhelmed the Cerberus redoubt? Where do you find self-sealing caves?" He tapped at the walls as he spoke.

"Ullikummis," Lakesh breathed, the name coming out like a curse. The monster controlled rock, and so he could shape a place like this, form it from the stuff about him.

Lakesh allowed himself a little smile then. He was beginning to understand what was going on.

Like all scientists and men of reason, he knew that

knowledge was the thing that would set them free.
Knowledge was the most powerful weapon they had
against their mighty foe.

Chapter 25

The stone door to Kane's cell slid back once again, and Dylan stood there in the eerie orange glow of the corridor.

Kane brought his hand up to his face, shying away from the light for a moment.

"How are you feeling?" Dylan asked, a sense of pride in his voice, pride and something else that Kane could not yet pinpoint.

"Hungry," Kane replied after a few seconds' thought.

Dylan smiled, the yellowing teeth flashing within the shadows of his hood. "You now stand on the precipice of utopia, Kane," he said, proffering his hand. "Welcome to the future."

Kane took the ex-farmer's hand, pulling himself up from the floor with the help of that strong grip. Dylan's words seemed different than they had before; they seemed almost like pleasing scents that tickled the nostrils. Somehow the stone inside Kane was responding to Dylan's voice, a receiver for some hidden, mystical broadcast.

"So what do we do now?" Kane asked. "What's the agenda?"

"There's a whole army here, waiting for a leader," Dylan said as he led the way from the cell into the rock-walled tunnel beyond. "Troops all over, each one in need of a leader, a general."

Kane looked behind him for a moment, taking in the claustrophobic proportions of the cell he had spent almost three days locked within. It stank of sweat and human waste. Kane felt a twinge of shame at the thought. Above, at the topmost arch of the low ceiling, a magma light glowed continuously, pulsing subtly brighter as he admired it.

Dylan stopped, turning back to Kane with an ingratiating smile. "Don't tell me you're going to miss it?" he joked.

"That? Nah," Kane replied, shaking his head. "I'm part of the future now, right? And things like prison are best left in the past."

"Not prison," Dylan corrected. "Life camp. This is Life Camp Zero, prototype for the system that will be used to reeducate the world."

"Reeducate the world?" Kane repeated, raising his eyebrows in surprise.

"Did you ever think that the baronies were weird?" Dylan asked, leaning closer as if voicing something conspiratorially. "They were a model, but they didn't work. Too many exclusions, too many people left in the Outlands beyond ville limits. Hell, I never lived in a ville, just made a living outside their walls, far from the barons' reach. The model didn't work, Kane—nine baronies set up across the country, little enclaves of rules in a land of no-one-gives-a-shit.

"Lord Ullikummis saw this and he said that it must change. He said that the future must start, that man must be freed from the shackles of the barons."

"The barons are dead," Kane said. "They upped sticks and disappeared. The villes are falling apart—I saw the wreckage of Beausoleil blowing away in the wind."

The pair walked down the tunnellike corridor, the

faint glow of magma ebbing from inset pods in the walls and ceiling and floor. "The barons may be gone," Dylan acknowledged, "but their model remains, holding people static, keeping them in their simple little roles."

"But Lord Ullikummis," Kane elaborated, "he's changing the game plan. He's setting people…free?"

It seemed a strange thing to say, for Kane knew that this ghastly Annunaki prince had as much interest in freeing humanity as a spider would a fly snagged in its web. Yet somehow, inside his head, he felt that this was the case, that Ullikummis—Lord Ullikummis—was benevolent. Kane recognized the mind trick, the double-think, even as the words tumbled from his lips. He almost believed it. If Rosalia hadn't tweaked the living stone inside him maybe he would have believed it entirely, never thought to question it.

"It's a war for freedom," Dylan explained. "Isn't that what you always fought for, Kane?"

Kane nodded in silent agreement. It felt strange walking beside this man, hearing the words he spoke. It was like hearing a voice double-tracked, a singer providing his own backing on an ancient recording. First Priest Dylan was speaking, and yet there was a second voice, subtler, hidden within his words. It made the bearded man seem charismatic, made his words hold more weight than they rightly should.

Kane followed as Dylan led him down another corridor, passing several hooded sentries before they reached a bank of elevators. Kane looked at them in fascination. The gleaming steel doors seemed so out of place amid the rough rock from which the complex appeared to be carved. For the first time in three days, Kane saw himself, his image reflected there in the dull sheen of the elevator doors. His hair was standing on end, tufts poking in all directions from his sleeping restlessly on the cavern floor. His hand moved to his jaw, feeling the dark stubble that had formed there. It was no longer stubble, in fact, but the beginnings of a definite beard. The man in the reflection wore scruffy clothes, the torn remains of a shadow suit, black strands pulled across his chest, arms and legs, rips showing the scarred flesh beneath. Kane glanced down at himself, saw the ruined suit he wore. It was smeared with blood and dirt, caked sand clinging along one side.

Dylan waved his hand at the wall in a gesture Kane couldn't quite follow, and a moment later the middle set of elevator doors slid open. Kane followed Dylan through the doors, marveling at the presence of the elevator in the way a primitive might, he was so taken aback by it. Inside, the elevator seemed standard enough. In fact, it reminded Kane of the ones they had used in the Cerberus redoubt, only its walls were marred with stretching fingers of stone, reaching down from the ceiling like snowmelt.

Kane watched as Dylan selected a floor on the rock-obscured panel and the doors closed. With a pleasing whir of motors, the elevator ascended and a moment later the doors opened once more to reveal another cavern tunnel. There were low walls here and there, dotted seemingly at random along the length of the route Dylan chose. Some of the odd barricades jutted from the walls themselves, sticking out like pointing fingers, blocking their route in such a way that Kane and Dylan had to shuffle sideways to pass them. They didn't seem like natural formations, yet Kane could not imagine their purpose.

"Where is this place?" he muttered, curiosity finally getting the better of him.

Dylan smiled as he turned back to the ex-Mag. "It's everywhere," he said. "Ullikummis is everywhere."

As Dylan said those words, Kane felt the tingling in his hand, his arm, the place where the stone had been embedded before Rosalia had blocked its progress. It was a giddy feeling, like falling in love. Kane felt sick.

Together, the two men walked down the tunnel, the low ceiling overhead giving Kane a sense of claustrophobia once more. He was becoming more conscious of such things since spending so long trapped in the doorless cell, he knew, yet he couldn't shake that terrible feeling of being caged. A moment later, he found himself in a wider tunnel, the roof higher than the service tunnels they appeared to have been using up until now. The corridor stretched far off into the distance, and Kane saw several robed and hooded figures walking along its length, moving off into side tunnels much like the one he and Dylan had just exited. Almost twenty feet above them, the rocky roof was decorated with mean-looking stalactites, their spikes reaching down like arrows aimed at the people beneath.

Turning left, Dylan led the way briefly along the tunnel until they reached a wide archway carved into the rock. Through this, Dylan pointed to a large cavern located beyond its mouth. Kane looked inside, saw the vast, high-ceilinged cave there. People were busily working in this room, checking paperwork and maps they had laid out across two waist-high, curved ridges of rock that ran the full width of the cavern.

"The nerve center of Life Camp Zero," Dylan explained. "We're still setting things up, but we plan to coordinate everything from here. Utopia begins."

Kane peered into the cave, his interest piqued. Over in the far corner he saw smoked glass amid the struts of rock, a burnt-orange color beneath the illumination of the bubbling lava lights. "You have a mat-trans," Kane stated.

Dylan nodded. "We have a few modes of transport now," he said. "Each has its part to play. Maybe you'll use them all in your campaign against Enlil."

Kane recalled then just why he had been recruited into Ullikummis's army. He was to be a general or a sergeant, leading a force into battle against the hated enemy he knew only too well—the Annunaki overlord called Enlil. "When does this campaign begin?" Kane asked.

"Your troops are still being amassed," Dylan told him. "Some are here, held in cells as you were, but there will be others soon enough. Recruiters are spreading out among the people, offering salvation."

Salvation. On any other day, Kane would have scoffed at the misuse of the word. Yet right now, as he stood with Dylan, the first priest somehow made it all seem so plausible, inevitable even. The obedience stone was inside him, Kane knew, making him susceptible to the overtures of the strange priest. It was all hypnosis, fooling people into believing that this was what they had wanted all along.

Kane's mind drifted back to the discussion he had had with Lakesh and Baptiste several months earlier, when they had tried to unlock the secret of the weird architecture of the Ullikummis-built Tenth City. The use of giant sigils, vast structures designed to take thought away, to make people comprehend things only in the way the overlords chose. That was the nature of Tenth City, but its design had occurred again and again throughout history, shaping every major city on Earth. If the hidden history of the world was one dictated by alien intervention, then the design of the cities formed an insidious part of that history, shaping the minds of the human race. The more civilized humanity became, the more humankind became trapped in the web of subjugation.

Kane peered around him once more, looking at the mat-trans in the corner, the low walls all around it. Perhaps the walls were part of the pattern, designed to affect a person's mind in infinitely subtle ways. He didn't know.

He turned back to Dylan, running a hand over his stubbled chin as he addressed the priest. "You know," Kane said, "I feel like hell right now. Maybe I can get washed up and changed, and then we can start figuring out the battle plan."

"Of course," Dylan agreed, his voice once again emitting some strange musical pull that Kane could not quite put his finger on. "There's a simple changing area on the floor below where you can clean yourself up. I'll take you there and order delivery of fresh clothes."

Kane nodded, feeling obliged.

Dylan dealt with some issue that had been raised by one of his people, and Kane felt sure that the man was the prison warden here, his authority absolute. He was Ullikummis in the absence of the stone Annunaki himself, and his word was law among these people. Kane needed to put him out of commission fast, stop whatever he was broadcasting from affecting the minds of those around him.

Once Dylan was done, he led Kane back to the bank of elevators and they descended to a lower floor. Then First Priest Dylan showed Kane to the washroom and left him there, promising that someone would be along shortly with clean clothes. He left Kane alone, trusting with absolute certainty that the obedience stone would stop him from trying anything rebellious.

There was a wall of mirrors behind three washbasins. Kane looked at himself in the nearest, saw the dark circles under his eyes, the shadow of beard across his chin. There was no denying that he looked rough, and for a Magistrate to appear this untidy somehow shamed Kane, his old life kicking in. There was a small hunk of soap in a dish, and a razor blade had been left beside it. The blade glinted beneath the soft orange lighting that swirled in the ceiling and walls.

Kane moved across the room, pushed open a door of one of the stalls. He was dehydrated and he hadn't eaten for over forty-eight hours, but still he needed to use the toilet. His body ached with the need to clear itself, and his muscles twinged with the pain of exhaustion. He took his time, gathering his thoughts as he sat there, letting his body do what it must. The expulsion left him feeling drained, washed out. He needed to eat and to rehydrate himself.

Finally he exited the stall, made his way back to the washbasins, ran his hands under the water until it became steaming hot. Then he turned the faucet, letting in cold water and running it over his hands, feeling its coolness wash between his extended fingers, cleaning the dried blood and skin from beneath his fingernails. He cupped his hands under the flow, brought the cool water to his face, splashed it over his tired features. He repeated the motion, this time drinking water from his hands before splashing the remainder over his face in an effort to revive himself. Then he leaned down and drank directly from the faucet, his mouth feeling as if something had died inside it.

Finally, Kane reached forward again, fixing the stopper in the basin and pressing on the faucet until a jet of warm water filled the bowl. He stripped off the ruined top of his shadow suit and lathered his face. Then, as the water steamed in the basin, he began to shave, cutting away the growth of beard and making himself presentable once again. It was cathartic in its way, a re-creation of the old Kane that preceded his capture and incarceration. He looked at himself in the mirror as his familiar features reappeared, smiling as he began to feel the old determination—the old fire—return.

Kane splashed water on his face, not caring that it was cold now, relishing the feeling it brought him, that sensation of being alive. The buzzing in his head was abating, but he remained ravenous with hunger. He looked down at his left wrist, searching for evidence of the stone buried there. It was sending signals through his nervous system, he knew, making him respond differently to Dylan's words. Kane was no scientist; he didn't know how it worked. Attached to his nervous system, the stone might exude an enzyme, pump endorphins to his brain, maybe. He couldn't tell.

There was a noise behind him and Kane turned, his keen eyes searching the darkness of the communal washroom. A person was walking past the screen that stood by the door, one that blocked a direct view of the room from the tunnel-like corridor beyond. Kane tensed, old instincts returning, as whoever it was navigated around the stone screen and entered the main area of the washroom. Apparently tall and slender, the figure's physique was disguised by the shapeless robe. The person carried a bundle of material, carefully folded, and Kane realized that here were the "fresh clothes" Dylan had promised.

"Just leave it there," Kane said. "Thanks."

The hooded figure stopped, placed the spare robe beside the basin closest to the door. "You dolt, it's me," she said, her voice an irritated hiss.

Kane watched the woman push back her hood, and recognized Rosalia's familiar face looking up at him, her silken hair and dark eyes glowing in the magma lighting.

"Well, well," Kane said, "fancy meeting you here, Rosie."

"Put on the robe," she instructed, "and hurry. They'll send someone along in a minute to check on you. We want to be out of here by then."

Kane reached for the robe, shaking it out and turning it upside down as he placed his bare arms in the sleeves. "What's the rush?" he asked.

"I cuffed the guard who was bringing this to you," Rosalia explained. "Didn't want you straying too far without me."

"I can believe that," Kane muttered as he pushed his arms through the sleeves and brought the hood down over his head. The robe fell about him, rough against his skin and ending just a few inches above the soles of his boots. "I feel like a monk," he griped.

Rosalia was back at the stone door, pushing at it and peeking outside. Kane saw the dark shape of her mutt standing guard, patiently waiting for its mistress to reappear.

"You want to know what happened to your friends?" Rosalia asked, turning back to him for a moment.

Kane nodded.

"Good. Let's go sightseeing," Rosalia said breezily. Then she pulled the door wide and skipped outside, the mongrel dog at her heels and Kane bringing up the rear.

He knew somehow that this was it—he had just taken the first step to freedom from this awful place.

But of course freedom wears many faces....

Chapter 26

Alone in the cavern once more, Brigid sat in the seat that had formed her prison for so long. She was free of it now, of course, yet she found she naturally gravitated to it, resting there as the only comfort in the vast cave.

Seven hours had passed, but Ullikummis had not returned since running the rock spike through the sand rendition of the girl. The spike remained, poking from the floor of the cavelike a stalagmite, just two feet across at its widest diameter. Brigid looked at it, ahead of where she sat on the stone chair. The sand remained strewed about the cavern, now just particles rising from the floor and dancing in the air on the light current that blew through the room. They had dried out, as the moisture that held them together had evaporated. Even if Ullikummis had not split the bust apart, the girl's face would have crumbled in time, the sand figure breaking apart as it dried. Brigid wondered if this had been the real answer here, if the impermanence of sand would have taught her the same lesson no matter what had happened.

Ullikummis had spoken to her, told her how the world was not so much different as bigger. Her own time with Cerberus had shown her something similar, she supposed—that the things people misunderstood had many levels, and were hidden in plain sight. The Annunaki, then, were not gods.

This was nothing new. Brigid knew their history, knew

how the Annunaki had traveled from the stars thousands of years before, had appeared as gods to the primitive peoples of Earth. But what Ullikummis had told her, about the mirror and the eclipse, suggested there was a deeper conspiracy here, a trick she hadn't even begun to suspect.

In the nineteenth and twentieth centuries, there had been advertising and public relations. This was how products were popularized, Brigid understood, and those products might be carbonated drinks or they might be politicians. The advertising men created little fabrications, worlds that people wanted to buy into and be part of. Before Cerberus, Brigid Baptiste had been an archivist in Cobaltville, and part of her job had been to smooth over history, to make the past look "right," to make it more palatable. She, too, had been a PR flack, designing false worlds with which to fool the public.

She looked around her, saw the cavern with its rough walls, its rock floor, the recessed pods of magma that provided just the slimmest of light. The cave was real; she was sure of that much. But everything else...

Ullikummis had made her sit in the dirt and craft a face, an imagined face of a fictitious girl. Brigid had done it because he had promised to set her free once she completed the task. With no other avenues of escape open to her, she had grasped at this possibility as her lifeline, her one way to freedom.

"The Annunaki," Brigid muttered, "are a blending of reality and mythology, of fact and fiction. They are a story that we fight, but the reality is something different, something we're never meant to see."

The girl Abigail—she, too, was a fiction, a story and nothing more. And Brigid's work with the historical division in Cobaltville had been a blending of fact and fantasy, too, creating new fabrications, new myths.

The titian-haired archivist and Cerberus warrior reached an inevitable conclusion then, the words forming on her trembling lips. "The Annunaki are us," she whispered. It made no sense, and yet it seemed to finally open something in her mind that she had never noticed before. Yes, the Annunaki were alien, they were the different. But the way they acted, the things they hid, were stories, tricks of simple good and evil to hide their true nature.

Ullikummis had mocked her, told her that the way she and her fellow rebels had understood the Annunaki carried no more depth of insight than observing players in masks on a stage. "They have a permanence we cannot comprehend," Brigid murmured aloud. "The games they play are moments which we perceive as lives."

She rested back in the chair, wondering at what this revelation told her, how it could help her. The defeat of the Annunaki lay in their own trickery. If that could be turned against them, they would wither and die.

Brigid smiled, remembering an ancient theological argument that had been repeated over and over: Satan's greatest trick was convincing the world he did not exist.

"If I were to become invisible," Brigid whispered, "then I could defeat the Annunaki. That's the key. By stepping outside their rules, I can stop them."

A noise came from behind her, and she recognized the sound of rock scraping against rock. A glimmer of magma glinted by the wall, reflected in the mirror that was propped there. Ullikummis was with her, striding across the shadowy cave.

"You have questions," he said.

Brigid shook her head. "No," she said. "At first I thought I did, but I realize now that I do not."

Ullikummis looked at her with approval. "If you have no questions, then you must only have answers," he observed.

Brigid nodded, a thin smile forming on her lips. "I think so. Do you have questions, my lord?"

"Just one," Ullikummis acknowledged. "I gave my word that I would set you free when you completed your task with the sand. When did I set you free?"

Brigid's emerald eyes met his, proud in understanding. "When the sand crumbled," she said. "But that was inevitable. Truthfully, you had set me free when you gave me the task, knowing I was ready."

"And what does your freedom tell you?" Ullikummis asked.

Brigid's eyes searched the sand about his trunklike feet, roving across the debris there. Finally, she glanced back to his face, realization dawning. "It tells me that freedom is a state of mind," she said.

Pleased, Ullikummis reached forward and placed one hand to either side of her head. "My father created me to be his tool of hate," he said. "Hate takes many forms, Brigid."

She looked into his burning eyes and felt herself falling, her stomach flipping. This creature had such power. His every movement seemed to command her, his every gesture to instruct her. His eyes swirled with magma, mesmerizing her, dulling her brain. Like so many of the Annunaki, Ullikummis seemed able to command with just a thought, his merest presence enough to make humans cower and obey.

The Russians had realized this, had understood that the greatest threat that aliens posed to humanity was not physical domination but mental. They had used uncharted areas of the human mind, like new continents where weapons could be hidden.

"Did you believe in God, Brigid?" Ullikummis asked. The question startled her, sitting as she was, staring into a would-be god's eyes.

She shook her head. "I don't know," she admitted.

"The Annunaki were your gods," Ullikummis explained. "For many years, they were worshiped for their superiority, their infinite brilliance when compared to man."

"They created that situation," Brigid said.

"No," Ullikummis corrected. "Encouraged, no doubt, but the desire was there in man to worship something. Before the Annunaki it was clouds, insects, weather patterns. Man has a capacity to worship that sets him both above and below other races."

"But they are false gods," Brigid replied, her voice heated with irritation. Ullikummis's hands were still at either side of her head, caging her, blocking her in.

"Would you recognize a true god if he came to you?" Ullikummis asked. He let the question hang, leaving her to ponder it a moment, watching her face with fascination.

Brigid turned the thought over in her head. *"Did you,"* she muttered. "You asked '*Did you* believe in God?' Not 'Do you?' Why?"

"What do the gods believe in?" Ullikummis replied, a question for a question. "Did you ever wonder that?"

"The Annunaki, you mean?" Brigid clarified. "They believe in…hate, rivalry, subjugation of others."

"In badness, then," Ullikummis stated. "Is that what you are saying? You believe this race so pure that they could only have evil qualities and nothing good?"

"No," Brigid said, "there was one called Enki. Your father's brother. He tried to help mankind. It's said that he's the reason we're here, because he saved us from the Great Flood."

"Enki cut off my feet. And what did Enki believe in?" Ullikummis asked.

"I don't know," Brigid admitted, feeling confused, almost punch-drunk by his questions.

"If you are to be elevated to the status of Annunaki, you had better find out," Ullikummis told her.

Brigid stared at him, feeling the hypnotic pull of his swirling magma eyes. He was tricking her, feeding her mind with information that spun upon itself, questions that came only as questions, problems that existed solely to baffle and confuse.

He's trying to get into my brain, Brigid realized.

"You are free now," Ullikummis said, drawing his hands away from the chair and taking a step back. "You have intelligence and knowledge and a capacity for learning that is exceptional among those of your race. With your help, Enlil can be dethroned and the world can move forward."

"So that you can take his place?" Brigid asked, the question laced with suspicion.

"Each step forward changes the next one you must take," Ullikummis replied. "Upelluri taught me that."

Brigid felt his presence in her mind then. He had spent so much time with her, concentrated his energies on her for so long, determined to change her way of thinking. And she saw it, an ink blot across her mind, her old thoughts becoming smaller, irrelevant to her. No, that could not happen. That must not happen.

Ullikummis had changed her through the softest of coercion, made her see things that weren't there. She looked up, past him to the shining thing that waited at the edge of the cave. She was believing in things that did not exist as anything more than reflections on the surface of the mirror, Brigid realized.

It occurred to her then that she could not possibly hope to halt this thing's progress in her mind, could not possibly hope to survive intact as it overwhelmed her. She could do nothing but embrace the mental might of Ullikummis, scion of the Annunaki, and in so doing become one with them, commune with their very way of thinking. And, in doing that, she threatened to lose Brigid Baptiste forever.

There had been a trick to it before, Brigid recalled. Gold on blue—green and red. The weaving threads of destiny.

"My father required a weapon," Ullikummis said, "a physical expression of his hatred."

The words seemed to echo in Brigid's mind as she remembered the multicolored threads. She was losing the continuity of memory, fragmenting into something less than she had been before.

"I was that weapon," Ullikummis continued. "I was the hatred that my father unleashed upon his enemies."

Brigid concentrated, remembering the colors and the pattern they created.

"And now I need a weapon of hatred, too," Ullikummis told her. "A weapon so devious, so powerful, that it can shape the future."

Brigid concentrated on the colors, the familiar pattern that the threads wove, even as she sank into the mental embrace of the great god Ullikummis, knowing she could no longer fight him.

Chapter 27

Kane walked with Rosalia down one of the seemingly never-ending tunnels that made up Life Camp Zero, her nameless mongrel following at a discreet distance. The walls glimmered with the recessed pods of swirling magma, and Kane saw similar pods located at haphazard intervals in the ceilings and occasionally beneath his feet in the rough-hewn rocky floor. There were low walls here and there, hunks of rock jutting out like barricades. At first, Kane had taken these to be random, the result of whatever erosion had created the dense collection of tunnels, but after a while he realized there was a pattern to the juts and hurdles, and the pattern was repeated in each new tunnellike corridor.

"What is this place?" he asked, keeping his voice low.

Rosalia shrugged. "Ullikummis shaped it," she explained. "He can manipulate rock, you understand."

"Yeah," Kane agreed. "I've seen him do that a few times. But this—life camp, prison, whatever you want to call it—this is a huge operation. It must have taken months to construct."

"No," Rosalia told him as her dog trotted along behind them, "it's an adaptation. He builds on old things to create new ones."

"The same way mythology does," Kane mused. "Build-

ing new faith out of the ruins of the old. Typical Annunaki."

Kane stopped in one of the rock-walled tunnels, peering behind for a few seconds to make sure they weren't
being observed. Reassured, he turned to Rosalia. "So,
where are the other prisoners?" he asked.

"All around you," Rosalia said, indicating the solid
walls.

Kane glanced where she indicated, shook his head. "I
don't see them," he admitted.

Rosalia shot him a fierce look. "You think you were
the only one they kept in a cell with no door?" she challenged hotly. "You really think you're so special?"

Brushing a hand through his hair beneath the hood,
Kane had the good grace to look self-effacing. "First
Priest Dylan gave me the impression that…" He stopped,
shaking his head ruefully. "Not so smart, believing your
own press, huh?"

"Not so smart believing a liar," Rosalia told him dis-
missively. "You want to keep that in mind, Magistrate
man, if we're going to get out of here alive."

Looking apologetic, Kane peered around the tunnel
again. The walls were closely packed, claustrophobically
so in parts where lumps jutted out in those strange barricades. If he stood on tiptoe and stretched, he could reach
the arched ceiling, brushing it with his knuckles. Other
than himself, his beautiful companion and her dog, the
corridor was empty.

"Well?" he encouraged. "Can't stage a jailbreak without knowing where the cells are, now, can I?"

Rosalia reached a slender hand behind Kane's
neck, pulling him close as if to kiss him. "Watch," she
breathed.

He looked down to see her other hand brush against

the rock wall to his right, at about the height of his belt buckle. The wall appeared blank at first glance, but Kane could see a shadowed recess there no bigger than his thumb, surrounded by a little ridge that stood out about a quarter of an inch from the uneven rock surface. A keyhole, he guessed, or a sensor that did the same job as a keyhole, anyway.

Rosalia swept her hand across the recess in the rock, barely touching it with the pale, inner side of her forearm. There came a rumbling then, a deep vibration as if an earthquake was happening, and Kane felt the floor shake beneath his feet. She pulled him a pace back as the wall began to part, and suddenly the rectangular shape of a doorway formed, seamless to the rock wall itself, yet distinct.

The rock panel shuddered aside, merging with the wall to its right. Kane took a step forward, gazing at the door, which had disappeared from view. There was no visible mechanism to operate it, and it seemed to run on invisible tracks, sinking into the substance of the wall in some unfathomable manner.

Tentatively, Kane took another step forward, entering the tiny cave that lay behind the door, checking over his shoulder to make sure Rosalia wasn't about to try anything. The cell was six-by-eight, the same size as his own had been, and a single magma pod glowed faintly in the ceiling, its swirling contents shifting subtly as Kane watched. Lying on the hard rock floor of the cell was a slender woman wearing the familiar white jumpsuit of the Cerberus staff. The suit was torn and scuffed, and even under the faint orange glow of the overhead light, Kane could see streaks of dried blood marring its once vibrant material. The magma light caught the woman's hair, making it appear red, and for a moment Kane's heart leaped as he thought she was Brigid Baptiste. Then he stopped himself, breath catching in his throat, as he recognized her. Not Baptiste, but…

"DeFore? Reba DeFore?"

The woman looked up through the curtain of her blond bangs, and Kane saw glistening streaks down her face where tears flowed freely. "Lakesh?" she asked.

Kane pushed the hood of his robe back as he bent down to speak with her. "No, Reba, it's me," he said. "It's Kane."

"Kane?" DeFore sounded uncertain, frightened. Kane recognized her altered mental status from his days as a Magistrate in Cobaltville, where prisoners had sometimes gone stir-crazy, suffering mental breakdowns. "Is that really you?"

"It's me," he said, his voice tender and reassuring. "It's okay, it's me. It's not a trick."

"Where are we?" she asked, then peered over Kane's shoulder and saw the other figure standing there, the slender woman in the rough robe. "Who's that? Is that Brigid?"

"No," Kane said, glancing over his shoulder and, with a quick nod, encouraging Rosalia to enter the room. "This is Rosie. She's a friend."

"Kane, what's going on?" DeFore asked. "It feels like I've been lying here for so long."

"I know it does," he said, "but I'll have you out soon enough. Just hang tight, be strong."

DeFore reached out then, brushing the side of his face with her fingertips. "Kane," she snickered. "As I live and breathe, it really is you."

He nodded again. "It really is. Now, you're going to have to stay strong for just a little while longer, Reba.

I need to get things in place before I can get you and everyone else out of here. Okay?"

The Cerberus medic looked mystified, like some senile old woman being told she had already eaten, yet having no memory of the meal. "Are you leaving?" she asked. "Are you leaving me again?"

Kane rested his hand on her shoulder, held it firmly as she lay there on the cave floor before him. "Be strong, Reba," he reiterated. "It won't be long now."

Then he stood, watching the broken figure of Reba DeFore as she slumped on the floor of the tiny cave, tears flowing down her cheeks.

Rosalia preceded him out of the cell, showed him how to close the door. "You need to brush here," she said, "like a swipe card." She held Kane's left wrist in a tight grip and drew his hand across the sensor. The door grumbled a moment, then slid back into place, sealing Reba DeFore in her cell.

Kane nodded. "I see."

Then he peered down the ill-lit corridor, seeing more of the recessed sensors hiding in plain sight, each one poised uniformly at waist height. There were over a dozen lining the walls that Kane could see, and he briefly tried to calculate how many prison cells might be here in this vast, eerie complex. There could be hundreds, he realized, more than enough to hold all the captured Cerberus personnel. And if that was the case, then it meant one thing—Brigid Baptiste must be here somewhere, trapped behind one of these hidden doors.

Rosalia's hand reached up, stroking him gently across his cheek. "What are you thinking, Magistrate man?" she asked.

Kane looked at her. "How do we get out of here?"

"The main exit, but it's blocked and guarded," Rosalia told him.

"Any other way that you know of?"

"There's another exit," she informed him. "Cuts through a vehicle hangar, opens out lower down in the complex. I use it to walk the dog, let him get some exercise."

"Why isn't that entrance guarded?" Kane asked.

"The route there is," Rosalia told him, "but think about it—who's trying to escape?"

Kane nodded. "The cells lock themselves," he reasoned, "making escape almost impossible."

"No 'almost' about it, Magistrate man," Rosalia corrected.

"There's always a way," Kane told her, and he raised his arm, examining his wrist. There was no scar, but there seemed to be a puckering of the skin, as though his flesh had buckled where the stone had embedded itself. "How long do I have?" he asked.

"We'll fix it in time," Rosalia assured him. "You trust me, right?"

Kane wasn't so certain, but he reluctantly gave his assent as he followed Rosalia down the tunnel toward an intersection. She moved on, checking left and right as she led the way through the vast maze of caverns, the dog trotting along at her heels, tongue out. They passed several groups of hooded figures, the people Kane had come to think of as prison guards, and Rosalia acknowledged them with a nod or a quick word, keeping to her path through the tunnel-filled complex.

After a while they reached a wider tunnel, this one littered with low walls like hurdles.

"Main exit is that way." Rosalia indicated the far end of the tunnel.

Kane looked, recognizing where he was. Dylan had brought him here. The operations center was off to his left. The ceiling was high and covered in spiky stalactites that reached down like witch's fingers, sharp nails clawing at the air above him. It was uneven, something formed over centuries of erosion. Kane saw magma pods here and there, spaced irregularly along the vast length of the corridor, most on the ceiling but a few located along the walls or embedded in the solid stone floor. At the far end, a distance of perhaps three hundred yards in all, Kane could make out figures standing patiently, sentries guarding the life camp's main exit.

Rosalia ran her wrist across a sensor eye in the wall, and a door melted aside. Beyond, Kane saw a flight of stairs carved from the rock, stretching down to lower levels of the prison. Rosalia motioned him forward, and Kane followed her and the dog as they walked into the strange stairwell, gesturing behind him with a sweep of his arm to close the entrance.

Inside, the rocky stairwell echoed, carrying the sounds of their footsteps back to them in staccato bursts. The dog's panting seemed louder here, too, echoing in Kane's ears from the hard surfaces that surrounded them. Like the rest of the prison, the stairwell was lit by lava pods hidden in recesses, and he marveled at the economy of design. Supposedly spaced at random, the glowing pods cast enough light to see by, and their orange tint gave the whole life camp the feeling of living inside a furnace, painting everything in a fiery glow.

Rosalia led the way down the steps, moving gracefully and silently. The dog scampered behind her, and Kane followed them both until the svelte woman stopped at another wall and brushed a sensor with her wrist. A door opened, revealing another poorly lit tunnel stretching away from the stairs. The walls here were rough, with jutting bumps sticking out at head height, forcing Kane to duck.

"Kind of monotonous design sense you have here," he observed sarcastically.

Rosalia shot him a look so fierce he almost backed away. "Keep your mind on the job," she told him, "and stop trying to dazzle me with small talk."

Contritely, Kane agreed. "Reba seemed pretty messed up," he said, returning to the subject at hand. "I don't know how much use she'll be in a firefight. Is she typical?"

"This place is designed to break the spirit, Kane," Rosalia told him. "They've starved the prisoners, giving them only enough to keep them alive. Sometimes not even that."

Kane felt the emptiness in his own stomach as she spoke, reminded of how little he had eaten in the past sixty hours. Ahead, Rosalia approached one of the hooded guards, constructing some cock-and-bull story about having to check on the vehicle bay for signs of welding equipment.

"You need a hand with that?" the sec man asked, his face hidden in shadow.

"That's okay, I brought my own muscle," Rosalia said, gesturing to Kane. Despite the shapelessness of the robe he wore, it was clear that he was well-muscled, his shoulders wide in the narrow rocky corridor.

Kane nodded to the sentry, looked across at his bored partner. The second man was working a coin over his knuckles, running it back and forth between his fingers in a show of dexterity. After a moment, Kane noted it wasn't a coin. It was a smooth, flat rock, one of the smaller missiles that he had been on the receiving end of when he had battled these people just a couple of days before.

Rosalia brushed her hand against the door sensor, and the rock gate trundled backward, revealing a vast cave that waited beyond. The woman walked ahead and Kane followed, marveling at the size of the cavern they now found themselves in.

Kane estimated that it was sixty square feet, high-ceilinged, with the usual array of stalactites clawing down from above. Pods of orange light glowed along the walls and floor, both of which undulated with the roughness of the stone here.

As Rosalia resealed the door behind them, Kane spotted something glinting in the magma glow of the lights. He hurried over to get a closer look, recognizing it immediately. It was a Manta, the sleek wings of the aircraft finished in a burnished bronze, with cup-and-spiral designs marking its hull. Kane reached up, running his hand along one of the wings, touching it as if to make sure it was real. Even as he did so, he saw a second Manta docked on the other side of the vast room, its burned-gold shell shimmering in the volcanic light.

"Mantas," Kane breathed. "They've got Mantas."

Rosalia looked at him quizzically. "Is that good? You fly these?"

He nodded. "We get one of these up and running and I can get back to Cerberus, bring reinforcements and shut down this hellhole."

"You're forgetting something," Rosalia told him. "In two hours or so that stone will kick in full force. Then you won't care about any of this."

Kane was about to argue, but stopped himself.

"Truth sucks, doesn't it?" she said, raising a dark eyebrow in challenge. At her heels, the dog whined as if in sympathy.

Kane's mind was racing, trying to work out a way to use this discovery to his advantage. With a Manta at his command, he could fly anywhere, recruit help and stage a massive jailbreak. "If I could get to New Edo, I could speak to Shizuka, come back here with her Tigers of Heaven," he reasoned. "They'd overrun this place in no time."

"Are they that much better than your people," Rosalia challenged, "or are you so inferior?"

"Listen, sweetheart," Kane snarled, jabbing a finger in her face, "Cerberus was ambushed. Before we even knew what was happening, your new friends overran the place…."

"They caught you napping, you mean?" Rosalia said. "A big, strong military facility and they caught you on the one day you were all asleep."

Kane made a fist in frustration, biting back a reply.

"This is bigger than you, Kane," Rosalia told him reasonably. "You can't defeat this in one move."

"Then…what?" he asked.

She pressed her hand to his arm, squeezed the biceps beneath the fustian robe. "Let's look outside," she said gently.

Together, they made their way across the vast hangar, heading toward the little door that Rosalia had found to the side of the main exit. Kane saw other vehicles stored in the shadows as they strode across the echoing bay. The exit itself was locked, sealed with more of the living stone. Kane eyed it for a moment, saw it would be wide enough to bring both Mantas out side-by-side if he needed to. That was good to know. Once everything went ballistic, a rapid escape wouldn't be impossible.

Rosalia brought her hidden stone into play once again, swiping it over a recessed port until Kane heard a lock click open. Then the beautiful woman reached ahead, placed both hands on the uneven rock and pulled until the seemingly solid rock wall began to move toward her. It was a swing door, Kane saw, nothing more complicated than that. He felt fresh air on his face as the door swung toward him, and narrowed his eyes as the bright sunlight struck his face.

The mongrel went running ahead, brushing the side of the door with its flank as it hurried outside and went charging off into the forest beyond. Rosalia followed, with Kane a few paces behind her.

Outside Life Camp Zero, Kane blinked, drinking in the fresh air with deep breaths. Rosalia glanced at him and smiled before turning her attention to the dog hurrying ahead of them. The animal stopped at the verge of trees, looked back once with imploring eyes, then ran off into the tree cover with a single bark.

"He knows where he's going?" Kane asked, nodding toward the dog.

"He'll be fine," Rosalia said. "He never strays far."

"What's his name?" Kane asked, still squinting in the brightness of daylight. The sky was overcast, with silver clouds moving rapidly overhead as the wind picked up. Still, the brightness of the reflected sunlight was dazzling after being inside the dim prison for more than two days.

"He doesn't have a name," Rosalia said. "I never gave him one."

"How long have you had him?" Kane asked.

"Six months maybe." She was watching the dog as it pelted through the brush, sniffing at rabbit holes it found.

"You have a dog six months and you don't give it a name?" Kane asked, taken aback.

Rosalia turned to him and smiled enigmatically. "You give things names and you get attached to them," she said, "Magistrate man."

"Touché," Kane said, nodding in resigned agreement.

As they spoke, he looked around more closely. They were in a little clearing, high up on a mountain slope. The immediate area around the door was flat, with dusty soil marking a place where the trees had been cleared, presumably to let the Mantas take off. Five paces away, the steep slope of the mountain was covered with trees, a vast forest that filled the ravines and valleys all around. There was something nagging at Kane as he took in that vista through squinting eyes, something awfully familiar about the whole thing.

For a moment he stood still, peering at the mountains around them, the forest that blanked the area far and wide. Rosalia was standing two steps ahead of him as she watched her nameless dog sniff at one of the nearby trees, cock its leg and begin to urinate.

Kane turned then, glancing behind him at the open doorway, the rocky line that showed where a larger door for vehicles would open into the hangar. The smaller door was set within the larger one, Kane realized now, seeing how it all fit together. And he knew this place. This place was home.

In a swift movement, he reached forward, grasping Rosalia by the arm and pulling her off balance. He bent his face close to hers, spoke through gritted teeth.

"Why didn't you tell me?" Kane snarled. "Why didn't you tell me we're still in Cerberus?"

Chapter 28

"Would you have believed me if I had told you?" Rosalia asked, her dark eyes meeting Kane's as he loomed over her.

Beyond the plateau, the dog peered up at the sound, barked once in excitement.

Kane glared at the mongrel. "Stay," he commanded.

The animal whimpered, turned to run, then seemed to think better of it. It waited, watching from the relative safety of the tree cover.

Kane turned back to Rosalia, anger flushing his cheeks inside the shadowy hood. "Explain it to me," he growled. "Everything."

"Let me go," she responded. "I'm not your enemy, Kane. Now let me go."

"I was just beginning to trust you," he snarled, "and I find out this."

Rosalia tried to shake off Kane's grip, but he held her tighter, grasping her other arm with his free hand.

"Explain it to me," he repeated, his tone brooking no argument now.

"We came here under the cover of night," Rosalia related, "with Ullikummis at the head of the group. There must have been fifty, sixty people, Kane. He said he wanted to overwhelm this place, to strike hard and to hurt those within."

"How did you get in?" Kane asked.

"He had people on the inside," Rosalia told him. "Obedience stones embedded within them, dormant in their bodies, grafted to their central nervous systems."

"Players on the inside," Kane murmured, seeing the picture unfold before him.

"We waited in the woods," Rosalia continued, "and he called to them. Ullikummis called to them, a mental signal like a song you can't stop humming. I heard it, too, vibrating inside me. We all did. The stones are like a part of him, and they send signals to his people, not instructions so much as emotions. Once the stone is inside you you have to learn to block them, look past them."

"Or what?" Kane demanded.

"Or they drive you insane, Kane," Rosalia told him, "make you one of them. A firewalker."

Kane nodded, taking the information in. "What happened then?" he asked.

"At the signal, we attacked this base," Rosalia said. "Your Cerberus, whatever you call it. I didn't know it was yours, Kane, I didn't know you would be here."

"I wasn't here," Kane told her. "My crew was out in Louisiana when you attacked. When we got back here the whole place was in disarray.

"What happened then?" he demanded, tightening his grip on the woman's arms.

"Your sentries didn't see it coming," Rosalia said. "How could they? They were the very people Ullikummis had recruited, and they didn't even know it. It didn't take long to take over this rat hole, enclosed and undermanned as it was. You make it easy for people."

"That's a point of contention," Kane snarled. "You shouldn't have been able to just walk through the doors."

"You put up a fight," Rosalia said with an approving

smile. "I saw you. You gave that monster a good run for his money. I wanted you to succeed, Kane—you have to believe that."

Still holding her arms, Kane shook Rosalia angrily. "Then why didn't you help me?"

"I was in the enemy's base, surrounded by armed subjects loyal to that monster," Rosalia said with a laugh. "You don't know when to pick your battles, Magistrate man, but I do."

Kane considered that, and his grip on Rosalia's arms eased. Finally he let her go, stepped back a pace and looked out over the mountainous vista that surrounded the Cerberus redoubt. There were guards high above, stationed beside the thick pillars of stone that blocked the main door. "Is this you picking your battle now?" he asked.

Contritely, she nodded, her dark eyes fixed on his.

"Go on," Kane encouraged. "Tell me what happened once I was down."

"Ullikummis placed his hand on the wall," Rosalia said, "like this." She pressed one hand to her breast, the fingers spread wide. "Then there was a rumbling, and the place began to change, like a bug shedding its cocoon. The rocks seemed to grow like mold, forming before my eyes, reshaping and entwining with one another like a lover's embrace.

"He speaks to rocks, Kane," Rosalia said. "He tells them to do things. It makes no sense, but I see him do it."

Kane gazed off into the distance, watching as the silvery clouds sailed by overhead like boats on a stream. "It's a form of telekinesis," he told her. "Psionics. Baptiste figured he had something embedded deep inside him, some tool that could reach out and do these things."

"You met him before?" Rosalia asked.

"Couple of times," Kane told her. "First time was Tenth City up in the north. He built it literally from the ground up, pulling rocks out from the soil, turning them into buildings, nightmarish architecture that twisted and turned. Baptiste called it a sigil, a magical symbol of power. She said it could affect people's way of thinking, make them more susceptible to his instruction."

At the edge of the trees, the dog was sniffing the air, and it turned back to Kane and Rosalia and barked.

"What's that—he sense something?" Kane asked.

She shook her head in irritation. "Stupid mutt, jumping at shadows. He'll get us both killed."

Kane ran his hand over his face, putting pressure there as if to awaken himself. He was trying to work out a map of the complex in his head, figure out how the place they called Life Camp Zero related to the Cerberus redoubt. "The cells are the living quarters," he speculated, "but he's boxed them in somehow, filled them with rock."

"I don't know your home well enough," Rosalia admitted as he looked at her.

"We'd need to open the cells all at the same time," Kane proposed. "Release everyone at once."

"And then what?" she challenged. "You saw the woman, Kane—you saw the state she was in. Nobody's going to fight with you. You barely have the strength to fight yourself."

"Grant and Baptiste," Kane said with a smile. "Release them and we'll have a fight on our hands. You'll see."

"So that's your great plan?" Rosalia said contemptuously. "Open the cells and let the great unfed fight a losing battle against superior odds? Even you can't be that foolish, Magistrate man."

But Kane was still thinking, figuring out his game plan. "You said you heard music when you were near Ullikummis," he said. "I heard the same thing when I was near Dylan, niggling in the back of my skull like an itch I couldn't scratch."

Rosalia's dark eyes flashed beneath the hood as she looked at him. "Yes, I feel that, too, even with my stone blocked. Your point?"

"Architecture that affects people's minds," Kane stated, using his fingers to tick off each point he was making. "A broadcast system hidden in the shapes of the rocks. A signal sent from Overlord Ullikummis, or maybe from the chosen devotees to his cause. Dylan's broadcasting the boss's instructions, somehow. Maybe a bigger stone, something like that."

Rosalia smiled wickedly, seeing Kane's reasoning.

"Take out his stone and the system's got nothing left to broadcast," Kane concluded. "And in the subsequent confusion, even a half-starved army of Cerberus personnel could potentially overpower your stone-chucking friends. Am I right?"

Rosalia reached forward, placing her hands on Kane's biceps in unconscious imitation of the way he had held her just a few minutes before. She leaned close to him, her voice low. "It's possible, but how are you going to shut down Dylan's broadcast stone?"

Kane fixed her with a no-nonsense stare. "The only way there is," he said. "By force."

The dog trotted back to them, and Rosalia offered it soothing words of encouragement. Then she looked at Kane. "You've fought these people before," she said. "Do you remember?"

He nodded.

"They're strong, Kane," Rosalia reminded him. "Not

all of them, but the one with stones in their heads, here—" she brushed her finger on Kane's forehead, just above his brows "—they can tap into something, become like stone themselves."

"So that's what it was," he grumbled. "I half thought I was imagining things. They shrugged off my bullets, got up and just carried on."

Rosalia looked at him with pleading eyes. "We could run, you know? Get away from here. I'll get that stone shit out of you once we're clear."

"I won't leave my friends, Rosie," Kane said. "You don't know me well, but you do know that, don't you?"

She knelt down, stroking the dog's coat over and over until it settled beside her. "Your concepts of honor and responsibility are so quaint," she told Kane.

He shrugged. "Right is right. Now, these stone people, how do they become invincible like that, do you know?"

"Concentration," Rosalia told him. "I don't know how, but the stone works in concert with them. They're still human beings, but they can switch, make their flesh solid for brief bursts. They just concentrate."

"So, if we broke their concentration…" Kane began, an idea beginning to take shape in his mind.

"Yes?" Rosalia prompted.

He reached for the belt he still wore beneath his robe, running his finger along the pouches until he found what he was looking for. "You're going to need these," he said, handing her the things he had removed from his belt.

The beautiful dark-haired woman smiled. "Simple and brilliant," she said with an appreciative nod.

Together, the two refugees began to work out the details of their audacious plan.

TWENTY MINUTES LATER, Kane found himself wandering alone through the tunnels of the eerily remodeled redoubt. Despite the surface changes, the complex was still recognizable, and now that Kane realized where he was he navigated with ease. Rosalia had left him at the doors to the hangar bay, agreeing to her part of the plan with surprising good grace. Kane needed her to free the prisoners using the stone located under her skin, while he took Dylan out once and for all.

"Keep your head down," Kane had advised her. "No point getting killed by the guards around this place until… Well, just don't get killed."

Rosalia had laughed. "Oh, Magistrate man, you can be so naive. It's almost sweet the way you care for others." She'd pinched him on the arm then, before turning down the ill-lit tunnel and disappearing into its shadows, the pale-eyed mongrel trudging along at her heels.

While Rosalia headed down to the remodeled living quarters that now served as cramped cells, Kane trotted along a service tunnel, searching the monotonous surface of the wall for the door he knew must still be there. He spotted the vertical ridge that marked the position of the door, used his obedience stone to unlock the rock coating, making it roll away into the skin of rock all around it. Inside, he found the locker he wanted, and the emergency survival equipment stored within, just as he had expected. Kane pushed the first-aid kit aside, reaching farther into the cupboard, where the flares were kept. He wouldn't need them, either, just the thing that was stored beside them. Picking it up in one hand, Kane removed the little cylindrical device and hid it beneath the folds of his robe.

He continued on his way, heading back to the ops room. He realized now that this was the Cerberus operations center, that the bands of rock had been constructed over twin aisles of computer equipment. The room had acted as the nerve center for the Cerberus team, and it made a kind of perverted sense that it would be the setting for Kane's overthrow of this terrible new regime.

He halted at the arched doorway, eyes scanning the cavernous room beyond. A dozen robed operatives were working there, and Kane concluded that they were now patching together the computers, trying to get the systems operational for their own arcane purposes or those of their leader, Ullikummis.

Dylan was sitting near the rear of the room, where Lakesh's desk had stood just forty-eight hours earlier. Parts of the desk remained exposed, poking through the rocky veins that had clawed over it in thick, branchlike lines. Kane scanned the equipment there, searching for what he needed. The computer was almost entirely gone, hidden beneath the rock skin, but that didn't matter—Kane wouldn't need it. He fidgeted for a moment, feeling the weight of the thing he'd nabbed from the emergency survival kit.

Dylan looked up at his approach. "Feel better?" he asked, pushing aside the report he had been mulling over. Again Kane was aware of some second level of meaning, some trick that subliminally changed the man's words, made him somehow more appealing.

"I need to eat," Kane said.

"Of course," Dylan agreed. "I'll get something brought down while we discuss battle tactics. Lord Ullikummis wants to move swiftly on this project. Now that you're on board I see no reason for delay."

"How do they work?" Kane asked, standing over the man's desk.

Dylan looked baffled, his brows knotting in confusion.

"The stones," Kane growled impatiently. "Tell me how they work."

"The stone we placed in you simply helps you embrace the new world," Dylan said, "opening your mind to it."

"What about the endurance of your people?" Kane asked. "I remember them shrugging off bullets."

"They're your people now, Kane," Dylan reminded him. "You're one of us."

Again, a wave of pleasure swept over Kane at the priest's words, a mother's lullaby. Kane shook his head, willing the effect to pass. Rosalia had blocked his stone, but had said he only had a couple of hours before it bonded completely with him. Once that happened, Dylan's words, and those of chosen servants like him, would cage Kane, alter his personality, making him a pale imitation of what he had been. He needed to break the control right now.

"Can anything hurt them?" Kane asked.

"Why would you want to hurt your brothers?" Dylan asked reasonably.

"If they're to be my army," Kane said, leaning his hand on Lakesh's desk as he bent closer to Dylan, "then I need to know their weaknesses as well as their strengths. Don't I."

Dylan nodded. "It's a level of strength created by an individual's concentration," he explained. "So long as a warrior remains focused, he or she can assume the incredible properties of our stone savior."

Kane pulled back, his hand brushing something on Lakesh's desk. Somewhere beneath the stone cladding a green light flickered on, indicating that the public address system was engaged.

"Don't let it worry you," Dylan reassured Kane. "They won't crack under pressure."

"It's not pressure I'm thinking about," Kane said as he whipped the small cylindrical object from its hiding place beneath his robe. "And I'm not the one who should be worried."

Then Kane yanked the pull tab from the cylinder in his hand, and for a moment Dylan stared in horror, thinking that the ex-Magistrate was detonating a grenade. But instead of an explosion, the foghorn unleashed a deafening squeal, fiercely loud in the confines of the cavelike ops room. Before Dylan could even begin to react, Kane shoved the horn against the pickup microphone of the public address system, and its angry ululation reverberated down the tunnels and caverns of the redoubt-turned-life-camp.

TWO FLOORS BELOW, Rosalia smiled as the hideous banshee wail blurted from the speakers lining the redoubt's walls. Many of the speakers had become buried beneath the rock coating, but they still howled with the annoying echo.

At her side, the dog yelped in irritation at the deafening racket, the poor beast especially sensitive to the hideous noise. Rosalia ignored its cries, having already placed the earplugs Kane had given her into her ears, and hurried forward with determination. All around her, hooded guards were looking about in confusion, and one man dropped a tray of food he had been taking to one of the prison caves.

Rosalia brushed her wrist against the hidden sensor

panel of the nearest cell, striding on even as the door began to shudder back on its hidden tracks.

Kane's plan was in action. It was time to release the prisoners.

Chapter 29

As Rosalia swept her wrist against the fourth sensor along the wall, one of the guards finally noticed what she was doing.

"Hey," he shouted, struggling to be heard over the wailing sound of the alarm being piped over the PA system. "You can't do that. The prisoners will—"

Without hesitation, Rosalia struck the man in the face with her fist, knocking him back against the rough rock wall.

"I am stone," the man growled, clenching his fists.

This was it, Rosalia knew. This was the moment where she would find out if Kane's plan had worked.

She kicked out, sweeping her foot high into the air until it struck the hooded guard a vicious blow to his jaw. He cried out in pain, staggering back against the wall again as one of his teeth flew from his mouth with a bloody spray of torn gum. The guard looked stunned as Rosalia kicked out a second time, striking him in the chest with the ball of her other foot. With a blurt of expelled breath, he sagged backward.

"You're not stone anymore," Rosalia told the guard as he fell. The sirenlike noise echoing through the tunnels had seen to that.

Up ahead, Rosalia's dog ran toward the next guard, leaping into the air with its teeth bared.

All around, prisoners were emerging from their cells.

Grant's broad-shouldered form staggered out of one doorway, a look of consternation on his face. He grabbed at the robed guard who was just hurrying past the open cell door toward Rosalia, snagging the man's loose-fitting robe and hurling him into the wall. The guard slammed against the wall with a crack of bones, sagging limply to the floor.

Grant looked around him, utterly confused. "What the hell is going on?" he shouted over the whine of the alarm.

Rosalia turned, pushing back the hood of her robe. "No time to explain, Magistrate man," she said.

Grant's brows furrowed as he took in the figure before him. He had met with Rosalia months ago, out in the open desert around the fishing ville of Hope. He didn't quite know what to make of her appearance here now.

"What?" he spit, bewildered.

"I'm on your side," Rosalia told him. Then she gestured to the ceiling, indicating the racket that was still playing over the public address system. "This is Kane's doing. We're closing down this shit hole."

Grant scratched at the close-cropped hair on his scalp as he saw Rosalia part another of the stone walls that hid the cells.

"This is going to take some big explaining when we're done," he muttered. But for now, he was happy to go with the flow, turning his attention to another of the robed guards even as the man plucked a slingshot from his belt.

IN THE OPERATIONS ROOM, Kane found himself surrounded by a group of hooded warriors. The horn continued blaring into the microphone, the reverb sounding like some hideous scream in the cavelike space.

"I don't know what the hell you think you're doing," Dylan spit, "but this is not the right way to welcome the future."

Kane glared at him. "Oh, this is the only future you're getting," he snarled. Then his fist struck out, smashing into the jaw of the nearest guard. The man fell, collapsing onto the rocky ledge that had grown over the aisle of desks.

Dylan looked astounded, realizing for the first time that his warriors no longer had their remarkable stonelike abilities of defense. A highly trained Magistrate, Kane worked through the untrained warriors in a matter of seconds, tossing them aside and breaking arms and legs with a succession of well-placed blows. He didn't have long to do this, he knew. It would be only a matter of moments until Dylan shut down the shrieking foghorn and his people could gather their wits once more, turning concentration into physical endurance.

A hooded woman stood before Kane, muttering the mantra he had heard a dozen times before: "I am stone."

Kane drove his fist into her face, collapsing her nose in a single, bloody strike.

"No, you ain't," he growled.

Then he grabbed the front of her robe with both hands and threw her aside even as she cried out with the pain of her shattered nose.

Dylan was at the PA system now, and he snatched up the shrieking cylinder, pulling it away from the microphone. The awful wailing noise dwindled from the overhead speakers, but the foghorn kept blurting out its angry song in the first priest's hand.

Kane turned on his heel, knowing full well he would need something more powerful than his fists once the noise abated. He had dispatched nine of the personnel in the room in those brief instants of respite, leaving just Dylan and two of his hooded guards standing.

As Dylan shut off the irritating horn, Kane sprinted through the archway, hurrying out of the room toward the nearest stairwell. A moment later, Dylan and his people were trotting swiftly down the corridor in pursuit.

ON THE LEVEL of the redoubt that had once held the living quarters, Rosalia, Grant and a handful of other Cerberus personnel battled valiantly as a second wave of guards tried to retard Rosalia's progress. She was unlocking each cell in turn, swiftly using her hidden stone to tap the sensors and make the doors slide open.

Abruptly, the sound from the public address speakers ceased, accompanied a moment later by cries of relief from several of the prisoners.

"No," Rosalia hissed, "you don't understand. Without the noise, they'll be able to concentrate again."

Even as she said it, that eerie battle cry seemed to echo the length of the tunnel they found themselves in:

"I am stone."

"I am stone."

"I am stone."

"I am stone."

"COME ON, COME ON," Kane muttered to himself as he pressed his wrist to the sensor and heard the armory door unlock.

A short way down the corridor the stairwell door groaned open and First Priest Dylan led his two hooded guards out into the tunnel-like space beyond.

In an instant, Kane had shoved the rock-covered door back on its hidden tracks and ducked inside. Even as he disappeared into the armory, he heard Dylan calling, identifying him as he rushed out of sight.

"Perfect," Kane muttered.

Most of the guards were down. Now all he had to do was figure out a way to stop Dylan from broadcasting instructions to Ullikummis's people. Without him, their brainwashing should abate.

As swiftly as possible, Kane reached back, brushing his wrist against the hollow in the wall, commanding the door to seal.

The armory had changed. Where once had stood sleek shelves lit by bright fluorescent overheads, now the ceiling had lowered, and sharp stalactites pointed downward like icicles from its rocky surface. The familiar magma lights were dotted all over, casting their warm orange illumination, leaving much of the armory in shadow. The shelves were still there, and Kane recognized that their pattern remained unchanged. Yet they looked different, covered in a shinglelike skin, as if moss had encroached on the room, clambering up the shelving units with its sticky growths. Whatever Ullikummis's touch had done, it had altered the Cerberus redoubt on a molecular level, changing the fundamental nature of things Kane had previously taken for granted.

Frantically the ex-Mag looked around him, trying to get his bearings in the half-light of the orange magma glow. Shelves of ordnance stretched out across the vast room, ammo clips, gun barrels and cases glinting beneath the soft orange lights. This had been Henny Johnson's domain, Kane recalled. Ex-U.S. Army, Henny had delighted in the storage and cataloging of all this ordnance. Right now, Kane needed to find a weapon that would work against Dylan and his people.

Behind him, Kane heard the stone door trundle open once again: Dylan.

Hurrying down the aisles between the shelves, Kane spotted the unit holding Sin Eater pistols, their familiar wrist holsters stored in a flip-top box on the shelf above. Kane reached into the box, snagged one of the leather holsters with one hand.

"Kane?" Dylan's voice was close to the only door. The sound played over Kane like something warm and friendly, like treacle. "What are you doing in here?"

"Saving the future," Kane muttered under his breath as he shoved the voluminous right sleeve of his hooded robe back and strapped on the holster, tightening its straps. Then he snatched up one of the Sin Eaters and a plastic bag full of ammunition before running deeper into the storage complex.

"He's down here," one of the guards was saying. It was a woman's voice, and Kane turned just as a rock hurtled toward him, cutting the air with a familiar whine.

Kane leaped out of the projectile's way, slapping his empty palm against a nearby shelf as he used it for cover. The rock zipped past, continuing its path into the armory before crashing against a display of grenades. Kane winced as one of the shelves fell from its housing, spilling grenades all over the floor. Thankfully, nothing went off.

Swiftly, Kane loaded the Sin Eater, ramming home a clip from the plastic bag and shoving the rest into the pouch at his belt, bag and all. The pistol was still locked in its clamped-shut position, and Kane placed it in the wrist holster, securing it with practiced familiarity. With a flinch of his wrist tendons, the pistol would launch into his hand and he could dispense justice to these infiltrators.

Another flurry of stones hurtled toward where Kane hid, smashing a tray of combat knives on the nearest shelf. Their points cut through the air, missing Kane by just the smallest of margins, like some insane circus act.

"Show yourself, Kane." Dylan's taunting voice echoed through the armory, the depth of his words feeling like a physical thing. "It's time to stop all this nonsense and finally embrace the future."

"I'll give you a future you won't forget," Kane murmured as he searched the armory for something with more firepower.

While it appeared that Dylan himself was not armed, Kane needed to knock those stone throwers out of the picture or he was doomed. The obedience stone inside him would take control and the fight would simply drain out of him. Even now he could feel the weird effect that Dylan's presence seemed to have, his words washing over Kane's senses like waves on the shore.

"Spread out," Dylan ordered his followers. "Find him and bring him to me."

Kane heard running feet as the two soldiers came hurrying to find him, both rapidly checking each aisle as they sought their prey. In the next aisle over, Kane spotted a rack of Copperhead subguns. Remembering the damage the Copperhead had caused Ullikummis, Kane dashed across the opening, grabbing for one of the powerful blasters even as another hail of stones hurtled toward him. One of the stones clipped the hem of his robe, and Kane stumbled, correcting his balance automatically. A moment later he was rolling, dodging between another set of shelves before the hooded figures could catch up to him.

Safe for the moment, his back pressed against a shelving unit filled with flares, Kane checked the ammo on the Copperhead with growing annoyance, knowing full well that Cerberus protocol was to keep weapons unloaded while they were held in storage. He searched his memory, overlaid his mental map of the storage facility with the way it looked now under its new rocky layer. The ammo should be four units over, held in a locked cupboard.

Snatching up one of the flares, Kane primed it and tossed it where he guessed his foes were searching. There was a sudden flash of brilliance as the flare ignited, and Kane heard a grunt of surprise as the guards were momentarily blinded.

"Come on, Kane," Dylan called. "You're behaving like a child, and Lord Ullikummis has promised we will all be reborn."

"Rebirth sucks," Kane muttered to himself.

Something in his mind warned him of danger then, that miraculous point man sense, and he turned just in time to see one of the hooded figures sneaking up on him from the near end of the shelving unit. Kane whipped out with the Copperhead, swinging it like a baton at the guard's legs, sweeping his feet from under him. The man fell to the floor, a handful of small stones dropping from his grip.

Kane was on him instantly, commanding the Sin Eater into his hand and blasting a fierce burst of 9 mm bullets into the guard's face.

A noise from behind him alerted Kane to his second assailant, and he ducked automatically as one of the vicious little stones was fired at him from the sentry's slingshot. It was a woman, Kane saw, and then the realization came. It was Helen Foster, his old colleague, the one he had met with in the redoubt's main artery prior to facing Ullikummis less than three days earlier. Her face was fixed in a grimace and Kane saw the scarring across its right side, where he had blasted her in their previous meeting. On the one hand, he was pleased she had survived, whatever her altered mental state might be, but on the other it disturbed him to learn that the devotees of Ullikummis seemed to be almost invincible, somehow able to recover from any wound.

Tossing the Copperhead subgun through the gap between shelves, Kane scurried up the unit before him, using its shelves like the rungs of a ladder even as Helen snapped off another rock at his retreating form. The sharp shard of flint clipped the shelf by Kane's right hand, igniting a shower of bright sparks just beside his face.

For a moment Kane was dazzled, and black spots swam before his right eye as he hurried up and over the shelving unit, brushing aside its contents so that they rained down on his opponents. Then he was over the top, leaping across the open aisle to the next unit, easing himself down its side with a swift hand-over-hand movement.

As dropped, Kane saw Dylan walking briskly toward him, his hood pushed back from his face as he searched the aisles for the renegade.

"Come now, Kane," Dylan said smoothly. "This is madness and you know it. Accept your new master's willing embrace. Accept the future."

Kane commanded the Sin Eater into his grip, smiling as he felt its familiar weight there. He snapped off a burst of gunfire, sending twelve bullets in quick succession at Dylan as he loomed at the end of the aisle. The man didn't even flinch, merely raised his right hand and swept it through the air, flicking the bullets aside.

"What the hell are you?" Kane growled.

"I am the future," Dylan told him. "Ullikummis promised me utopia, made me a superman. I am stone, Kane, and soon you will be, too."

The words seemed almost melodic to Kane's ears, touching something inside him. The stone, he realized. Dylan's words—his very presence—were affecting the stone within him.

Dylan took another step toward Kane, arms spread as if to give the ex-Mag an embrace. Kane's feet pounded against the floor as he turned away, running for the end of the aisle.

On the far side, Kane retrieved the Copperhead assault weapon, then sprinted down the next aisle toward where he was certain the ammunition would be stored. A rock wall stood before him, and Kane scanned it for several seconds, searching for the aperture where the sensor would open the hidden door. He swept his wrist past the scanner, heard the hidden lock snap open.

Running feet slapped against the rock floor behind him, and Kane turned even as his hand fumbled with the stone-clad cupboard door. Both Foster and her hooded companion were running down the aisle toward him, their slingshots poised to unleash another hail of the vicious little stones. Kane pulled at the ammunition cupboard's door even as two flat stones cut the air where he stood. One cuffed him across the left shoulder, while the other crashed against the cupboard door two inches from where his hand pulled at its rough surface.

The unit was open now, an array of ammunition waiting within. The shelves inside had changed from how Kane remembered them, still rigid and uniform, but with a smattering of sand and pebbles sprinkled across their surfaces as if something washed up on a beach. Whatever Ullikummis had done, however his touch had metamorphosed the Cerberus redoubt, his effects had been strange and absolute, touching even the most hidden areas. Kane wondered for a moment how the ventilation system must look, whether the air flow itself had been disrupted, blocked as in a cancerous lung.

Kane's hand whipped inside the ammunition cupboard, snatched up clips for his Copperhead as the hooded man ran at him, fist raised. Kane turned, blocking the savage punch and bringing his elbow low so that it jabbed into the man's chest. His opponent tumbled a step backward and Kane brought up his other arm, swinging the length of the Copperhead once again like a nightstick and whipping him across the jowls.

As the man staggered back, Kane slammed the clip into the Copperhead and, without a moment's hesitation, pumped the trigger, drilling titanium shells point-blank into his chest at a rate of seven hundred rounds per minute. In less than three seconds, the hooded figure toppled backward, crashing into another shelving unit and bringing its contents—twin attaché cases—down onto his prone form.

As the man fell, Kane saw Helen twirling the slingshot in her hand, whipping it around to generate the momentum required to launch its stony contents like bullets at his face. Kane turned away, leaping behind the nearest shelf even as she tossed the stones. Behind him, they cut a tattoo against the doors to the ammunition cupboard, but Kane was already running, heading back toward the single entrance to the huge armory.

He ran onward, glancing over his shoulder to see Helen reappear, the hood of her robe low over her face. That made it easier, Kane thought as he squeezed the Copperhead's trigger and sent two dozen bullets in her direction. Rather than avoiding them, she held her hands up over her face, and Kane watched in awe as the bullets struck her as if striking a wall. When she brought her hands back down, she was unscathed, standing as she had before the assault. Relentlessly, she began whipping the slingshot around once more, launching another of the sharp flat stones at Kane's retreating form.

"Dammit," he muttered. "Looks like I'm gonna have to go shopping for something bigger."

As he spoke, he swerved into the next aisle, letting the disklike stone cut uselessly past him. He threw the Copperhead aside, searching the shelves for something with more kick. The Copperhead was fine for close-up work, but he couldn't waste any more time point-blanking these abominations. He needed to finish them, cut Dylan out of the loop and destroy the signal that the first priest was broadcasting from his hidden stone.

Kane's hands brushed over a box of stick grenades as he ran down the aisle, knowing he would be foolish to detonate one in this space, especially with all the live ammunition that lined the walls. Up ahead he saw a bank of a half-dozen dragon launchers, antitank weapons that could be operated by a two-man team. Arms pumping, Kane ran toward the aisle, dropping low and sliding across the rock floor as he spotted Dylan just three aisles across from him, staring this way and that.

Then Kane was at the bank of missile launchers, grabbing one by its carrying strap. Almost three feet long, the dragon launcher was a compact tube designed to fire guided missiles. The unit bulged at its back end, with a bulky sighting unit atop a metal cylinder approximately six and a half inches in diameter. The units were steadied on a drop-down, front-mounted tripod.

As Helen Foster hurried around the corner of the aisle, Kane swung the bulky launcher, striking her in the stomach with the force of a battering ram. The woman grunted, sprawling to the floor in a flurry of robes.

Kane turned, frantically searching for the storage unit that contained the dragon's missiles. He spied it a second later, the warheads racked horizontally on wide rock struts that had once been metal.

Kane snatched one of the missiles as Dylan appeared at the end of the aisle, a smile on his insufferable face.

"What are you doing, Kane?" the first priest asked. "You know you want to submit. Give your will over to the future."

Kane scampered backward, hurrying down the aisle, putting a little distance between himself and the ex-farmer.

"It's all over, Dylan," Kane shouted. "Your sick future's about to go up in smoke."

Then he crouched down, loading the missile in the dragon launcher with a determined shunt. There were explosive materials all around, he knew—which meant things were about to get very dangerous. He just hoped that Rosalia was keeping up her side of their agreement.

ON THE INCARCERATION LEVEL of Life Camp Zero, Rosalia and the half-dozen freed prisoners found themselves surrounded by hooded guards with the physical property of stone. As one, the guards pulled slingshots from their belts and loaded them with the stones they carried in ammunition pouches at their waists.

Rosalia had expected Kane's distraction to last longer, or had at least hoped he'd find a way to keep it going. But now her hand was revealed, and for what? To die at the whim of Ullikummis's loyal subjects, stoned to death?

The robed figures clashed with the people around Rosalia, and Grant used all his strength to force one of the group back into the others, knocking them over. Beside him, Domi was struggling with another hooded figure, driving rabbit punches into the man's side as he swatted at her. Reba DeFore and Mariah Falk struggled with yet another guard, each grabbing an arm and trying to spin him, as if playing some schoolyard game. For a few seconds, the corridor went quiet as both groups assessed one another. It was a momentary respite at best, as the hooded figures were amassing at both ends of the rock-walled corridor. There was no escape.

Rosalia looked left and right, searching for an exit even as she brushed her wrist against another sensor, unlocking another cell door. Inside, Cerberus director Lakesh struggled to his senses, holding his hands up against the stronger light that seeped in from the corridor.

As the hooded guards tossed a clutch of stones at Rosalia and the prisoners, her dog leaped forward, bounding down the corridor with an angry bark. Rosalia watched in amazement as the canine—that stupid, useless mutt—ripped into their foes, a blur of teeth and sharp, stubby claws, like a thing possessed.

Rosalia and the prisoners watched as the dog took on all comers, jaws clamping down on outstretched hands, yanking at fustian robes and pulling their wearers to the floor. Each touch, each bite, seemed to drop another of the figures, and they sank to the floor with screams, the battle utterly and eerily forgotten. There was something uncanny about the whole scene; the dog's touch seemed almost fatal to the people affected. In the flickering lights of the magma pods, the dog seemed almost to expand, to double or triple in size with a ghostly image about it—a dog with three heads.

Rosalia knew nothing of her dog's history, had no

inclination of the forces hidden within its matted and un-assuming form. At that moment, all she knew was that any contact appeared to burn the devotees of Ullikummis in the way the cross was said to burn vampires of myth.

It was the turn in the tide of battle that the prisoners needed. Suddenly rejuvenated, they struck out, beating back their hooded captors, and Rosalia fought among them.

DOWN IN THE ARMORY, Kane was kneeling on the rocky floor, loading the dragon missile launcher he had acquired from one of the nearby racks. According to the manual, using the M-47 Dragon antitank rig should be a two-man operation, but Kane concentrated on his purpose, loading the tube with grim determination. At the far end of the aisle, farmer-turned-religious-zealot Dylan was trudging toward him, the folds of his coarse robe billowing out around him.

"You thought you were going to inherit the future," Kane muttered as he pushed the missile into place, "but all you're getting is a handful of ashes."

Still kneeling, Kane hefted the tubelike hunk of metal over his right shoulder, letting its leg struts fold out automatically until they rested in place in front of him. He held his eye to the sight and engaged its guidance system, watching the figure of Dylan at the far end of the aisle. He was close. He was *real* close.

As Kane prepared to fire the missile launcher, Helen Foster leaped from a gap beyond the shelving unit he crouched beside, swiping at his head with a flat, disklike rock. Kane ducked back at the noise, and the stone missed his skull by barely an inch, brushing against the folds of his hood. He snapped out with his fist, punching Foster high in the leg—the nearest place he could reach from his crouch. The dragon launcher rolled from his shoulder and fell to the floor with a loud clatter.

Helen stood there and took Kane's blow, not making a noise. He saw her face then, saw the strangely vacant look in her eyes, and he resigned himself to what he'd had to do all along. Whipping up his right arm, he engaged the Sin Eater once more, driving a continuous stream of shots into Foster's figure as she loomed over his crouching form. The bullets struck at her groin, chest and, finally, her face, knocking her off her feet. She crashed into the shelving unit and Kane shoved. The unit rocked and Foster fell, flailing in a pile of toppling debris from its shelves. She was trapped.

Kane ignored Helen's thrashing form, automatically sending the Sin Eater back to its hidden holster as he snatched up the dragon launcher once more. In a heartbeat, the M-47 dragon launcher was resting on his right shoulder, as Kane sighted down its length at the approaching form of Dylan.

"Kiss the future goodbye, little man," Kane snarled as he depressed the firing stud of the antitank weapon.

There was a blaze of fire in the ill-lit room as the missile launched, powering across the short distance and slamming into Dylan's body as he took another step. The force of the launch powered through the dragon unit, and Kane relaxed as it pushed against him, letting himself topple backward and roll away even as Dylan was knocked in the other direction.

Kane pressed his face toward the shelving unit as the warhead exploded just thirty feet away from him. The calamitous explosion was followed immediately by a rush of smaller rumblings as the ammunition nearest to Dylan and the exploding shell went off. Kane covered his head with his arms, leaning into himself as ammo was set off all around him, popping and bursting in fiery blooms.

As the smoke thinned, Kane turned his head, searching the length of the aisle for whatever remained of the first priest. The rocky shelves were awash with smoldering debris, and the floor and ceiling had blackened with the series of explosions. For a moment, all Kane could see of the far end of the aisle were the dark, churning vapors of smoke billowing from where the missile had hit. Then, to his astonishment, he saw something moving amid the wreckage.

Smoke pluming from his body, the ex-farmer called Dylan pulled himself up off the floor. His robe had been burned away, just a few flaming tatters remaining across his back and shoulders as he stood. His flesh was a ruddy red from the heat of the explosion, and his dark beard had vanished, leaving patches across his chin, and several flames still licking at his lips.

"It's impossible," Kane muttered. "No one could possibly survive—"

Dylan fixed him with an angry glare, pacing down the aisle and picking up speed as he neared the ex-Magistrate who had attacked him. "You'll never understand, will you?" Dylan spit. "I am stone. Ullikummis promised a utopian future, but we are its architects. We, his supermen."

Kane struggled to his feet, still reeling from the cacophony of explosions that had run through the shelves all around him. Dylan rushed at him, the flaming remnants of his robe disappearing in fizzing bursts of fire and smoke.

Kane brought his arm up as the first priest drove a punch at his head, flames still licking down his arm. The blow struck with incredible force, knocking Kane off his feet even as he tried to deflect it.

"You'll embrace the future soon enough," Dylan told him.

Kane knew the man was right. The stone inside him was beginning to overpower his thought process, making even Dylan's most lackluster proclamation seem like nectar from the gods. Kane needed to drop Dylan and do it now, take the threat he represented out of the picture once and for all as the armory burned all around them.

He dropped to the floor, kicking out with a swift leg sweep designed to bring Dylan crashing down. His foot caught the farmer-turned-priest behind his knee, and Dylan wobbled slightly where he stood, but didn't fall.

"I am stone," Dylan spit, glaring at Kane, "and stone is the future." He lunged forward, hands outstretched.

Commanding the Sin Eater back into his palm, Kane directed a stream of bullets right into the man's face. The bullets struck Dylan, knocking him back, yet they failed to pierce his flesh. Somehow, Kane realized, Ullikummis had changed his key warriors, altering their genetic makeup with his pebblelike seeds. Dylan's chant was not an idle boast; he had somehow acquired the physicality of stone.

As Dylan stumbled backward, Kane's Sin Eater clicked on empty, and his mind raced as he reached for the pouch at his belt and struggled to reload. Six feet before him, Dylan was pulling himself away from a burning shelf, a determined, manic gleam in his dark eyes. Kane's fingers delved into the waterproof plastic bag that contained the spare cartridges for the Sin Eater, and then a devilish plan formed in his mind.

Without hesitation, he tipped the contents of the bag to the floor, discarding the ammunition clips he had snagged from the armory. At the same moment, he commanded the Sin Eater back into its hidden recess beneath his sleeve. With an animalistic howl, Kane ran at Dylan even as the ex-farmer turned to face him once more.

As Dylan brought his arms up in a gesture of defense, Kane leaped in the air, kicking off the uneven rock floor, the plastic bag clutched in his left hand. Dylan tracked Kane as he sprang, bringing his hands up to grab the onrushing figure. He snagged a handful of Kane's robe, tearing it away as Kane barreled at him.

Then Kane was on him, his hand going to Dylan's face as his weight drove the priest backward. Dylan fell back, his feet kicking out as he keeled to the floor. Kane's hands snapped the plastic bag out straight, placing the five-by-seven-inch pouch of clear plastic over his opponent's mouth and nose.

Dylan collided with the floor with a crunch, his skull smashing hard against the rocky surface. Kane was above him, fighting to hold the man down, pressing all his weight against Dylan's singed body as he sprawled before him. Nearby, another ammo case exploded as flames touched it.

Kane shoved, holding the plastic bag over his enemy's mouth and nostrils, driving it against the man's face as he struggled.

Dylan fought, pushing against Kane's chest. His angle was wrong; he couldn't seem to get the leverage to throw Kane despite his struggles. Kane rode the man like a rodeo pro, clinging tight with his powerful thighs as he pressed the bag over the first priest's face. The clear plastic began to mist over where Dylan breathed against its surface, two jets of white appearing beneath his nostrils, a fog of moisture around his mouth.

"Bullets, missiles, explosives—all useless to a man

who can assume the qualities of granite," Kane said, fixing Dylan with a fearsome look.

Dylan continued to struggle, his voice muffled by the bag as he tried to break free. Trapped beneath Kane's powerful form, he writhed, frantically trying to free himself as his breath misted against the shield of plastic.

"Guess I finally figured out the one thing that can stop you," Kane growled as he stared into Dylan's eyes—eyes now wide with fear.

Dylan pounded against Kane's sides, but the blows were coming weaker now, and Kane endured them with a grunt. The first priest reached for Kane's wrists then, realizing too late that his only hope was to pull Kane's hands away from his face, to free himself of the obstruction to his breathing. Kane pushed down harder, holding the bag in place over the man's darkening face.

"Whatever Ullikummis told you, whatever he promised," Kane snarled, "even the future has to breathe, Dylan. Take that away and all his promises of the future and of being a superman mean nothing."

Dylan continued to struggle for almost three minutes, sprawled there before Kane on the hard rock floor of the armory. Finally, his face darkened to a deep red, darker even than the effect the explosion had caused, and the whites of his eyes turned pink. Then, as Kane held the plastic over his face, the man's eyes widened, became distant, and spittle formed across the clear underside of the bag. Finally, with a spasm that seemed to run through the length of his singed, near naked body, Dylan flopped on the floor. Then he ceased struggling, ceased moving at all.

Kane remained poised there for a long time, letting the minutes tick by as he held the bag in place over his foe's face, fires stuttering all about them. He needed to be sure that Dylan was dead, that the first priest could no longer project whatever it was that affected the stones implanted in himself and the others.

ONCE DYLAN HAD BEEN killed by Kane's hand, the battle for the redoubt became easier. Shortly thereafter, the guards ceased fighting, many of them genuinely confused to find themselves amid the strange network of tunnels. Rosalia's dog returned to her side as she went through the last of the cells, freeing the remaining Cerberus prisoners.

There had been a few casualties from the first strike. Clem Bryant, Daryl Morganstern and Henny Johnson were listed among the dead.

"There's something you should know, Kane," Lakesh said when the ex-Magistrate finally regrouped with his friends in the transformed operations room of the life camp. "There's no sign of Brigid—she's not here."

Kane looked steadily at Lakesh as he snacked on some freeze-dried rations that had been recovered from storage. "Don't say it, Lakesh," he warned, "because she's not dead. I'd know if she was."

"I've prioritized getting the transponder monitoring equipment up and running again," Lakesh explained hopefully, referring to the hidden biometric signal that every member of the Cerberus team carried. "Once we have access to that data, we'll be able to locate all our personnel. Brigid among them."

"Do that," Kane agreed brusquely.

He was tired and hungry and he wasn't happy about what he'd had to do to Dylan in the armory. The man was a farmer, misguided and fooled into joining a cult created by an Annunaki prince. Maybe he had deserved better.

"You look pensive," Lakesh observed.

"Just can't shake the feeling that something has gone horribly wrong," Kane said.

"The redoubt can be rebuilt in time," Lakesh reassured him, "and if Brigid's alive we'll find her."

"No, it's not that," Kane said. "It's something more fundamental. We were caught napping while the world changed. Now we're playing catch-up and we don't even know the rules of the new game."

Lakesh sighed. "I've instructed everybody to gather outside in twenty minutes," he said. "We'll work out our battle plan then, and I think the fresh air will do all of us some good. Don't you?"

Kane nodded. "There's more than one way to build the future, I guess."

Chapter 30

Wearing the torn remains of the hooded robe, Kane looked about him at the figures waiting on the plateau beyond the entrance to the Cerberus redoubt. Vast pillars of stone stood across the front of the door like the bars of a prison, blocking the entryway to anything wider than a man. His colleagues—his friends—were dotted about the sandy plateau, sitting on flat rocks or wandering about in little circles, taking in the fresh evening air. They looked dazed, and it put Kane in mind of the people he had freed from Tenth City all those months ago. Brewster Philboyd, Donald Bry, Lakesh—all of them looked like people waking up from a deep sleep, like people coming out of a coma. In a sense, Kane realized now, they were. Whatever had gone on in the place now called Life Camp Zero, it had been a far more subtle kind of infiltration than it had first appeared.

Lakesh called the team over and began addressing the operations people among the group in his stentorian voice. Lakesh looked like an old man, Kane realized with a start. Incarceration had been a terrible drain on him, more so than any of the others. Domi stood at the Cerberus director's side, propping him up as he took a head count and began organizing smaller groups. Domi had dressed in the bloody remains of her shorts and top, and her alabaster flesh was marred with scrapes and scratches.

Someone was missing, Kane knew, feeling it deep in his being, almost like a physical wound. His *anamchara*—Brigid Baptiste—was gone. Wherever she had been held, it wasn't here in the altered structure of the redoubt. They had searched the whole facility, and Brewster Philboyd and Reba DeFore had managed to jury-rig the transponder monitoring equipment via a recovered laptop. Like all the Cerberus personnel, Brigid had a subcutaneous transponder injected beneath her skin, instantly traceable via the Cerberus mainframe. When Brewster had run the diagnostics through the laptop he had come up blank. Brigid had simply disappeared from the system; her transponder was no longer broadcasting a signal.

Almost two dozen of the robed guards could be seen among the familiar Cerberus personnel, and they seemed just as confused as Kane's people. A kind of mass hypnosis had swept over the crowd, and the prison guards were as much victims as their prisoners.

From behind Kane, the familiar forms of Mariah Falk and Grant edged through the tight columns of stone, bringing with them loaded trays of food. Like everything else in the redoubt, the canteen had been overwhelmed with a lacing of rock, and its kitchens were in a state of ruin, most of the equipment unusable. Still, army rations had survived, and even the freeze-dried junk and canned gunk was better than nothing until Cerberus was up and running again.

Mariah was talking with Grant about theories she was already developing about the stones, her geologist training giving her a particular insight into their structure and characteristics.

"If we can find some way to negate their effects," Grant agreed, "then we'll be on the road to recovery."

Mariah nodded sadly. "I know it won't bring people back," she said, "but I guess we need to go forward now."

"It's the only place left to go," Grant told her. "Brave heart, Mariah—we'll get through this mess in time."

The two strolled straight past Kane, Grant not recognizing his friend in the hooded robe of the enemy, taking him for one of the recovering guards who were only now beginning to wake up from the mass hypnosis they had suffered.

Kane kept silent. There was someone else he needed to speak with first, before he could reacquaint himself with old friends. Kane scanned the group, searching for Rosalia. It would be just like her to skip out once things were quiet, he thought, disappearing like mist on a warm day. But no—there she was, standing at the edge of the plateau, tossing a stick out into the forest beyond for her nameless dog to chase, her long, dark hair billowing behind her in the wind, a pariah on the fringes of the group of friends.

Hood up, Kane made his way past the familiar Cerberus personnel, ignoring them. He received a few odd looks, dressed as he was as one of the enemy, but for the most part the Cerberus people were busy catching up, getting medical attention and forming a battle plan with Lakesh at their center.

"Rosie," Kane called as he approached the beautifully tanned woman at the edge of the clearing.

She turned to him, her hair whipping around her face in the wind until she pushed it away with a casual sweep of her slender hand. "I suppose you'll be wanting that stone of yours removed now, huh, Magistrate man?"

Kane nodded. "Yeah, but I wanted to say something."

Rosalia looked at him, her predatory eyes assessing the threat he might pose to her even now. Behind her, the dog came scampering out of the tree cover, the stick in its mouth. Kane watched as the mutt dropped the stick on the ground at her feet, panting eagerly for her to join in the game. Her expression fixed, Rosalia reached down and threw the stick off into the trees again, and the dog yipped as it turned, scurrying off through the bushes after it.

"You did good there," Kane told her, feeling a little uncomfortable in the woman's presence. "Helped free my people. Got me out of a jam. For what it's worth, I think you're a good person."

Rosalia shook her head. "You're so naive, Magistrate man," she muttered.

"Hey, I'm trying to pay you a compliment," he said, irritation creeping into his tone. "I owe you. You helped me and I wanted to say thanks. That's all it is, and you can decide for yourself if it's worth anything coming from a Magistrate man like me."

Rosalia peered over Kane's shoulder, looking at the pillars that occluded the entrance to the redoubt. "You going to rebuild?" she asked.

Kane shrugged. "I don't know yet. I'm not sure if it's going to be safe to stay here right now. We might have to move on till we can figure everything out."

"I looked around a little," Rosalia admitted. "You had a pretty impressive setup here. I'm sorry it got messed up the way it did."

Kane nodded graciously. "Cerberus has spent years lurching from one threat to the next, confident we could react to whatever showed up on the horizon," he said. "I don't think we ever realized we were in the war. This will change that—we can't just react anymore. We'll have to take the fight to Ullikummis now, and to Enlil and the other overlords. We're not Magistrates turning up to fix problems. We're soldiers right there in the trenches as grenades are landing at our feet."

Rosalia reached forward, pushed the hood from Kane's head and looked into his steely gray-blue eyes. "You did good, Magistrate m—" She stopped. "You did good, Kane. Better than I—"

The dog barked, cutting into her words. Kane looked down and saw that the mongrel had returned with the stick, dropping it at their feet, tail drumming playfully. Kane leaned down and took the stick, pulling his arm back and launching it off into the trees once more. The dog scampered off, tail wagging.

Kane turned back to Rosalia, looking at the beautiful woman as she pushed the hair away from her face yet again. "Than you what?" he prompted. "You were saying."

She smiled enigmatically. "You came through all right," she told him. Then she reached for his left sleeve, pushed it back as Kane turned over his arm. "Shall we do this, then?"

He nodded. "I'll go find someone to take care of your dog," he said.

"He'll be fine," Rosalia assured him as she produced the little sewing kit from the folds of her robe. "You sit down. This will hurt, but you'll be fine. I did it to myself a couple times, before I figured out how the stones worked."

"You still have one inside you," Kane stated as he sat down on the dirt.

"I'll keep it for now," Rosalia told him, pulling a needle from her kit. "May be useful in this brave new world Ullikummis is creating."

Kane nodded. "It's an alien artifact, you realize."

Rosalia looked at the ex-Mag for a moment, her dark eyes flashing with mischief. "I have it under control,

Kane," she promised: "You need to stop worrying so. You're like an old woman."

"Yeah," he muttered as she dug the needle between the veins of his wrist. "I get that a lot."

Rosalia probed with the sewing needle, wiggling its point beneath Kane's skin until she located the little coin-size stone that had affixed itself to his insides. Kane winced as he felt the needle scrape against the thing buried inside him, felt Rosalia begin to pluck it out of his body the way one plucks at a splinter.

"Come on, brave Magistrate man," she goaded. "Big boys don't cry."

Kane grunted, keeping his arm still as Rosalia worked. It took almost fifteen minutes of probing and scraping, but finally she pulled the hidden stone to the surface, worked it through a split she had made in the skin. It emerged covered in blood, with threads of flesh still attached to the surface. With the point of the needle, Rosalia flicked the stone away, and Kane watched as the bloody object rolled a few feet across the ground.

Kane held his right hand against his wrist to staunch the flow of blood that trickled downward. Rosalia wiped the needle on the material of her robe and replaced it in the little pocket sewing kit she carried. Her dog had returned and it sniffed at the bloody stone, whined and turned away as if disinterested.

"That's one weird dog," Kane murmured.

"One of a kind," Rosalia agreed. "You okay?"

Kane pressed his hand harder against the open wound. "I'll be fine."

"You look a little pale," she told him.

"Careful," Kane warned. "You're starting to sound like you care."

"Well," Rosalia said noncommittally as she replaced the sewing kit in the hidden pocket of her robe.

Kane watched the proud woman as she ran her hand over her dog's head until it whimpered with affection. The canine looked at Kane with its strangely expressive face, pale eyes peering into his.

"So, what are you going to do?" Kane asked. "Just ride off into the sunset?"

"Something like that," Rosalia agreed.

"It's a dangerous world out there," Kane said. "More dangerous than it's been in a long time."

"Good. Let's keep it that way," Rosalia spit. "More opportunities."

Kane didn't know what to say to that. The woman was stubborn, proud, a loner. But she had helped him, helped everyone in Cerberus, whatever her ultimate reasons for doing so. Plus she was smart, a solid fighter. Right now, with the team depleted and the redoubt in ruins, someone like Rosalia was just what they needed. He gazed out at the evening sun as it sank toward the horizon, its warm colors reminding him of the dismal magma lights that had illuminated the redoubt, and of Brigid Baptiste's vibrant hair. Baptiste was still among the missing, and without her, Kane knew, their side would struggle against the threat of Ullikummis.

"Why don't you stick around?" Kane proposed suddenly, still gazing out at the evening sun sinking over the forest.

Rosalia looked at him, staring at his strong profile in the fading light. "I'm a free agent, Kane," she told him. "I go where I please."

Kane fixed her with a look. "There's safety in numbers," he said. "Doesn't need to be permanent, just a temporary arrangement until we work out all this mess. We'd appreciate your help, Rosalia. *I'd* appreciate your help."

Rosalia chuckled. "Oh, Magistrate man, are you going misty on me?"

Kane pushed himself up off the ground, brushing dirt from the robe. "Hey, the offer's there," he said. "Now, I'd better go see what kind of brouhaha Lakesh is working up."

As Kane walked back toward his friends, Rosalia looked at the dog before her, wagging its tail, tongue hanging out. "Well, I know what you'd do," she told it. "You'd go where the food is, stupid mutt." After a moment, she stood up, glancing across the plateau toward the group that had gathered around Lakesh. "Screw it, let's go make some new friends," she said, glancing down at the animal. "Don't you look at me like that—I have the sense to go where the food is, too. Food and shelter and maybe a noble Magistrate man to put his life on the line and keep me safe."

A moment later, Rosalia and her pale-eyed dog joined Kane at the edge of the crowd listening to Lakesh outline their plan. Kane turned, looking at the dark-eyed woman as she stood beside him, and he raised a quizzical eyebrow.

"What?" she challenged. "You'll get yourself killed without me, and we both know that's true, so don't give me none of that Magistrate bullshit you spout."

Kane inclined his head, turning his attention back to Lakesh as the Cerberus leader revealed their next move. They would leave the redoubt, Lakesh explained, for it was too dangerous to remain here right now. Instead, the Cerberus team would scatter to the four winds, go underground and infiltrate Ullikummis's strongholds, try to track down and halt this monster's advance. As Kane listened, Rosalia tucked an arm around his waist and leaned her head into him, pressing against his chest.

From where he stood on the other side of Kane, Grant peered over, surprised at the choice of dark-haired companion Kane had found. Still, Kane knew what he was doing, Grant thought—in Grant's experience, his partner always did.

Before them, Mariah Falk took center stage and began explaining what little she had extrapolated about the rocks.

Things had changed, but that wasn't so bad. After all, Cerberus was an organization, a mind-set, a calling, not just a headquarters hidden inside a mountain.

It was a new world, and a new team of heroes would emerge to strike out for the freedom of all humankind.

THREE DAYS BEFORE it had all been so obvious to Ullikummis. He had stood there in the main artery of the Cerberus redoubt, poised over the fallen forms of Kane and his teammates. Kane had put up a valiant fight, but he was doomed from the very start.

Ullikummis turned, ignoring his fallen foe, searching the floor for the one that truly interested him. There, with her vibrant red-gold hair like the rays of the setting sun, lay Brigid Baptiste, the apekin who had tricked and subsequently expelled him from the Ontic Library. Baptiste had a memory like no other. Her ability to file and recall facts was truly exceptional, even to one of the Annunaki, whose shared memories reached countless millennia back to the dawn of their race.

Ullikummis had turned then, the final vestiges of the hydrochloric acid still burning at his face and chest, scanning his loyal subjects as they stood over the group of captured Cerberus rebels. Infiltration had been easy, their defeat a matter of time rather than in any sense a challenge.

Dylan had stepped forward at the stone god's beckoning, bowing his head in subjugation to his acknowledged master. Dylan, who had taken the title of first priest, was a man easily impressed with simple favors, meaningless tributes from the ones he considered his betters.

"You shall be tasked to turn them," Ullikummis had explained, his voice rumbling through the tunnel. "A life camp, whose role is to open their minds to the new lives they will lead." Then he had indicated the unconscious woman with the red hair. "All except this one," he said. "She is something special—she will form a key part of the future."

Dylan had nodded once with reverence, acknowledging his master's instructions in silence. Ullikummis had foreseen even then that Dylan would be replaced, his position as first priest coming rapidly to its end.

Now Ullikummis stood on the windswept shore on his self-raised island of Bensalem, staring out across the crashing waves of the Atlantic, the woman at his side. She seemed small in comparison to him, her figure a slender mixture of curves, where his was rough surfaces, jutting spikes. She had changed her clothes, dressed in some ensemble she had found among the discarded raiment of his new slaves. She stood now in black, appropriate enough in its connotations to human beings and their primitive fear of the dark. She was a dark creature now, the black leather clinging to her like a second skin. Her fire-red hair whipped around her head in the wind that blew in from the sea, and a cape of fur was cinched around her shoulders, the pelt of a dead thing.

"My father conceived me as his hand in the darkness," Ullikummis said, "his all-consuming hate made manifest."

The woman watched the sea with emerald eyes that seemed to mirror the color of the waves, her hair echoing the red-gold rays of the sunset.

"Now I have you, my own hand in darkness," Ullikummis continued, "my own hate made flesh."

The woman with the fire-red hair nodded, a thin smile on her lips as the waters of the Atlantic sloshed against the jutting rocks of the island, crashing there in big, foam-tipped breakers.

"Brigid Haight," she agreed, the smile widening on her stone-hard features.

* * * * *

The Executioner®
Don Pendleton's
TRIAL BY FIRE

A Congo rescue mission turns into a deadly game of hide and seek.

When a plane with American cadets is shot down in the Democratic Republic of the Congo, Mack Bolan is sent to find the group. With terrorists tracking them, the rescue mission becomes a dangerous game of escape. The Executioner's primed for battle—and ready to teach everyone a lesson in jungle warfare.

Available September wherever books are sold.

GOLD EAGLE®

AleX Archer
THE ORACLE'S MESSAGE

**Men would do anything for it...
but one woman will determine its fate**

The Pearl of Palawan is rumored to grant a power long
coveted by mankind—immortality. Out of curiosity
archaeologist Annja Creed
finds herself drawn into a
group of German divers
looking for the fabled pearl.
The race is on but no one
realizes the true nature of
the artifact, or the danger
it poses to them all.

*Available September
wherever books are sold.*

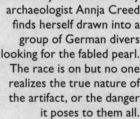

GRA32

James Axler
Outlanders®

INFESTATION CUBED

**Earth's saviors are on the run as
more nightmares descend upon Earth…**

Ullikummis, the would-be cruel master of Earth, has captured
Brigid Baptiste, luring Kane and Grant on a dangerous pursuit. All
while pan-terrestrial scientists conduct a horrifying experiment
in parasitic mind control. But true evil has yet to reveal itself, as
the alliance scrambles to regroup—before humankind loses its
last and only hope.

Available November wherever books are sold.